D0249909

Prai...

"You can alwa...
ravishing rom...
until the wee hours of the morning." —Teresa Medeiros

"Julianne MacLean's writing is smart, thrilling, and sizzles with sensuality."   —Elizabeth Hoyt

"Scottish romance at its finest, with characters to cheer for, a lush love story, and rousing adventure. I was captivated from the very first page. When it comes to exciting Highland romance, Julianne MacLean delivers."   —Laura Lee Guhrke

"She is just an all-around wonderful writer and I look forward to reading everything she writes."
—Romance Junkies

. . . and her bestselling romances

"Sparkles with life and emotion . . . delightful."
—Jo Beverly

"A sizzling treat."   —Karen Hawkins

"Brimming with incredible passion." —Cathy Maxwell

"It takes a talented author to segue from a lighthearted tale of seduction to an emotionally powerful romance that plays on your heartstrings . . . a very special, powerful read."   *—Romantic Times Book Reviews*

Mᴏʀᴇ . . .

The Prince's Bride

JULIANNE MacLEAN

St. Martin's Paperbacks

This is a work of fiction. All of the characters, organizations, and events portrayed in this novel are either products of the author's imagination or are used fictitiously.

THE PRINCE'S BRIDE

Copyright © 2013 by Julianne MacLean.

All rights reserved.

For information address St. Martin's Press, 175 Fifth Avenue, New York, NY 10010.

ISBN: 978-0-312-55281-7

Printed in the United States of America

St. Martin's Paperbacks edition / May 2013

St. Martin's Paperbacks are published by St. Martin's Press, 175 Fifth Avenue, New York, NY 10010.

10 9 8 7 6 5 4 3 2 1

PART I
The Abduction

Chapter One

This was wrong, so very, very wrong. . . .

She was a villain tonight, there could be no denying it, but any guilt was somehow eclipsed by the unexpected pleasure of this wicked and very sinister charade.

The passion is not real, Véronique reminded herself as she took hold of Prince Nicholas's gloved hand, met his gaze with a mischievous look of desire through her half mask, and allowed him to assist her into the coach.

Quickly, before he joined her, she glanced around at the cushions placed just so, the bottle of champagne in the corner, and breathed in the subtle scent of rosewater, which she had splashed onto the dark green velvet upholstery a few hours ago, before she'd entered the ball.

The coach lamp flickered wildly as the night breeze wafted in through the door. With graceful, controlled movements, she sat down and reclined seductively.

Prince Nicholas, her quarry, followed her inside and closed the door behind them.

At last, they were completely alone.

As he slid onto the seat beside her, the lamplight

reflected off the brass buttons of his royal regalia and sparkled in his enticing blue eyes. His mask covered most of his face, but not those luscious full lips. Not that the disguise made a difference. She already knew what he looked like. He had been shown to her the day before, pointed out like a partridge in the wood.

"Look, that's him down there—in the black coat. That's Wellington beside him. Viscount Castlereagh, the British foreign secretary, is wearing the gray hat." Pierre Cuvier handed her the spyglass. "Will you be able to pick him out in the crowd?"

Leaning out over the rail of the stone arch bridge that spanned the Seine, Véronique shut one eye, peered through the lens, and peered down at the three men standing on the bow of the boat as it passed beneath them.

She had been briefed about Prince Nicholas's extraordinary good looks, but had not expected to nearly lose her breath as she caught him in her sights.

She'd also been warned about his notorious reputation with women. According to Pierre, he was a flagrant charmer and heartbreaker. A scoundrel of the highest order.

Now that she had seen him in the flesh, she understood why he could get away with such behavior. Not only was he a royal prince of Petersbourg—a small but powerful European nation on the North Sea—but he also had the face of a Greek god, with jet black hair and blue eyes, a teasing smile that could charm all the angels out of heaven, and a strapping muscular build, unquestionably fit for a throne.

Though he would likely never wear the crown, for his brother's wife, Queen Alexandra, had recently given birth to a son.

None of that concerned Véronique, however. She had

a job to do, and she must stay focused on the task at hand.

"Yes, I will be able to pick him out," she replied as she snapped the spyglass shut and handed it back to Pierre.

"He'll be wearing a mask," he warned.

Véronique turned to walk back to the coach. "Don't worry. It won't be a problem."

Yet here she sat this evening, reclining on the soft upholstered seat in the overheated coach, smiling at her captured prince with tempting allure, wondering how much time she had. How long would they be alone before the laudanum took effect? Five minutes? An hour?

Her desire for him was alarming, and she realized she may not be in full control here. She supposed she had known that before she stepped into the coach, for everything had turned rather warm and hazy in the ballroom when they first met. Something very potent had sparked between them, and now she was caught up in a delicious sexual current, which she feared might sweep her off her feet.

"I didn't expect this tonight," Nicholas said in a low, husky voice that heated her blood. "It was supposed to be a night of political debates and endless arguments."

"You've all been arguing for days," Véronique replied, referring, of course, to the fate of Napoléon, who had been defeated at Waterloo less than a month ago, and had just surrendered to the British. He had boarded the HMS *Bellerophon* at the port of Rochefort, but no one could agree on what to do with him. "Haven't you had enough?"

Nicholas slid closer, slowly removed his gloves one finger at a time, then cupped her chin in his hand. "Enough talk of politics, yes, but not nearly enough of *you*."

There it was . . . the famous charm. She would have liked to believe she was immune to it, for *she* was the seducer in this situation, but when he spoke to her in that velvety voice and touched her with those strong, gentle hands, she melted like every other woman who found herself blinded by his impossible charisma.

Keep your head, Véronique. It won't be long now. . . .

"Are we going somewhere?" he asked while his gaze dipped to her parted lips. "Or did you invite me to your coach for some other decadent purpose?"

She raised an eyebrow. "Such as?"

The corner of his mouth curled up in a devilish grin. "I'm not sure, darling, but you seemed rather determined to lure me out of there. Where do you live? Is it far? Or do you have some other plan for me? A hotel perhaps, or a long, leisurely drive through the city?"

The coach lurched forward and pulled away from the curb.

Prince Nicholas's eyes remained fixed on hers, and he smiled. "A drive it is, then."

With a simmering look of desire, he kissed the side of her neck, and the moist heat of his lips lifted her into a dreamlike cloud of arousal. Letting her head fall back on the seat cushion, she laid her hands on the gold epaulets on his broad shoulders and closed her eyes. How relaxed she felt in his arms.

It wasn't supposed to be like this. She wasn't supposed to let it go this far. . . .

Nicholas continued to lay a trail of hot kisses across her collarbone and down to her cleavage. "You taste sweet, my darling," he whispered. "Like honey."

Then he lifted his head and gazed intently at her for a heart-wrenching moment.

Slowly he reached up and pulled his own mask away.

Tossing it to the floor, he said, "I am glad I found you tonight, and that you dragged me out of there."

Seeing his whole face for the first time in the golden lamplight caused a shiver in her heart—a sudden twinge of uncertainty. Or perhaps a better word was regret, for what she was about to do to him.

What was it about this man? she wondered frantically. Was she foolish to think there was something more between them than a devious plot on her part, and a casual sexual seduction on his? Perhaps he made all women feel this way when he held them in his arms, as if there were something deep and profound between them. True love at first sight, so to speak.

She didn't love him. No, of course she didn't. To her, he was just a means to an end.

"May I have the pleasure of removing your mask, Véronique?" he asked. "I would like to see your face."

She laid her gloved fingers upon it to hold it securely in place. "But isn't this part of the allure?"

Her voice was full of a confident, teasing melody, but she felt her lip twitch at the dishonesty, for they were alone now, like true lovers. She reminded herself that she was being paid to seduce him, and very soon the mood in the coach was going to take a severe turn.

He surprised her then, by sitting back, slouching in the seat, and grasping her gloved hand. He looked down at it with curiosity as he weaved his fingers through hers. "You still haven't told me your full name. Why ever not? Do you feel you must keep secrets from me? Is it because of who I am?"

A ball of heat caught fire in her belly. "I didn't think the details of my identity—or yours—should matter to either one of us tonight. Napoléon will soon be dealt with, and for that reason, you won't be in Paris much longer. Besides, I am no fool. I know your reputation. You want a single night of pleasure with me, no strings attached, isn't that right?"

He paused. "Is that really what you think of me? Of *this*?"

She chose her words carefully. "Am I wrong?"

He said nothing while he rubbed the pad of his thumb over the back of her gloved hand. Then he raised it to his lips.

"I don't know what has been happening to me lately," he confessed with eyes closed. "I am not myself."

"How so?"

He shook his head as if he had no answer to give; then he looked at her. "Perhaps it is the end of this bloody war. The world seems different somehow. Or maybe it's the fact that my brother now has a wife and a son, and my sister has gone off to become a married woman as well."

"Do they seem happy?" Véronique asked, curious about his perceptions of the world, and his illustrious family.

"My brother is happy. I am not sure about my sister. She is in Austria now, and I worry for her."

"She is married to the future emperor. I am sure she will be fine." Véronique looked out the window and wished she did not have to do what she must this evening. She wanted things to be different. "I heard that her husband was wounded at Waterloo."

"Yes, but the archduke is on the mend. Thank heavens for that." Nicholas was slouched very low in the seat with his head tilted back. He closed his eyes again. "Did you lose anyone at Waterloo, Véronique?"

She remembered certain days of the war and thought it would be best to avoid that painful subject. So she turned toward him again, her body at an angle, and rested her cheek on a hand. "We lost a neighbor—a young man who had been a playmate for my sister and me when we were young."

Nicholas opened his eyes and regarded her in the dim lamplight. "You have a sister? Younger or older?"

"She is nineteen and in love with a gentleman who cannot marry her."

He frowned. "Why not?"

"His parents will not approve the match. They have threatened to disinherit him if he makes a promise to her. They do not consider our family worthy enough for their son. He is a viscount," she explained with a sigh. "My father owns a lovely piece of property. It borders theirs, but he has no title, and money is . . ." She swallowed hard. "The war was hard on us."

A shiver moved through her, and as the coach rolled on, she found she could not avoid the truth after all.

"I did not tell you everything just now," she continued. "We lost more than a neighbor. Both my older brothers . . . very early during Bonaparte's campaigns."

Nicholas's dark brows pulled together in a frown. "So your family . . . they are Bonapartists?"

She shook her head. "Not anymore. It's been years since that Corsican tyrant had a single shred of loyalty from us. We are relieved the king is back on the throne, but my father—" She paused again. "—he is not the same man he once was. He has taken to gambling and drinking."

Nicholas raised her hand to his lips and kissed it tenderly. "I am sorry to hear that, Véronique. I know what it's like to lose someone."

Her heart warmed at the kindness in his words, and for a moment she forgot what she was doing here. All that seemed to matter was the way he made her *feel*—like a woman who was meant to be loved.

By him.

But this was not love.

Still . . . there was something strangely enchanting about this encounter.

"You are referring to your father, the king?" she asked, in response to his last comment, for it was a well-known fact that the king of Petersbourg had been lethally poisoned the previous year.

Nicholas continued to kiss her hand and began to journey up her wrist while she tingled all over with pleasure. "And my mother died when I was very young. They say I took it hard."

"You don't remember?"

He seemed lost in thought, or very sleepy. . . . "I remember everything."

The coach rocked back and forth as they made their way to the outskirts of the city.

"God, I'm tired all of a sudden," he said as he reached out to pull her into his arms. "Come here, I want to hold you."

She snuggled closer and rested her cheek on his shoulder.

"You smell good," he whispered as he kissed the top of her head.

He smelled good, too. Véronique turned her face into the crimson wool of his jacket, which was decorated with a navy sash and a black belt with brass buttons. Closing her eyes, she inhaled in the delectable scent of his body.

He was a handsome royal prince, and his clothes smelled clean and regal, like nothing she'd ever smelled before.

She wanted to know so much more about him. If only they could continue talking this way, but the drug was taking effect. Soon he would be unconscious, they would reach the little farmhouse on the outskirts of the city, and everything would change. He would not say caring words to her when he learned what she had done to him.

She sat very still for the next few minutes. She did not move a muscle, nor did she initiate any further conversation. When the sound of his breathing grew slow and even, she carefully lifted her head to study his profile.

What a beautiful man he was. His dark features were perfectly sculpted. He had the enticing aura of someone born to be a woman's dream lover, her Prince Charming in every way. It was almost comical that he was a true prince.

In that regard, his brother, King Randolph, would no doubt take notice of his mysterious disappearance from the Paris ball and leave no stone unturned in the quest to locate him and punish those responsible for the abduction.

With a sudden pang of dread for all that she would face in the coming weeks, Véronique carefully disentangled herself from Nicholas's embrace, placed his arm gently upon his lap, and slid across to the opposite facing seat.

She watched him for a long time and wondered what he would think of her when he discovered her treachery.

She regretted it already, for there had been something truly extraordinary between them this evening. It was both sexually exciting and surprisingly intimate in a way she had not expected. As a result, this mercenary task had become a secret indulgence. For a while, she had forgotten that this was wrong, and that she was a corrupt, false-hearted charlatan.

If things were different, she would not have chosen this path for herself, but she was duty-bound to her family. She could not allow their entire world to come crashing down around them. Véronique would therefore do what was required and pray that somehow she would emerge unscathed.

The coach pulled to a halt, and she peered out the window.

The door flew open suddenly and banged against the outside panel. Véronique frowned at her sister, Gabrielle, who wore a black cloak with the hood pulled up to hide her fiery red hair.

"For pity's sake, be quiet," Véronique whispered. "We must be careful not to wake him."

Gabrielle grabbed hold of the rail and swung into the dimly lit interior. She took a seat beside Véronique and stared with fascination at Prince Nicholas, who was sprawled out on the opposite seat like a gorgeous work of art. He slept soundly.

"How long has he been out?" Gabrielle asked.

Véronique removed her mask and gloves and rubbed her fingers over her cheeks where the stiff fabric had been too tight. "Not long. Ten minutes perhaps?"

Gabrielle inclined her head and leaned a little closer. "Upon my word, he is deadly handsome. How in the world did you keep your head?"

"It wasn't easy, I assure you."

"Did he kiss you?"

Véronique let her memory take her back to those first few moments. . . .

"Not on the mouth."

Gabrielle's eyebrows lifted. "Not on the mouth?" She spoke as if scandalized, but Véronique knew her sister was thrilled at the possibilities. "Care to explain?"

"No," Véronique said. "There's no time for that. I don't know how long he will sleep. Did you bring the rope?"

Gabrielle pulled it from her cloak—like a rabbit out of a hat. "I've got it right here. Which one of us gets to do the honors?"

Véronique immediately snatched the rope from her sister. "I caught him," she said, "so it's only right that I get to bag him."

Chapter Two

Nicholas woke to an excruciating pain in his head—a state that felt worse than death.

Not that he knew what death felt like, but it was probably better than this. He tried to sit up.

Lord help him. . . .

His brain was throbbing in his skull like a hammer on a bass drum, and his stomach was churning like the Baltic. He shut his eyes and lay back down, very still, knowing that if he tried a second time to sit up, he would likely retch up the contents of his stomach, and he needed to get his bearings first.

Which direction should he roll to hit the chamber pot? Or at least to avoid a bed partner, if there was one.

He remembered enough about the night before to know that he had left the ball with Véronique.

Véronique . . .

He opened his eyes and blinked up at the green silk canopy in the bright morning sunlight. Was he in her bed? Or had she taken him to a hotel? Why couldn't he remember?

Swallowing hard over the intense wave of nausea

that rose up in him at the mere idea of moving, he pressed the heels of his hands to his forehead and shut his eyes again. A dizzying, throbbing sensation engulfed him. The bed was spinning like a top.

Nicholas carefully glanced in the direction of the pillow beside him, but found it to be vacant. Thank God for that.

Squinting in the blinding sunlight streaming in through the windows, he finally managed to lean up on an elbow and look around the unfamiliar bedchamber. The walls were papered in a busy floral pattern, and the bed itself was an ostentatious display of extravagant French opulence. It was ornately sculpted with images of leaves and cherubs, and covered in shiny gilt. Positively sickening.

The windows were trimmed in heavy silk drapes and valances in a blue floral fabric to match the walls. The patterns were more blinding than the sun.

The furniture was also very French, with a showy parade of silly china knickknacks and vases on top of every surface.

He looked down at himself as well and saw that he was still wearing his clothes from the night before. Minus his sword and boots.

Where the devil was he? And where was Véronique?

He took another moment to recover from his uncomfortable awakening and managed to toss the covers aside and sit up on the edge of the bed.

The room began to spin faster, and his brain throbbed.

He glanced around for the bellpull. Ah, there it was, on the opposite side of the bed. Slowly, he lay back and managed to roll in that direction, then put his feet on the floor and stood, never letting go of the corner bedpost.

At last he reached the velvet-covered rope and tugged

it three times. Then he lay back down again and closed his eyes to wait.

A half hour must have passed, maybe more. He wasn't sure. No one came.

Again, he struggled to his feet and tugged harder on the bellpull. God, he felt like a decrepit old man. He could barely stand up straight.

Spotting a pitcher of water on the washstand, he made his way to it and poured a glass, which he sipped slowly.

Still in a terrible state of agony, he walked to the window to look outside.

Down below, an impressive manicured garden and rectangular pond with an enormous fountain in the center provided a spectacular view. Beyond that, in the distance, he could see what he guessed to be the English Channel. How far had they driven last night?

The water sparkled turquoise in the sun. There were a number of ships moored in close proximity to one another, not far from a port village.

Nicholas frowned as he wondered if Bonaparte was on one of those ships. Perhaps it was not the English Channel. Perhaps it was the Atlantic. Was this Rochefort?

Dammit. He needed to know where he was.

Forgetting his headache and swimming stomach, he stalked to the door and grabbed hold of the knob, only to discover that he was locked in.

He rattled and tugged at it, then slammed his shoulder up against it, but to no avail. The exit was impenetrable.

The realization that he was a prisoner in this room struck him rather violently, but he swept the notion aside, for surely that could not be. Perhaps Véronique only meant to keep his presence here in her bedchamber a secret, for he was, after all, a royal prince, and they had sneaked out of a ballroom together for a dalliance that could hardly be called proper.

Feeling ill again and deciding that he should not sound an alarm just yet, he walked unsteadily back to the bed and collapsed on top of the covers to wait for her return. Hopefully by that time, the headache would have subsided and a servant would have brought him some breakfast.

He pulled the pillow over his head and fell back to sleep almost instantly.

Véronique was just about to spear her roast lamb with a fork when Gabrielle came bursting through the door.

"He is awake, and he is not happy. You had best come quickly. He is causing a ruckus."

Véronique set down her utensils, removed her napkin from her lap, and tossed it onto the table. Her dinner had been brought to her private chamber by the butler only a few minutes earlier, and she wondered if anyone else had heard the commotion.

She and Gabrielle had been placed in this very remote wing of the house to watch over the prince. Why hadn't she heard anything? Perhaps she would need to move to a closer room.

Following Gabrielle out into the corridor, she fought to calm her heart and prepare herself for Prince Nicholas's wrath. She would have to answer any questions he had through the door, for she'd received very strict instructions to keep him contained until Lord d'Entremont arrived on Tuesday.

That was three days from now.

As she hurried down the wide carpeted corridor, the ruckus grew louder and more violent. It sounded as if she and Gabrielle had trapped some sort of wild beast. He was pounding against the door and shouting like an ogre.

Bang! Bang! Bang!

"I've had enough, damn you! Open this bloody door before I break it down and tear someone's throat out!"

Véronique stopped dead in her tracks and met Gabrielle's stricken eyes. "Good heavens."

"What did I tell you?" Gabby replied. "He is not pleased. What if he *does* break down the door? Perhaps I should fetch a weapon."

Véronique held up a hand. "We must remain calm. I'm sure there will be no need for weapons. I will talk to him."

Bang! Bang! Bang! "Who's out there! Open the f——ing door!"

Véronique gasped and stepped back in horror, then recovered from her shock and strode forward to pound her own fist on the door. "Watch your tongue, sir! There are women out here!"

Her retort was met with silence, while her heart pummelled her rib cage and fired her blood through her veins like a white-hot flood of terror.

"Is that you, Véronique?" he asked in a much calmer voice.

She inhaled shakily. "Yes, it is, Your Highness, and I apologize for the locked door. Are you all right in there? Do you require anything?"

Again, her words were met with silence. She glanced at Gabrielle, who took hold of her hand as she used to do when they were young girls and she needed comfort and reassurance for some reason.

Véronique squeezed her hand and nodded to convey that everything would be fine. In all honesty, however, she felt as if they had captured a lion, and the only thing standing between them and its sharp teeth was this single wooden door.

"I'm well enough," he replied, sounding surprisingly polite after the rather disturbing vocal display mere seconds ago. "But why is the door locked, darling? Do you not have a key?"

She stepped closer. "I am sorry, I do not," she explained, and said nothing more.

He was quiet again, and she could well imagine that he was struggling to make sense of things while listening carefully up against the door.

She nervously cleared her throat. Her body was buzzing with awareness. She felt extraordinarily alert.

The silence went on and on.

"Your Highness?" she said. "Are you there?"

Of course he was there. He was locked inside.

The floorboards creaked on the other side of the door. "*Why* is the door locked?" he asked, and she recognized the height of his agitation.

"Because I am not supposed to let you out. You are to remain here until Tuesday, when Lord d'Entremont arrives. I believe he wishes to speak to you about something. If you will notice, there are fresh clean clothes for you in the wardrobe."

"Who is Lord d'Entremont? And where are we?" Nicholas asked, ignoring her reference to the clothes.

"He is a French marquis, and this is his house. We are near Dieppe."

He paused. "Have I met him before?"

"I do not know."

Another pause. "What does he wish to speak with me about?"

"I am sorry . . . but I do not know the answer to that question either."

The sound of Nicholas's heavy footsteps pacing back and forth behind the door caused her to look sharply at the doorknob. She was expecting him to break through at any second, and was tempted to open the door to avoid such a calamity, for she was not equipped to do battle with him physically. But she could not risk that he might flee before d'Entremont arrived.

"What is your relationship to the marquis?" he asked.

Gabrielle squeezed Véronique's hand. "I am simply—" She hesitated, for she wasn't sure how to explain it. "—I am his courier, so to speak."

The pacing stopped. "Are you telling me that you were hired to deliver me here? That he is paying you?"

She saw no benefit in lying to Nicholas. He was not a fool. He was already seeing this plot for what it was, and he would only grow more frustrated if she withheld information from him. She would therefore reveal as much as she could.

"That is correct," she said, "but I have not yet been paid. I will receive nothing until he arrives and speaks to you."

"On Tuesday," Nicholas added.

She labored to keep her breathing steady and under control, even while this strange conversation from opposite sides of a locked door was taking a dreadful toll on her nerves.

"Yes."

Again he was quiet, then: "You are aware—I hope—that what you have done is against the law. It is kidnapping, Véronique, and I am a person who will most definitely be missed. I am a prince of Petersbourg, here in France for diplomatic purposes. When my brother finds out what has occurred, there will be serious consequences. Are you sure you want to be involved in such a plot? If you unlock this door now and take me back to Paris tonight, I give you my word that I will not press charges against you. I don't even know your last name, for pity's sake. Let me out of here now, take me back to Paris, and I will allow you to simply walk away from this. No questions asked. Then I will deal with d'Entremont separately."

Her mind was now swimming in panic, but she would not be deterred. She had promised the marquis that she would deliver and hold Prince Nicholas here until Tuesday, and she would not let anything keep her from doing so, for they had an agreement, and she needed the marquis to fulfill his part of it.

"I am sorry, Your Highness, but I cannot take you back to Paris. You must remain here."

His angry footsteps approached the door, and he banged so hard on it that it rattled in the jamb. Both she and Gabrielle jumped back to the opposite wall, as if he were coming at them with a knife and there was no door to protect them.

But there *was* a door, and they were safe. At least for now. She must not lose her courage.

"What does he want to see me about?" Nicholas asked again.

"I told you before, I don't know."

"Does it have something to do with Bonaparte?"

Véronique gave no answer, for she did not know the marquis's intentions, nor did it matter. She only wanted her house back.

"Does he want me to negotiate for the emperor's freedom? Because I assure you, he will be wasting his time discussing such a thing with me, especially if he means to get what he wants through barbaric methods such as this."

"Please believe me, Your Highness. I have no idea

why he wants to see you. He did not share that information with me."

Gabrielle leaned close to her and whispered, "You don't think the marquis will harm him, do you?"

Véronique immediately put her finger to her lips to hush her sister.

"Who is that?" Nicholas asked. "Who is with you?"

"No one," Véronique replied. "I was talking to myself."

He was quiet for a few heated seconds, and all Véronique wanted to do was flee. She didn't want to have anything more to do with this, but she must weather it. She must.

"Whatever he is paying you," Nicholas said, "I will double it."

Gabrielle raised an eyebrow.

Véronique shook her head and mouthed the word *no*.

Gabby rolled her eyes and shrugged in defeat. Then she took hold of Véronique's arm and pulled her down the hall, farther away from the door. "Why can't we just put a bullet in his brain?" she whispered.

"I hope you are not referring to the prince," Véronique whispered in reply.

"Of course not. It's Lord d'Entremont who needs to be murdered. Or locked up—and somewhere a lot worse than this. Where can we find a dark dungeon with rats?"

Again, Véronique lifted a finger to say *hush*, and returned to the door.

"I can hear you whispering," Nicholas said. "I know you are not working alone, so I will ask again. Take me back to Paris tonight, and I will triple whatever he is paying you."

Véronique sighed heavily. "I told you that we cannot accept your offer. Again, I apologize for this, Your

Highness. We do not mean to cause you any distress or discomfort, but you must wait for Lord d'Entremont. Do you have everything you need? Are you comfortable?"

Silence again. Then: "Am I comfortable? *Are you bloody insane?*"

Véronique stepped forward and placed her open hand flat on the door. "Please be patient, sir. I will make sure dinner is brought to you posthaste, and I will try to make this as painless as possible. You must trust me."

She didn't feel quite right speaking those words, however, because she had no idea what the marquis intended to do with Prince Nicholas when he arrived. Or why he had wanted him brought here in the first place.

"What I'd really like to do is wring your neck," Nicholas said in a quiet, threatening voice that caused her blood to run cold in her veins.

The memory of their thrilling encounter at the ball danced through her mind. She closed her eyes and rested her forehead against the door as she recalled the touch of his lips on her neck, and the way he spoke about the loss of his father, and other intimate things. He probably regretted all of that now. Regretted ever setting eyes on her, which filled her with sadness, for there would never be another flirtation with this man, nor any more intimate conversations.

"I would like to say that was uncalled for," she replied, "but I suppose I deserve it."

"Yes. That and a whole lot more. You're making a mistake, Véronique."

She had a knot in her stomach the size of a turnip, but she could not let her emotions steer her away from this task. She had been warned that Prince Nicholas was a handsome and charismatic rogue who enjoyed sexual conquests. She could not allow herself to fall for his charms—though he was hardly charming at the moment when he expressed such an urgent desire to wring her neck.

"I will have a meal sent to you now," she said, stepping away from the door. "And you are correct. I am not working alone, so there is no point trying to break down the door and escape. There are guards here," she lied, "and no one will care if you continue to shout and pound on the door. You will only tire yourself. I therefore suggest that you make yourself comfortable and read one of the books on the shelf by the window. I was told that Lord d'Entremont selected those books for you personally. They came from his private library."

"Are you suggesting I should feel honored?"

Véronique wiped the back of her hand across her perspiring forehead. "I am simply trying to make this as painless as possible for you, sir. Now I must go and arrange for your dinner."

Turning away, she met Gabrielle's concerned gaze and signaled for her to follow quickly.

Véronique was surprised that her prisoner offered no further protest. She and her sister were able to escape to the staircase—without hearing any more angry or profane demands.

Bloody hell, he wanted to do far worse than wring her neck. . . .

Nicholas backed away from the door and curled his hands into tight, murderous fists.

When he thought about how Véronique had smiled at him from beneath that bejeweled mask when their eyes first met at the ball—how she had appeared so demure and innocent—he wanted to spit. Every detail of their encounter had been part of this sinister plot to lure him to her coach, drug him, and abduct him in the dead of night to the French coast.

Was Véronique even her real name?

Damn it all to hell.

Nicholas turned away from the door, stalked to the window, and looked out at the Channel.

God help her when he found a way out of this room, for he would not rest until she was rotting away in a prison somewhere, just as Napoléon would soon be doing.

Chapter Three

A supper tray arrived through a secret compartment in the wall, which enraged Nicholas to a heightened degree after he'd spent a full hour waiting at the door, listening for footsteps, while brandishing a vase over his head.

Nevertheless, when he heard the sound of a sliding door and the switch of a latch behind a picture frame, and discovered a hot dinner of roast lamb with spiced gravy and a full bottle of fine French wine, he was not entirely disappointed, for he needed his sustenance if he was going to deal with his captors effectively.

And who were his captors, exactly? he wondered as he wolfed down the tender meat and enjoyed more than half the bottle of wine, followed by a dessert of flaky raspberry pie and a selection of sweet biscuits and cream.

As soon as he finished the meal, he slid the knife into his breast pocket and set the bottle on his bedside table.

When the sun went down he found matches on the mantel, briefly considered setting the bed on fire to force someone to open the door, but decided against such a drastic escape strategy in case everyone decided to save themselves and leave him to burn.

Instead, he lit the lamp on the desk and inspected the collection of books that had been selected for him by the mysterious marquis himself.

Who the hell was he, and why did he think he could abduct a prince and live to tell about it? It's not as if the marquis was anonymous. Nicholas knew where he lived.

Ah, Christ. That did not bode well.

What the devil was the man up to? What did he want?

Véronique woke the following morning to the sound of glass smashing and a woman screaming outside.

Tossing the covers aside, she leaped out of bed and ran to the window. Down below on the flagstone terrace was a desk and chair, both smashed to bits, and her sister, Gabrielle, was looking up at Prince Nicholas's window and shouting. *"Are you mad? You could have killed me!"* She pointed a finger at him. "Go ahead and try. Unless you have wings, sir, you'll fall to your death!"

Was he trying to climb out the window?

Not bothering to pull on a robe, Véronique dashed to the door in her nightdress and flew into the corridor. Her hair was fluttering about her shoulders when she reached the prince's door and banged on it with a fist.

"Prince Nicholas! What have you done? You mustn't endanger yourself! And please do not vandalize the marquis's property! I hear he values his furniture."

Values his furniture? Oh, that was convincing. She grimaced at herself.

"Please come to the door and talk to me," she continued in a calming voice. "How can I help you?"

She heard the terrifying sound of his heavy boots pounding across the floor and experienced a renewed surge of panic.

Again she found herself recalling those first few moments in the coach when he'd kissed her—when she feared she might forget her purpose and allow him to ravish her.

She could not imagine being alone with him now. He was a beast with a dangerous roar.

Shaking away such imaginings, she laid her open hand on the door and listened. "Are you there?"

"Yes, I am here," he replied from the other side. His voice was low and wrathful, very close to the door.

"You shouldn't have done that," she said. "You could have hurt someone."

"Like your sister?" he replied. "And don't pretend that's not who she is. The resemblance is obvious, except she has red hair and you are very blond."

Damn him. She had hoped to keep Gabrielle's presence here a secret, but it was too late now. He knew. They would have to be very careful when this was over. They would have to hide for a while.

"Yes, that was my sister," she confessed. "I do not appreciate you frightening her like that."

"*Frightening* her?" he scoffed. "She didn't appear the least bit frightened. In fact, she has quite a colorful vocabulary. She called me a despicable rogue—among other things—which was wholly unfair, since I am the victim here, not she."

"Two steps to the left and she would have been victimized quite mortally," Véronique argued. "That was very dangerous, sir. Do not do it again."

"I'll do whatever I damn well please, Véronique— and worse—if you do not open this door in the next three minutes."

Véronique swallowed over her rising impatience. "I cannot do that. Not until Lord d'Entremont arrives."

When at last Nicholas spoke, his tone was only slightly less threatening. "Are you afraid I will try to escape?"

"Yes," she replied. "That is my main concern. If you are not here when the marquis arrives, I will not be paid what he has promised me."

"It cannot be money that you want," Nicholas said. "Otherwise, you would have accepted my offer to triple the amount. Does he have some sort of hold over you? Is it blackmail?"

Véronique could almost feel the heat of her unease burning through her veins, for it was no small matter to have a powerful prince asking about her welfare, as if he actually cared.

She did not dare tell him anything, however, for she could not be sure he was not simply manipulating her to get what he wanted. She could not be sure he would not use it against her somehow.

At the same time, she wanted desperately to confide in him and reveal Lord d'Entremont's cruelty and unfairness. She wanted to say horrible things about the marquis, confess her loathing, and drag his name through the mud, but she could not. Not now, when her home hung in the balance, and he held control of everything.

"I do not wish to say one way or the other," she carefully replied.

"Well, that is as good as a yes." Nicholas was quiet for a moment; then he scratched a finger against the door, which made her draw back in surprise.

"What if I promise not to leave?" he softly said. "What if I give you my word as a gentleman that I will remain here inside the house until Tuesday?"

His voice was soothing, and she found herself listening to his request, considering whether or not she could trust him. Then she struggled to knock some sense into herself. "I cannot take that chance."

"Why? Do you not trust my word? Do you believe I would endanger you? All I ask is to be treated like a guest, not a prisoner."

"You just threw a desk out the window, sir. That is hardly the behavior of a proper guest."

He paused. "I was at my wit's end. I needed to do *something* to get your attention."

There was a spark of flirtation in his tone, which filled her with mistrust. Véronique knew that he wanted something from her—namely his freedom—and he would likely say anything to get it.

"I am sorry," she firmly said. "You must be patient and wait until Tuesday. Is there anything else I can do for you? More books perhaps? Do you have a set of playing cards in there?"

She heard the sound of something going *plunk* against the door. His forehead?

Oh, she was not enjoying this. She didn't want to keep him locked up. She wanted to open the door and see him. Talk to him. Apologize for flirting with him, and slipping laudanum into his champagne glass.

"Please, Véronique," he said. "I am begging you. If you unlock the door, I promise I will behave."

Her heart squeezed painfully in her chest, and again she had to remember that he was a seductive genius. He knew how to play women like musical instruments.

"Try to think of this as a holiday . . . some much-needed time to yourself to do nothing but lie around and daydream. Surely a man in your position rarely enjoys such a luxury."

She heard his finger scratch the door again and moved closer to press her ear up against it. She could hear him breathing.

"I wish you would trust me," he whispered, so close, only an inch away, as if he knew exactly where her ear was resting.

Her body grew warm. It felt as if he were close enough to touch. She could almost feel his breath on her neck.

"What does he hold over you?" Nicholas asked. "Tell me. I can help you. You and your sister."

She forced herself to back away. "No, I don't think you can."

But that wasn't entirely true. He was a prince. He could do anything. She simply wasn't sure that she could trust him to follow through on such a promise. Not after what she had done to him.

"Please do not make this more difficult than it already is," she said. "Just wait for the marquis."

"Fine," he replied. "If that's the way it must be. But I will ask something of you in return."

"Yes?"

A few seconds passed. Did he even know what he wanted to ask?

"I promise not to destroy any more furniture," he said, "or throw anything out the window—myself included—if you will come again and talk to me, to help pass the time. Perhaps bring a chair and stay awhile."

Véronique wasn't sure if he genuinely desired her company, or if this was a clever scheme to trick her into eventually opening the door for him.

It didn't matter, she supposed, because she wasn't

going to break. She had come this far. The hard part was over. She'd be a fool to throw it all away now.

"Fine," she said, "I will return in a short while after I am dressed."

"You're not dressed?" he inquired, almost playfully. "You arc truly bent upon torturing me, aren't you?"

Véronique couldn't help but chuckle at the flattery, even while she suspected it was another form of trickery.

"You're wasting your time if you think you'll be able to charm me into setting you free," she told him. "I know your reputation, remember?"

"I remember a lot of things."

Dear Lord. He was impossibly charming when he wanted to be. Just the sound of his voice sent her spinning back into the excitement of their brief encounter in the coach, when he had touched her so enticingly.

But she must be sensible. There could be no further intimacies between them.

"I will return later," she said decorously as she turned to go. She stopped, however, when she spotted Pierre at the far end of the corridor, leaning one shoulder against the wall, picking at his teeth with a small stick as he watched her.

Pierre . . . who had driven the coach and helped carry Nicholas to this room. Pierre . . . who held the key to the lock and was the only person who could open the compartment to deliver meals to the prince. . . .

Suddenly conscious of her improper state of dress, Véronique gathered her collar in a fist and closed it about her neck as she approached him.

"What are you doing here?" she asked. "And how long have you been listening?"

"Long enough," he replied. "After the commotion on the terrace, I had to check on His Royal High and

Mighty. The marquis won't be pleased when he finds out about that desk."

Véronique raised her chin. "Do not look at me as if it is my fault. The marquis will have no one to blame but himself. I would consider it the proper cost of locking a man up against his will."

Pierre always seemed to wear a permanent scowl on his face, and this morning was no different. "Someone's going to have to clean that up," he said, "and it ain't gonna be me."

She squared her shoulders. "Why *not* you? You're as much a part of this as I am."

"I have to go fetch him his breakfast."

She narrowed her eyes. "Then I suggest you alert the butler. Though I suspect he's already aware of the situation."

Pierre had made it clear when they arrived that he did not get on well with the servants. He worked among them, but considered himself apart—and above them. He wouldn't enjoy having to speak to the butler about such a matter, for the butler was an intimidating man and did not consider Pierre to be his superior.

Véronique tried to shoulder her way past Pierre, but he grabbed hold of her arm. "I've got my eye on you."

He gazed leeringly down the length of her body.

Véronique pulled her arm free from his grasp, gave him a fierce look of warning, and quickly headed back to her own chamber.

Chapter Four

Nicholas was pacing back and forth in front of the bed when the sound of the sliding door in the wall alerted him to the arrival of breakfast.

Immediately, he moved to the large portrait that swung open on squeaky hinges, and opened a second door that slid upward like a sash window. There, in the large compartment, he found a tray with eggs, toast, and coffee. The aroma filled his nostrils and fed his obsessive desire to find a way out of here.

After removing the tray, he set it on the nearby chest of drawers, then tried again to open the second sliding door at the back, but it was locked securely, as it had been the night before.

He had checked behind all the other portraits in the room to search for another means of escape, but found nothing. It was as if this room had been constructed for the purpose of keeping someone prisoner and delivering meals.

What sort of place was this, and what did the French lord want from him?

He would find out soon enough, he supposed. In the

meantime, he must keep up his strength and prepare for his meeting with the marquis. Or preferably, escape before that moment arrived. So he dug into his breakfast and ate heartily.

As he spooned some fruit preserves onto a slice of toast and bit into it, he considered his plan for the day. His best hope was Véronique. He would do what he must to win her trust before Tuesday. In fact, he would do whatever was required, for he didn't know what the marquis had planned for him.

It was going to be an interesting day, he realized, because despite all the charm he was about to send through that locked door, he still wanted to wring her bloody neck, and would take great pleasure in doing so, as soon as he had the chance.

"Slow down, you're going too fast," Gabrielle complained as she struggled awkwardly to help Véronique carry the blue upholstered chair down the corridor toward the prince's chamber.

"Try to keep up," Véronique replied, walking backwards. "Is that better?"

"Yes, but what are you going to do in this chair all day? What will he want to talk about? Does he want you to read to him, or sing to him?"

Véronique glanced over her shoulder to ensure she didn't bump into anything. "I'm not certain. All he said was that he wanted company to help pass the time."

Shuffling along in their heavy skirts, fumbling with the chair, they finally reached the prince's chamber and set their cargo down.

"Be careful," Gabrielle whispered. "He might have some dastardly plan in mind."

They both turned their heads at the sound of Nicholas striding across the floor inside the locked room.

"Is that you, Véronique?" he asked.

"Yes. I am here with Gabrielle. She helped me carry the chair."

"Were there no servants at hand to perform such a task?"

Gabrielle's eyes shot to Véronique's, and she frowned.

"There are plenty of servants here," Véronique explained, "but the marquis has instructed them to keep out of this wing until he returns."

"Ah, so my imprisonment is a secret."

"Yes, Your Highness."

He paused. "What about the driver who brought me here? Has he been sworn to secrecy as well?"

"Yes."

They were all quiet.

"Is your sister still with you?" he asked.

Véronique gestured for Gabby to reply.

"Yes, Your Highness," she said. "I am here."

Silence again.

"We have not been formally introduced," he said. "I am Prince Nicholas of Petersbourg. It is a pleasure to make your acquaintance."

Gabrielle couldn't help herself. She curtsied. It was all very strange. "It is an honor, sir."

"Yes . . . well, I must apologize for nearly crushing you with the desk earlier today. It was not my intention. I simply didn't see you there."

"Apology accepted," she replied. Then she darted a glance at Véronique and grinned like a schoolgirl before mouthing the words: *He's lovely.*

Véronique put her hands on Gabby's shoulders and turned her around to face the other direction. "My sister was just leaving," she said.

With a teasing smirk, Gabby headed back to their own chamber.

A moment later, Véronique sat down, while the sound of a chair being dragged across the floor inside the room kept her waiting. She heard Nicholas sit down as well.

"What do you wish to talk about?" she asked. All her senses drummed with awareness as she leaned forward. His chair creaked as he settled into it.

"You," he replied in a low voice. "Put your hand up against the door," he added. "Place it flat on the middle panel, halfway down."

"Why?"

"It's lonely in here, Véronique, and I have not been able to think of much else besides the other night when you lured me out of the ball. Have *you* thought about it?"

She tried to fight it, but was compelled to answer honestly. "Yes, I have."

Closing her eyes, she imagined his open palm on the other side, only an inch or so away, and ran the pad of a finger over the smooth texture of the wood.

"What specifically do you think about?" he asked.

Her heart fluttered like the wings of a bird, and it took some effort to speak in a steady voice. "Our conversations, mostly."

That was a lie.

He was quiet. "You don't think of how we danced? Or how it felt when we were finally alone together in the coach, and I held you in my arms? Or was the spark between us all an act?"

"It was not an act," she said. "But that is irrelevant, because we will not see each other again after this. Besides, I am not the sort of woman who routinely leaves masked balls with strangers. That part, at least, was an act."

"I see."

Her arm was growing tired, so she lowered her hands to her lap.

"Is there anything else I should know that was not real?" he asked. "You are not married, are you? Or betrothed to someone?"

"No, I am unwed."

"With no chaperone that night."

"The masks made it possible," she explained. "I entered without revealing my true identity to anyone."

"Not even to me," he replied with a sigh.

She heard him stand up and walk away. Leaning close, she listened carefully. . . .

"I am pouring a glass of wine for myself," he explained, as if he could sense her curiosity. "Pity you are not in here with me. I would pour you a glass as well." He returned to his chair. "But that would be improper— for me to invite an unwed lady, such as yourself, into the private chamber where I sleep. Unfortunately I do not have a reception room to make it respectable." He paused. "This is a rather odd room. Have you been inside?"

"Yes," she admitted, "on the night we brought you here. Pierre carried you in, and I made sure you were comfortable before we left you."

She heard him tap his finger three times against the wineglass. "Was it *you* who removed my jacket, shirt, and boots?"

"Yes." There was no point in being coy, especially when she was reminded of his beautiful half-naked form on the bed.

His chair creaked. She imagined him lounging back in it with his long, muscular legs stretched out before him.

"I find it rather unsettling," he said, "that there is a sliding door for the delivery of supper trays. I wonder how many others have been held captive in this room, and for what purpose."

"I could hazard a guess," she replied, "but I shouldn't speculate. I could always ask Pierre. He has lived here, in this wing, all his life."

"Is he related to the marquis?" Nicholas asked.

Sadly, she knew the whole sordid story of Pierre's history here at d'Entremont Manor. His presence was no secret in the village. It had been a source of gossip for years.

"He is, in a way," she replied, "for he is the illegitimate son of the marquis's younger sister. She fell in love with one of the grooms when she was only sixteen. When it was discovered that she was carrying his child, the young man in question was found floating dead in the fishpond. She was locked up in the house during her confinement, and perhaps this was her room. Regrettably, she died on the birthing bed, but the child survived. That child is Pierre."

"So he is the marquis's nephew. I thought he was a servant."

"He was always treated like one." Véronique laid her hand on the door again and listened for any sounds. "From what I understand, when the current Lord d'Entremont inherited his title and became master of the house, he was more generous with Pierre, for he loved his sister. That is why Pierre lives in this wing and not with the other servants. He serves the marquis quite faithfully as his driver and private secretary, though the marquis still refuses to recognize him as his nephew."

"It sounds like a scandalous French novel," Nicholas replied. "Does the marquis have any children of his own?"

Véronique hesitated, for she felt uneasy revealing details of someone else's private life, but supposed it was common knowledge here in France. Besides, she owed nothing to the marquis. To the contrary, he owed a great deal to her.

"Lord d'Entremont had three children at one time, but lost the two eldest daughters to consumption ten years ago. Then he lost his wife to some other illness a short time later."

"And the third child?" Nicholas asked.

Again, she hesitated, for this was personal information and was perhaps part of the reason for the abduction. She had suspected it, but was not yet sure. . . .

"He lost his only son a month ago at Waterloo," she said. "He was a leader in Napoléon's Imperial Guard."

"A very prestigious position," Nicholas replied. "Do you think that has something to do with the marquis wanting to see me? The Petersbourg cavalry was instrumental in Napoléon's defeat on that battlefield. Could it be vengeance?"

She swallowed uneasily. "I don't know. I suppose it could be."

Lord, what was she doing?

"Where is the marquis now?" Nicholas asked. "From where is he traveling?"

She knew then that she had indeed been brought here to be interrogated, not to help pass the time.

Véronique sat with her back ramrod straight, her hands folded on her lap.

"Véronique?"

"Yes, I am here," she quickly said, "and I do not know where the marquis is at the moment. I have been dealing mostly with Pierre since the initial deal was struck."

The chair creaked on the other side of the door. "You must understand that it is not easy for me to remain here," he said, "like a sitting duck."

"I do understand."

"Then why won't you help me?" he asked. "Whatever it is that you need, Véronique, I promise I can give it to you. If only you would offer me some assistance."

"To do what? Escape?"

The chair creaked again as he sat forward and spoke closer to the door. "Yes."

Her heart began to pound at the mere sound of his voice . . . so close to the door while she waited for him to continue.

"If you would only come to my rescue," he whispered, "I would see to it personally that you would be rewarded. Not only would you be exonerated from all charges concerning my kidnapping, but I would ensure that you would have whatever it is that d'Entremont is promising. Won't you please tell me what that is?"

All her instincts were screaming at her to confide in him. To accept his offer. To unlock the door and become his partner in an escape. But could he be trusted to keep his word, and was it even possible for him to help her and Gabrielle? Could he give her back her home if d'Entremont refused to part with it?

"Please come inside," Nicholas softly said. "I want to see you, talk with you. We could help each other."

"Nicholas, please do not ask me."

"But I must," he replied. His tone was silky with a veiled passion that aroused her senses, even though she knew it was a clever manipulation.

"There was something between us the other night," he continued. "Something quite wonderful, as if it were destiny that we should meet. I believed it at the time, and I still believe it now. There is a reason you were chosen for this task, Véronique. You imply that you are trapped by d'Entremont, which is why you agreed to this. But I know you are no villain. *He* is the villain, and I have the power to buy your freedom from him, and erase this crime you have committed. You are not my captor, Véronique. He is. You are my rescuer, and I am yours."

There was a sudden terrible clatter somewhere else in the house, as if a maid had dropped a silver tray on a marble floor. It caused Véronique to jump in her chair. Her gaze darted to the far end of the corridor.

"What was that?" Nicholas asked.

"I am not sure," she replied. "I don't think it was anything."

Then why was her heart pounding as if she had been caught in some secret act of thievery?

"Listen to me, Véronique," he said. "This can all work well in your favor if you will unlock this door and come inside. We can plan something together, find a way out of this. I cannot do it without you, and I do not believe you want to be a part of something as ugly as what this might become. I do not know what the marquis wants from me, but clearly it is not a friendly invitation. This is sinister. I feel it in my bones, as you must feel it, too."

She realized she was nodding her head. She had been uncomfortable about this assignment from the beginning, but had ignored any inclination toward feelings of guilt or doubt. She had intentionally steeled herself into a woman driven by necessity, duty, and love for her family—for she must get her home back from the marquis. Nothing else outside of that mattered . . . until now.

Prince Nicholas had become so much more than a mere package for her to deliver. He was a man—a handsome, regal prince who had aroused her desires and touched something inside her, even when she knew he was manipulating her to get what he wanted. What she felt was something quite unfamiliar, which she did not yet understand.

She didn't want this to turn ugly. That would be a terrible tragedy. She would never be able to live with herself if d'Entremont did something foul, and she did not trust him, for he was no gentleman.

"I do not have a key," she told Nicholas at last. "Pierre has it. But there must be another. The housekeeper would surely have one."

Oh, what was she saying?

"Could you get it from her without Pierre knowing?"

"I could try."

A heavy silence ensued while she considered all the possible consequences of this decision. Was she really going to do this? Was it the right course of action? Or was she letting her emotions, and her desires, rule her intellect?

"We do not have much time," Nicholas said. "D'Entremont will be here in less than two days."

Despite everything, Véronique found herself nodding her head again. "I will do my best. So I must leave you now. Expect me later, at dusk, after the supper trays have been delivered."

She stood up and turned the back of the chair against the wall, then heard the deep timbre of Nicholas's voice behind the door. "When you slip the key into this lock, Véronique, I should warn you about something."

She listened. . . . "Yes?"

His voice, though quiet, possessed a raw, ominous quality. "I *will* need to kiss you."

A sizzling, almost alarming spark of anticipation danced down her spine at the mere thought of being in this man's arms again and accepting his gratitude. She had spent far too many moments over the past two days conjuring him in her imagination, fantasizing about what might have occurred in the coach if she had not put laudanum in his champagne at the ball.

But could she trust him? *Should* she?

Surely this was madness.

"I will return at dusk," she said nevertheless in a steady voice. As steady as she could manage.

Then she hurried back to her room to talk this over with Gabrielle.

Chapter Five

"Are you certain we can trust him?" Gabby asked while Véronique paced back and forth across the thick red carpet. "What if he turns us in for kidnapping and refuses to honor the agreement? What would happen to Mother?"

Véronique stopped pacing and cupped her forehead in her hands. "That would be the worst possible outcome. But somehow, for some reason I cannot explain, everything in my heart is telling me that he will keep his word if we help him. I despise d'Entremont, and I know you do, too. How can we trust him more than we would trust Prince Nicholas, who has been most unfairly treated?"

"By *us*," Gabby reminded her. "*You* especially, when you drugged him and carted him off to parts unknown, bound and gagged like an animal."

"He was never gagged," Véronique corrected her. "Now you are just being dramatic."

"How can I help it? This is quite an unbelievable situation. Worse than any farcical play."

Véronique faced her sister. "Do you know if Pierre keeps the key on him, or would it be in his room?"

"Do you really intend to steal it?"

"Yes, if I can. If not, I will try the housekeeper."

Gabby crossed the room to meet Véronique at the foot of the bed. "I saw him slip it into his coat pocket after we locked Nicholas inside on the first night. I do not believe it's been used since then. It could still be in his pocket, or he may have hidden it in his room."

Véronique experienced a fluttery feeling in her belly, accompanied by an acute sense of purpose. "I will check his room this afternoon."

"Should I go with you?"

"No, but you could be my decoy. Go for a walk in the garden so that Pierre will follow to keep an eye on you, as he always does. He is very suspicious. It's warm outside. He won't likely be wearing his overcoat. With luck, he will leave it in his room."

Gabrielle hesitated.

"What's wrong?" Véronique asked. "Do you not want to do this?"

"It's not that," she replied as she moved to a chair and sat down. "I am just not feeling well this morning."

"You do look pale." Véronique crossed to her sister and placed the back of her hand on her forehead. "Your temperature seems normal."

Gabrielle pushed her hand away. "I am fine. It's nothing." She quickly stood up and reached for her bonnet, slipped it on, and tied the ribbons under her chin. "Very well, then. Off I go."

Véronique escorted her sister to the stairs, then returned to their guest chamber to watch from the window.

A few minutes later, Gabby strolled leisurely toward

the cherry orchard. Sure enough, Pierre appeared from the stables to follow her at a distance.

The door to Pierre's chamber was unlocked, and the rest of the wing was deserted, so it was an effortless undertaking to slip inside. Véronique quietly closed the door behind her and glanced around.

It was a comfortable room, well lived in, for Pierre had occupied this space for many years, since the death of the former marquis. Heavy, dusty-looking fabrics covered the windows, and the furniture was faded and threadbare in places. A bookcase was stuffed tight with clutter, where papers lay horizontally on top of books with the spines out.

Her gaze shifted to the wardrobe. She walked quickly to it, opened the door, and found the coat he had been wearing on the night of the abduction.

With fast-moving fingers, she searched the pockets, but found them all empty.

Véronique huffed in frustration, then searched all the other pockets.

After closing the wardrobe doors, she turned to peruse the room. Her gaze settled on the desk in the corner, which was buried under a mountain of books and papers.

Véronique walked toward it and pulled open each drawer. She gasped with surprise when the bottom drawer revealed a large collection of keys. Surely it contained every key in the entire manor house.

She searched through them and found them to be labeled according to each floor and wing, which made it easy to narrow it down to the correct set.

Gently, she closed the desk drawer before tiptoeing out of the room. On her way out, she spotted Nicholas's dress sword and belt leaning up against the wall. Grabbing hold of them, she ran out and shut the door behind her, then hurried back down the corridor to her own chamber.

Once there, she crossed to the window to ensure that Gabrielle was still leading Pierre away from the house. When she spotted her sister, however, a wave of panic rose up within her, for Gabby was running back to the house with Pierre in hot pursuit.

Véronique dropped the keys into a flowerpot on the windowsill and ran quickly to reach her sister.

By the time Véronique found Gabrielle, she was up against a tree behind the thick cedar hedge, slapping and punching at Pierre, who was fighting to restrain her while he tried to lift her skirts.

A violent shaking began in all Véronique's extremities, and her vision turned red.

"Stop!"

She bolted forward and launched her body sideways into Pierre, knocking him away from her sister. He stumbled and nearly fell, but managed to remain on his feet before wheeling around to return and smack Véronique across the side of the head.

Pain reverberated in her ears. She responded by kicking him between the legs. He doubled over, knees pressed together, and crumpled to the ground.

Staring down at him in shock—while her gut twisted fiercely and her muscles strained against her skin—she was about to kick him in the stomach when Gabby dragged her away.

"If you come near her again," Véronique shouted in a penetrating voice she barely recognized as her own, "I will kill you! Do you understand?"

Writhing in agony on the ground, Pierre gave no response, which was fortunate; otherwise, she might have broken away from her sister and followed through on that threat, right there on the spot.

As Gabby led her back to the house, a sudden dizziness swirled in Véronique's brain. She stopped and grabbed hold of the cement post at the bottom of the stairs.

Gabrielle stopped as well. Her cheeks were pale.

"Are you all right?" Véronique asked. "You look like you are about to be ill. Did he hurt you?"

Gabby laid a hand on her belly, turned away from Véronique, bent over the side of the cement balustrade, and retched into the rose garden below.

Véronique hurried to her side. "Everything will be all right now," she gently whispered. "He won't ever touch you again. I found the key to Nicholas's room, and thanks to Pierre—and what he did to you just now—any doubts I had about helping Nicholas escape are now completely forgotten. I will tell him what Pierre tried to do to you, and I am sure he will come to our aid in every possible way. I found his sword in Pierre's room. We will return it to him, and we will sneak away tonight."

Gabrielle recovered from her sickness and turned toward Véronique in the warm sunshine. Her face was gray, and there was a shiny film of perspiration on her forehead and upper lip.

"I am not sick over what he tried to do to me," Gabby said. "It is something else—something which has caused me great anxiety over the past few weeks. I should have told you before, but I thought I might be mistaken. Now, I do not think I am."

Moving away slightly, Véronique began to guess the truth. "Is it what I think it is?"

Gabby nodded somberly.

"You are with child?" Véronique asked.

Tears filled her sister's eyes. "Yes, I am so sorry. I know this is the worst possible time to tell you such a thing, when we are about to be tossed out of our home. You have more than enough responsibility, trying to manage this situation. I assure you, I did not mean for it to happen."

Véronique frowned. "Does Robert know?"

"Not yet," she replied. "I haven't told him, because I wasn't completely sure, but now I am. My worst fear is that he will think I did this intentionally to trap him."

Véronique inclined her head a fraction. "You didn't, though . . . *did* you?"

"Of course not!" Gabby replied. "I love him with all my heart and soul, and I know he loves me, too. We have been waiting so long, hoping his father would change his mind about allowing us to marry. We just couldn't wait any longer."

"Well, you *should* have!" Véronique sank down onto the steps and pressed her forehead into the heels of her hands. "Oh, Gabby. What have you done? He is not free to marry you. His father will not appreciate being backed into a corner. This will make no difference. In fact, it will only worsen your chances of winning his approval. I thought perhaps when we got our house back, Father would stop drinking, and Robert's father might feel differently about your marriage, but now . . ."

Véronique was only vaguely aware of her sister sitting down beside her, for her mind was swimming with images of disaster. Just when she thought it could get no worse—when her family was about to lose everything— her sister had thrown another log into the inferno.

Gabby laid a hand on her shoulder and squeezed. "Everything will be fine. Robert loves me. He would never abandon me."

Véronique could feel the veins straining at her forehead as she turned to meet her sister's gaze. "Are you sure about that? Even if it means losing his inheritance?"

Gabby sat back. "I have to believe it, for the alternative is unthinkable."

Looking across the lawn to where Pierre was hobbling back to the stables, Véronique rose to her feet. She then stomped up the stairs. "You had better be right about that, Gabby, because the alternative is indeed unthinkable."

"Where are you going?" Gabby asked. "What will you do?"

Véronique stopped and turned to look down the steps. "I am going to unlock Prince Nicholas's door and have a private word with him. You had best pray to God that he will be our friend and not our enemy when this over."

She picked up her skirts and hurried into the house to fetch the key.

Chapter Six

When Véronique unlocked Nicholas's door, she could barely contain the fear that was blazing in her bloodstream, for it seemed as if her whole world was falling apart.

All she wanted to do was see him, apologize for everything, pledge her loyalty, and put herself—and her family—in his capable, heroic hands. There was never a moment in her life when she needed a hero more than she did now.

God willing, he would repay her actions today by ensuring that her parents would not be evicted from their home and tossed out onto the streets like yesterday's garbage. And he would protect her and Gabrielle from Pierre's unwanted attentions.

Everything would be better from this moment on, she told herself. It had to be. Surely it was, as he said . . . *destiny*.

Quietly, she pushed the door open and stepped across the threshold. The bed was unmade and in shambles, and the window was open. A cool breeze blew the curtains in giant undulating puffs of movement. She felt a slight shiver run through her, and continued to gaze about the room cautiously.

A pile of books covered the floor by the upholstered chair in front of the enormous fireplace, as if the prince had cracked the spine of each one, found it lacking, and tossed it onto the floor to burn later.

She frowned at the stillness, and wondered suddenly if he had escaped out the window while she and Gabrielle were distracted on the other side of the manor, fighting off Pierre's lecherous attentions and discussing their hopeless futures.

Then a hand covered her mouth. She gasped with panic. An arm snaked around her neck, and she was dragged roughly around the back of the door.

Prince Nicholas violently kicked it shut with his boot and hauled her across the room at such speed, her feet barely touched the floor as she struggled to kick free and shout for help. Words were nothing but a muffled plea against his palm, however, while his grip tightened around her neck, choking the very life out of her.

Before she could fight back, he swung around and flung her onto the unmade bed. She landed in a sideways roll and ended up on her back, horizontal across the center.

She barely had a chance to catch her breath before his hand covered her mouth again. He leaped on top of her and straddled her hips with murderous rage in his eyes while his other hand braced her arm at her side.

She continued to kick her legs and tried to swing a punch at him with her free arm, but he leaned back and dodged the strike.

"Where's the key?" he demanded to know, ducking and darting to avoid her flailing arm.

She tried to speak but could only murmur into his

palm, which he still held over her mouth, so she bit into it instead.

He yanked his hand away and shook off the pain, then wrapped it around her throat to hold her down.

She gasped for air while she clutched at his muscled forearm.

"Tell me where the key is."

"It's still in the door," she ground out as blood rushed dizzyingly to her head.

His angry gaze darted to the door, but he did not release her. "Damn."

She bucked like an animal to free herself, and only then did he seem to realize that he might kill her—or she might kill him—if he didn't soon back away.

He let go of her throat but grabbed both her wrists and pinned them to the mattress over her head.

"I ought to let you choke," he said, "for what you did to me."

Véronique would have liked to respond with a few colorful retorts, but she was too busy sucking air into her burning lungs.

Finally she managed to utter a few words. "And I ought to stab you in the eye with that key!" Chest heaving, she glared up at him with ferocious intent, while he glared down at her like a lion with lips drawing back to reveal a sharp set of teeth.

For the longest moment they stared at each other willfully until Véronique shouted at the top of her lungs and bucked her hips in all directions. He was too strong and heavy, however. The fight was futile. He simply covered her mouth again with that stifling hand and held her down until she tired of the exertion.

"Are you finished?" he asked with growing impatience.

Out of breath and accepting the fact that she was

indeed conquered—at least physically—she shut her eyes and nodded, which was a humiliating moment and completely frustrating in all ways.

Slowly he slid his hand away, and his steely muscular body relaxed on top of hers.

She remained very still. "I thought I was your rescuer," she said, "and you were mine. Do you not remember that conversation?"

He almost smiled, but it was a bitter amusement that glimmered in those piercing blue eyes. "I remember. I also remember waking up after the ball with a pounding headache and no memory of how I came to be in this room. You lied to me, Véronique. You tricked me and betrayed me."

"I apologize," she said.

He shook his head as if he did not accept it.

"Fine," she said. "Hate me if you want. But where do we go from here? Are we enemies now? Will you tie me up and leave me here while you make a run for it? Or do we still have an agreement? And what about the kiss?" she asked foolishly. "Was that just a lie to win my allegiance? If so, did you actually think that it would sway me? Because I will have you know—I did not steal that key for a kiss from *you,* sir. I stole it because I believed you were a man of honor who would keep your word and help me get back what d'Entremont took from me."

"And what was that?" Nicholas asked, leaning over her on all fours. "You have yet to reveal it."

She felt suddenly overheated and wet her lips. "He took my home," she explained. "Or rather . . . he took my father's home. He won it in a card game, knowing full well that my father was flat broke and drunk, and had nothing else left to wager. He encouraged the bet, and when he won the hand, he did not give my father a chance to win it back. It's a large property not far from here, worth a great deal, and it has been in our family for generations. D'Entremont wanted it for his son. He was going to reward him with it after Waterloo. But now his son is dead. The worst part is that my mother is ill and they have nowhere to go. D'Entremont told my parents they must be out by the end of the month, and she cannot stop weeping. It breaks my heart to see her like that. She is a good woman with the heart of an angel. D'Entremont is a monster. He trapped my father at the gaming table because he wanted our land."

Nicholas's eyebrows pulled together in a frown, but there was no sympathy there. "That's quite a woeful story," he said. "And what has he promised you for the task of abducting me? Has he agreed to give you back your home? Do you have it in writing?"

She nodded. "He holds the deed of ownership, which is why I did not think you could help us. But if you could purchase it from him, or charge him with kidnapping and force him to give it back to us . . ."

Nicholas rolled off her. At last she could breathe freely.

He lay beside her on his back and cupped his forehead in a hand. "Ah, Véronique. There is a part of me that wants to drag you back to Petersbourg right now and throw you in prison for life."

She leaned up on an elbow and looked down at him. "But there is another part of you . . . ," she said hopefully, urging him to continue.

He dropped his hand to his side and gazed up at her. "The other part of me must honor the promise I made to you through that locked door."

"Because you are a prince and a gentleman," she added as her heart unwound with relief.

He regarded her coolly. "Prince? Yes. Gentleman?

Absolutely not. I am a rogue and a scoundrel. I will help you now only because I cannot have you sounding an alarm."

For a long moment she peered down at him in the fading afternoon light. "Well, that is disappointing—just when I was beginning to think your reputation was undeserved."

He sat up and looked at her with a dark note of warning. "I assure you, it is *completely* deserved. If there is a scandal in Petersbourg, I am at the center of it."

Véronique remembered that the key was still in the door, and he had not yet gone to fetch it. "Perhaps it is time to redeem yourself and prove everyone wrong by doing something heroic in this matter," she suggested. "You could save my family. If you did that, I would sing your praises, and so would my father and mother."

He rose from the bed to go and retrieve the key. She took note of the fact that he had changed into the clothes the marquis had provided for him—clothes she suspected belonged to his late son. He looked less like a prince. More like a normal man.

Nicholas slipped the key into the pocket of his waistcoat and moved to the window to survey the surroundings.

"Are there any guards out there?" he asked, ignoring her last comment, as if he did not care in the least about his reputation, and wanted only to narrow in on the most important issue at hand—his escape.

"No," she replied as she inched to the edge of the mattress and stood. "There have never been any guards except for Gabrielle, Pierre, and me. Even the servants have been kept in the dark about your presence here. Only the butler knows. This part of the east wing is usually deserted, except for Pierre's room, which is closer to the stairs. They have been informed about Gabrielle and me, but that is all. The marquis left instructions for Pierre, and no one else, to deliver meals to us while he is away."

"That is rather worrisome," Nicholas replied. "If no one knows I am here, it seems too easy for me to disappear without a trace, do you not agree?"

She nodded as she walked to the trapdoor in the wall, which was located behind a large gilt-framed portrait that swung open on hinges. The compartment for the dinner trays was empty.

"I honestly don't know what he has planned for you," she said absently, then stiffened with shock when Nicholas clasped a hand around her wrist and pulled her around to face him.

She backed up against the wall until she was trapped there by his lean, muscular body.

"There is something else we agreed upon," he said, "and I believe I will claim it now."

In a smooth, swift wave of motion, his mouth found hers. The kiss was firm and demanding, and before she could comprehend what might happen next, she wrapped her arms around his neck and began kissing him passionately in the last of the afternoon light.

As she drank in the exquisite taste of his lips and tongue, and the warm damp sensuality of a hard kiss she should *not* find pleasurable—she knew that he was not expressing passion, affection, or love. This, for him, was something else. Something vengeful. He wanted her to know that he would take what he wanted from her, whether she liked it or not.

She should have been outraged by this show of disrespect, but she had been dreaming of a kiss from him for days, and it was disconcertingly easy to remember those fantasies as he kissed her now, mere minutes after he had held her down and she had fought against him with all her might.

His hips pressed forward and pinned her snugly up against the wall while his hands cupped her face, then gracefully stroked down her neck to the tops of her shoulders, where he squeezed gently until she sighed with a delicious swell of satisfaction.

Her knees were just about to buckle beneath her when he drew back and rubbed the pads of his thumbs across her cheekbones.

At last she opened her eyes.

"Thank you for bringing the key," he said in a soft, husky voice.

Véronique felt a deep shudder in her core, caused by a flash of heat that raced through her senses. "Does this mean you will help me recover my home?" She would do anything—anything—to get it back.

He released her and stepped away. "I gave you my word and I will keep it. Once we are free from here, I will bring a hammer down on d'Entremont's head like nothing you've ever seen. Everything he owns, I will take from him, including his freedom, for I will have him arrested and charged, at the very least, for unlawful confinement."

She was surprised when the scorching vengeance she saw in Nicholas's eyes caused a spark of arousal in her core, for it was a vengeance that *she* wanted, too, with all her heart and soul.

She hated d'Entremont and she wanted him to pay for the pain and humiliation he had inflicted upon her family. The rage felt like a dark monster inside her, awakened by what Pierre had just done to Gabrielle, who was pregnant and in danger because the man she loved could not marry her.

D'Entremont had stolen everything from her family, and Véronique wanted to see him punished. She wanted to see it again and again until the marquis atoned for all the pain he had caused.

"I hate him," she said. "I did this to you only so that we could rid him from our lives forever. It wasn't anything against you or your country," she explained. "I should have thought it through and told you the truth sooner. Perhaps we could have been allies from the start."

"It doesn't matter," he said. "We are allies now." He moved to the door, carefully opened it, and peered out into the corridor. "Where is your sister, and can you both ride?"

"Yes," Véronique replied. "I could go to the stables and see about taking a few of d'Entremont's horses. If I can sneak them out, where should I take them?"

He closed the door and faced her. "No, do not attempt anything like that. You might be discovered. We will simply wait until midnight and go to the stables together while the servants are sleeping. If you are sure there are no guards."

"I am sure."

"Good. Here is what you will do: Find our best escape route from here. There must be a servants' staircase in this wing somewhere. Make sure that it will lead us to an unlocked exit. Tell Gabrielle about the plan and be ready to leave at midnight." He paused to think for a moment. "What about the driver, Pierre? Will he be asleep by then?"

"I am not sure. He is always skulking about, keeping an eye on us. I must tell you . . . he just tried to assault Gabrielle in the gardens. I do not trust him."

Nicholas tapped a finger on his thigh. "He assaulted your sister? Just now?"

"Yes, but I saw what was happening, and I stopped him."

"How?"

Her body tensed at the memory. "It's all a bit of a blur . . . but if you must know, I kicked him where he was most vulnerable. He crumpled to the ground like a wet rag."

Nicholas pondered that. "Well done." He then walked to the window and looked out again. "We must finalize our plan for later." He reached into his pocket for the key and held it out to her. "You'll have to lock me in again. Otherwise, Pierre may discover our plan. Can I trust you?"

"Of course."

Before handing the key over, however, he studied her carefully with hooded eyes. Then, at last, he relinquished it. "I don't suppose you have any laudanum left from the other night, do you?"

She understood his intentions instantly. "I believe I do. It would be in my reticule."

"Excellent. Now, one last thing, . . . do you know where my sword is being kept? I shall need it."

"I already have it in my possession," she told him. "I stole it out of Pierre's room just now."

Nicholas's eyebrows lifted, as if he was surprised that she had thought of it and accomplished so much already. "Good."

For a moment their gazes locked and held. No doubt, he was gauging whether or not he could trust her, as she was thinking the same thing. When he took in the full length of her body, however, she experienced an unexpected sensual thrill and remained fixed to the spot, inviting his intense scrutiny, feeling invigorated by thoughts of what would occur in a few short hours.

They would leave this place together and ride into the forest.

And d'Entremont would finally get what he deserved.

Feeling unnerved by the sinister arousal that coursed through her veins, Véronique turned toward the door, but Nicholas grasped her arm.

"Before you leave," he said, his voice quiet and low, "you should know that I still haven't forgiven you for what you did. But I am pleased that we are at least on the same side."

"As am I," she shakily replied, for her body was on fire beneath heat of his touch.

She pulled her arm free, quickly walked out, and locked the door behind her.

Chapter Seven

After the sun went down, heavy drops of rain began to fall from thick clouds in the sky. The wind blew hard and rattled the windowpanes.

Why must it rain tonight, of all nights?

Fighting a relentless impatience, Véronique paced back and forth across the carpet while Gabrielle sat in a chair, watching the flames dance wildly in the grate.

"Come and sit down," Gabby said. "You're making me nervous, and you're not making the time go by any faster."

Véronique shut her eyes and massaged her temples. "You're quite right. I must try to relax." She glanced up at the clock on the mantel. "Only one more hour . . ."

She wondered if Pierre had consumed the wine yet, for she had managed to wrestle his supper tray out of the maid's hands in the corridor, slip the laudanum into the decanter, and deliver it to him herself—under the pretext of speaking to him about what happened in the garden earlier that day.

She promised Pierre that she would not tell the marquis what he had done if he promised never to do anything like it again. He had agreed, of course, and she gave him his supper.

Now, as she sat down across from Gabby before the fire, she had to work hard to relax.

"Perhaps you should ring for some brandy," Gabby suggested.

Véronique shook her head. "No, I must have my wits about me tonight."

Especially when she slipped the key into the lock, opened the door, and found herself back in the presence of Prince Nicholas.

That kiss had rattled her brain. Whenever she thought about it, her body fairly trembled with excitement and desire.

She mustn't allow herself to become swept away by it, however. She was not helping him escape to satisfy her own pleasures, or to enjoy acting the part of a harlot. She was doing this for her family. Gabrielle, especially, who was now in a perilous situation.

The only way out of this was to rely on the generosity of Prince Nicholas, who had more power than their enemy.

The clock began to chime. Her gaze flew to the mantel. "It's eleven o'clock. Will you be ready to leave when the time comes?"

"Of course," Gabrielle replied. "I've been ready since the supper trays were collected. Will *you* be ready?"

Véronique slid her sister a sidelong glance.

"Of course you will be," Gabrielle added with a knowing look. "I daresay you've thought of nothing else since you walked out of his bedchamber this afternoon with your cheeks flushed the color of a ripe tomato, and your hair all tousled."

Véronique frowned. "What are you implying, Gabrielle?"

Her sister shrugged innocently. "Nothing at all, for surely you would tell me if there was anything important to relay. You would share your feelings with me, since we are sisters and so very close."

The windowpanes rattled in the storm. "I have *no* feelings about Prince Nicholas whatsoever," she insisted, but Gabby raised an eyebrow at her. "Fine, I do find him attractive, but you know I am not like you. I am not romantic. I am practical. His appeal matters not, for he is just a means to an end. He will help us get our home back."

"Just because you are practical," Gabby argued, "does not mean you feel no passion. I saw him with my own eyes, and I cannot imagine that you could fail to be affected by his looks and charms, and surely if you are concocting plans of escaping together, there must be some sort of bond between you. Do you want to talk about it? I may be younger than you, but I do have some experience with love."

"Love?" Angered by the suggestion—for she had no intention of feeling anything of the sort—Véronique stood abruptly. "This has nothing to do with love. He is handsome, but prince or pauper, he is also a notorious rake. I am not only practical, but I am *sensible,* as well, Gabby. All that matters to me now is our escape from this place, and the recovery of our home."

Footsteps pounded down the corridor. Both Véronique and Gabrielle turned their attention to the door.

"What was that?"

The footsteps passed by and continued down the hall toward Nicholas's room.

"Do you think it could be Pierre going to check on him?" Gabby asked.

Véronique tiptoed quickly to the door and pressed

her ear up against it. The footsteps stopped farther down, and she heard the jingling of keys.

Gabrielle joined her at the door. "What's happening?"

"I don't know," Véronique whispered.

The sound of a lock clicking and the turn of a knob struck Véronique with terror. Carefully, she opened the door a crack and peered out. "Oh no," she whispered.

Gabby touched her arm. "What is it? Tell me."

Véronique watched the end of the hall. "The door is open. Someone has gone inside."

Something clattered across the floor in Nicholas's room. Then an obvious scuffle followed. Véronique pulled the door open and dashed out into the hall.

Nicholas raised his hands over his head in surrender when the cold barrel of a pistol touched his forehead, square between the eyes, and the chamber cocked.

As soon as Pierre relaxed his shoulders, Nicholas knocked the weapon away and kicked Pierre in the stomach. He was about to dive for the gun, but the sound of a second pistol cocking from just inside the door halted him on the spot.

Pierre, who was doubled over in pain, glared at him with flaring nostrils.

Nicholas turned his gaze toward the second intruder—a well-dressed older man with silver-rimmed spectacles and slightly graying hair.

"Who are you?" Nicholas asked, his body tense and primed to fight.

"Good evening, Your Highness," the man said with a bow. "I am Jean Fournier, butler of the house. I am here to inform you that the marquis wishes to see you now."

Nicholas frowned. "The marquis is here?"

"Yes, sir. He arrived home just over an hour ago. I apologize for not rolling out the red carpet for you upon your arrival the other night, but I was instructed to keep your presence here a secret."

"So you knew about me."

"Indeed." The butler stared with loathing at Pierre.

Wondering what else this man knew, Nicholas fought to calm the raging fire in his blood.

"Now, sir," Fournier said, "if you will allow me to escort you this way, Lord d'Entremont will see you in the library and answer any questions you may have."

Nicholas considered his options as Pierre limped to pick up the pistol.

So much for a midnight escape, Nicholas thought.

He wondered if Véronique was aware of this.

At that precise moment, as the butler led him to the door, the sound of a woman's heels clicking down the long corridor in a frantic rush reached his ears.

Véronique and Gabrielle nearly skidded to a halt as he crossed the threshold with the two men brandishing pistols on either side of him.

Nicholas met Véronique's eyes and knew immediately that she had nothing to do with this. She was as surprised as he.

Then he set eyes on Gabrielle for the second time since the incident at the window. She was a pretty young girl with fiery red hair and a rather frightened-looking countenance. No wonder. Men in the corridor with pistols was not usually a welcome scenario.

"Where are you taking him?" Véronique asked.

"Good evening, mademoiselle," Fournier said.

"They are taking me to the library to meet d'Entremont," Nicholas explained as he passed. "He just arrived this evening."

Obviously, their plan was foiled, and he hadn't yet decided what to do about it. If something happened to him, he hoped Véronique would at least have the decency to send word to his brother, Randolph, in Petersbourg.

He wanted to tell her to leave now and report this outrage to someone, but then she would not be guaranteed the recovery of her home. He realized with regret that he could not trust her to put his needs before her own.

As he walked down the corridor with Pierre and the butler, he was keenly aware of the women following close behind—curious, no doubt, as to this unexpected unfolding of events.

The marquis had returned home early.

But for what purpose?

Chapter Eight

The hot fire in the cherry- and oak-paneled library was blazing in the hearth as Nicholas was shown inside. There were a number of candles lit on tall standing candelabras, and the room smelled of woodsmoke and spices.

He turned at the last minute to see the butler backing out, closing the double doors behind him, and shutting out Véronique, who looked as if she wanted to accompany Nicholas inside to act as a witness. But a witness to what?

The doors clicked shut.

Suddenly he was alone in the room with the crackling fire and the sound of hard, pelting raindrops against the windows.

Then he noticed a large high-backed chair facing the fire. It concealed the figure of a man. Nicholas saw only the top of his head and the toes of his boots.

A hand with a giant ruby ring reached over the armrest and beckoned him closer.

"Do not call me over like a dog," Nicholas bellowed.

"Stand up and face me, d'Entremont, and tell me the meaning of this."

The hand disappeared again while Nicholas waited for the marquis to reply.

At last he spoke in a low, gravelly voice. "I regret to inform you that I cannot stand, Your Highness, for I am a cripple. A weak, pathetic invalid. Come and see for yourself."

Nicholas felt a tightening in his chest as he comprehended the marquis's strange greeting, which was not at all what he had expected, based on Véronique's description of the man. Nicholas had imagined a towering, imposing figure.

Nevertheless, he knew better than to underestimate an enemy, so he moved forward cautiously, all his senses on high alert. As he approached, his gaze fell upon d'Entremont's legs. They were covered by a green woolen blanket.

Stepping around the high-backed chair, Nicholas finally beheld the marquis's face.

He was about sixty years of age with prominent dark features. His hair was thick and wavy with only a few traces of gray. His nose was slender and straight, his eyes hazel, his shoulders broad. Nothing about him struck Nicholas as weak or pathetic. Standing at his full height, d'Entremont had no doubt been an imposing figure at one time, but tonight, he did not get up.

"Would you care for a brandy?" the marquis asked. "It's my finest."

Nicholas was tempted to tell him to take his fine brandy and choke on it, but restrained himself. Instead he turned and spotted a sparkling crystal decanter and an empty glass on a table near the desk.

He crossed to it, poured himself a drink, then returned to sit on the matching chair that faced the fire across from the marquis.

"I am waiting for you to explain yourself," Nicholas said. "Why am I here, and why all the secrecy? If you wanted to see me, why not just send a letter and invite me?"

"I couldn't take the chance that you would refuse my invitation and return to Petersbourg," d'Entremont replied.

"Then why not come to Paris and call on me at my hotel? Clearly you knew I was there, for you had me abducted out of a private ballroom."

"I was farther down the coast," the marquis explained, "trying to arrange for a ship to America."

"For yourself?"

"No." D'Entremont regarded him shrewdly, as if waiting for Nicholas to guess the true answer.

"For Bonaparte?"

"Yes." D'Entremont pinched the bridge of his nose as if he were in pain. "Unfortunately, I was unsuccessful. The emperor has surrendered. He is now in the hands of the British."

Nicholas was relieved to hear it, but was no less on guard. To calm his temper, he took a sip of the brandy, which was indeed very fine. Perhaps the best he'd ever tasted. He hoped it wasn't laced with laudanum.

"So what do you want from me?" he asked. "To arrange Bonaparte's escape? I assure you, you're wasting your breath—and your fine brandy—if you think I will be pressed into helping that tyrant get away."

D'Entremont stared at him intently. When at last he spoke, his voice was quiet and solemn. "You have your mother's eyes."

The words sent a jolt into Nicholas's heart, and he frowned. "Did you know my mother?"

And what the devil did his mother have to do with anything? She had been dead for over twenty years.

"Yes," d'Entremont replied. "I knew her very well, which is why you are here now, Nicholas." He waved a hand dismissively through the air. "But I will not drag this out and force you to continue to ask why this is happening. I will answer your question now. I sent for you with such haste because I am dying. I will not be long for this world."

Nicholas cleared his throat. "I am sorry to hear it."

The marquis began to cough. He clutched his stomach, then recovered his composure. "As am I. You may or may not know that I lost my only son at Waterloo, which has caused me much sadness and grief." His voice quavered, and he paused.

"My condolences," Nicholas softly said.

The marquis sipped his brandy, set it down on the table beside him, then managed to continue. "When he fell on the battlefield, I lost my only heir. Now I must decide what to do with this estate and all my worldly possessions."

Nicholas thought of Pierre, the marquis's illegitimate nephew, but remained silent as he waited for d'Entremont to finish.

"That is why you were brought here, Nicholas. I wanted to meet you in person and explain all this myself."

"Explain what, exactly?" Nicholas sat very still as an ominous feeling settled into his stomach.

"That I wish to name you as my sole heir, with the exception of one small property near Paris, which I will bequeath to my nephew, Pierre."

"Why me?" Nicholas rubbed the back of his neck while the answer to that question was already filtering uncomfortably into his brain.

"Because the man you knew to be your father—King Frederick of Petersbourg—was not your real father. I must tell you now that that man is *me*."

A sudden coldness swirled in Nicholas's head as he stared speechless at the marquis. "No," he said firmly. "I do not believe that to be so." He rose from his chair and stood, then set down his glass and started for the door.

"Please come back," d'Entremont pleaded. "You must give me an opportunity to explain. Do you not want to know the truth?"

Nicholas halted with a tight grip on the doorknob while his gut churned with sickening anger over all that he had endured these past few days.

And now this . . .

Nevertheless, he let go of the knob and turned around to face the dying marquis, while the wind and the rain outside beat more violently upon the glass.

It had been more than an hour since Nicholas was taken to the library. Véronique waited impatiently in her chamber until at last, a knock sounded at the door. In a rush of movement, she leaped out of her chair and hurried to answer it.

"Who's there?" she asked, in case it was Pierre.

"It's Nicholas."

She pressed her hand to her breastbone and let out a breath of relief as she opened the door.

There stood Nicholas alone—unharmed and alive—in the corridor.

Her euphoria vanished, however, when she saw the look in his eyes. His brow was furrowed, and he was running a hand through his hair, as if he were lost and uncertain which direction to turn.

"What happened?" she asked.

He leaned in to see Gabrielle rising from her chair

before the fire, peering at him curiously. "I must speak with you," he said to Véronique. "Alone."

She immediately turned to her sister. "Will you excuse us?"

"Of course," Gabby replied, and sat back down.

Véronique followed Nicholas into the corridor and closed the door behind her.

"Come this way," he said, taking her by the hand.

His touch sent a current of energy through her body, and she found herself focusing all her attention on the snug, warm grip of his hand upon hers.

She was grateful that he was alive.

They came to the room where he had been held captive, and he led her inside. She noticed that the servants had been there, for the bed was made and a fire was burning in the hearth.

Nicholas let go of her hand and moved to the mantel. He found matches and lit five candles on a candelabra on the desk. The room brightened while the wind howled through the eaves outside.

Véronique hugged her arms about herself and shivered.

"Are you cold?" he asked.

"I am fine," she replied. She was eager to learn what had occurred in the library with Lord d'Entremont.

Somehow he knew she was lying about not being cold, for he glanced at the freshly made bed and reached for a wool coverlet that was draped over the footboard. He brought it to Véronique and wrapped it around her shoulders. "Is that better?"

"Yes, thank you."

Their eyes held for a moment. Her body grew warm, but not because of the coverlet. The heat was something else—a tingling brush of desire.

She was deeply attracted to this man—that was

obvious—but she realized suddenly that it was so much more than that. She truly, genuinely cared for his welfare, perhaps because she felt responsible for bringing him here.

"Are you all right?" she asked.

"I am not sure." He turned away and sank into the chair before the fire.

Véronique followed and sat down across from him. "What did he say to you?"

Slouching low, Nicholas rested his temple on a finger. "I doubt you'll believe it. I certainly didn't. Not at first, but now . . ." He sat in silence, then leaned forward until their foreheads touched. He covered her hands with his own. "I apologize for being rough with you today. That was inexcusable."

"It's fine, Nicholas. What did d'Entremont say?"

Without looking up, he answered the question at last. "He told me that he knew my mother many years ago, and that they were lovers."

Véronique drew back in surprise.

"D'Entremont said he loved my mother deeply and passionately, and that he never loved anyone else as he loved her."

Véronique shook her head in disbelief. "But he was married for almost twenty years and had three children with his wife. From what I know of it, it was a happy marriage until the day she died."

"Happy. Content. Yes. D'Entremont held his wife in the highest regard, but he never let go of the undying love he felt for my mother."

Véronique leaned closer. "Was this before she married your father, or after?"

Leaning back, Nicholas said flatly, "It was after."

Véronique paused and wet her lips. There was obviously a great scandal brewing here, and she was uneasy about pressing Nicholas for more information, but she had so many questions. . . .

"After my brother, Randolph, was born," he continued, "my mother spent time in Paris—a full year with distant relations while my father was immersed in the rising tide of the Petersbourg Revolution. He was a general in the army then, not yet king. According to d'Entremont, he and my mother met at a political assembly in Paris and fell in love, almost at first sight. Many months later, my father discovered her adultery and threatened to take Randolph away from her, and never allow her to see him again, if she did not return to Petersbourg immediately."

"What happened after that?" Véronique asked.

Nicholas leaned his head back on the chair and gazed up at the ceiling. "She went home like a proper, dutiful wife."

Véronique touched his knee. For a long while he did not move. Then he lifted his head and regarded her intently in the flickering light from the candles.

"She gave birth to me eight months later."

Véronique absorbed this shocking piece of news and considered what it meant for Nicholas. Not only had his mother betrayed her vow of fidelity, but his father had been ruthless in his desire to keep his wife's adultery a secret. For those reasons, Nicholas had never known that he was not a true blood royal, that the king was not his father.

In addition to that, his brother, Randolph, was only his half brother. The same would be true of his sister, Princess Rose. Nicholas was not only the wild and wayward middle child of a dead monarch; he was a secret bastard son. He had no claim to the throne.

He was also the son of a man she despised with every breath in her body.

"What will you do?" she asked, pulling her hand away.

Nicholas shrugged. "I have no idea. My brother knows nothing of this, nor does my sister."

She gave him a moment to consider the future, then could not help but ask the question that was screaming for an answer in her mind.

"Why did he tell you this now?" she asked. "Why did he kidnap you, like some primitive barbarian lord?"

Nicholas breathed deeply. "He was desperate. He wanted to see me urgently, and could not risk that I would refuse, or put him off."

"Why so urgently?"

Nicholas paused. "Because he is dying, Véronique, and he needs an heir."

She blinked a few times. Her astonishment, and the hatred she felt for d'Entremont, was making her feel rather nauseated. "He is dying?"

It was selfish of her, and she was ashamed of herself for thinking such thoughts, but she could not help but wonder what it would mean for her family. D'Entremont held the deed to her home and had agreed to sign it over to her upon completion of this task. She had brought Nicholas here, as promised. He must now sign the property over to her . . . he *must*. And quickly.

"Has he already named you as his beneficiary?" she asked.

"I do not know that yet. He said he wished to bequeath everything to me upon his death, but I have not accepted those wishes. I did not behave as a loving son should. I was angry and in shock. I told him I wanted nothing from him . . . that I did not want to be acknowledged as his son. Then I walked out."

Véronique folded her hands on her lap. "How sick is he?"

"I cannot be certain. He couldn't walk, though. Did you know that?" He regarded her inquisitively.

"No, I did not. The last time I saw him, he seemed in perfect health."

"When was that?"

"Four months ago, the day after he won our house at the card table. Since then, I have been dealing only with Pierre."

Nicholas was watching her steadily in the firelight, and she noticed again how blue and piercing his eyes were. "Why doesn't he name Pierre as his heir?" she asked. "He is his nephew, his dead sister's only child. Pierre has served him faithfully all his life."

"I asked him that question. D'Entremont said he does not believe Pierre to be a man of honor. He does not trust him, nor does he feel that Pierre deserves any of this."

"But he trusts *you*?" she replied. "Pardon my candor, Nicholas, but he doesn't even know you."

Nicholas held up a hand. "Do not apologize. You are quite right. Certainly my reputation does not represent me as a man of honor on any count. But I am his true blood son, and I suspect in these last weeks of his life, he is romanticizing the past and remembering the great love of his younger days. More important, he has just lost his only legitimate son on the battlefield at Waterloo. Now he wants the whole world to know that I am his."

Véronique fought to stay focused on the decision Nicholas must make, for it could impact her situation greatly.

"Your family—your father's entire monarchy—would be forever tainted if you allow d'Entremont to reveal this to the world. The scandal would be colossal."

Nicholas turned his head rather sharply to look into

the fire. "Scandal is nothing new to me. I've always had a reputation for it. Now I know why. My life makes perfect sense to me now, for I am the son of a scoundrel. No wonder my father hated me. I was not even his." He cupped his forehead in a hand. "Bloody hell."

She forced herself to touch Nicholas's knee, to offer comfort, even while she was reeling inside with the possibility that he—or Pierre—could become her landlord if she did not get her property back very soon. "What will you do?"

He paused. "I will think on it. Perhaps old secrets are better left in the past. Both my mother and father are gone now. What good can come of it, except to satisfy a dying man who is a stranger to me, and a villain to you?"

Véronique considered that, and knew that if he did not accept what was bequeathed to him, it would go to Pierre.

D'Entremont was right about one thing at least: Pierre was not an honorable man, and she doubted he would hold true to his uncle's promises if he inherited everything. He would never relinquish possession of her home. He would take great pleasure in keeping it just to spite her and Gabrielle. Or perhaps he would demand that one of them accept him as a husband in order for their family to continue living there. It did not bear thinking about.

She looked up and realized that Nicholas had been watching her for the past few minutes. Did he know she was thinking of her own troubles, not his?

"Thank you for listening," he said. "I needed someone to talk to."

All this was unimaginable. It hardly seemed real. Her heart was aching for Nicholas. She felt terrible for all that she had put him through, and she wanted—she *needed*—him to consider her as his friend.

She squeezed his hand. "Please, there is no need, not after what I did to you. I hope you can forgive me for that—and I am relieved it was not some other sinister plot, as we imagined it to be. I was worried while you were in the library. I did not know what was happening. I wanted to break down the door and go to your rescue with a horsewhip or some other weapon."

She was not lying about that. Despite her selfish deliberations just now, she did care for Nicholas. Far more than she should.

"I would have enjoyed being a witness to that," he replied with a hint of a smile that sent her heart sailing.

He was d'Entremont's son.

He was a rake and a seducer of women.

She must be very careful with her feelings, for she really did not know him at all. Yet every move he made . . . every sound . . . every glimmer in his eyes, was immensely spellbinding to her in more ways than she could fathom.

He ran his thumb over the back of her hand, and she felt that persistent, fiery spark of desire in the depths of her womanhood.

Heaven help her, she was already knee-deep in potential scandal, having kidnapped a prince, not to mention attending a masked ball without a chaperone. Now she was alone with this prince in his bedchamber at midnight, considering how she must behave . . . how she must feel about him.

He could end up as her landlord. It occurred to her that she mustn't incite his scorn or displeasure. She must make up for what she had done to him and win his allegiance. But what sort of alliance would it be? And how far would she go to ensure it?

"Perhaps I should leave now," she heard herself saying.

She should speak to the marquis, before it was too late. He must pay her what he owed her. Then she would be free of this sticky web.

This time, Nicholas squeezed *her* hand. "Please do not go yet."

He weaved his fingers through hers, and she found herself luxuriating in the intimacy of such a simple mingling of hands and fingers.

Another rush of desire heated her blood, and she forced herself to think of his reputation. He was a notorious libertine, and he had all the power here, especially if he was soon to be master of her father's property. The attraction she felt toward him made this a very dangerous situation.

He kept his intense blue eyes fixed upon hers as he leaned forward in the chair and brought her hand to his lips. "Stay," he whispered as he laid a few light kisses across the sensitive flesh of her knuckles. "Just for a little while."

His touch continued to disrupt her balance while her blood quickened.

"Why?" she asked, fighting to remain strong in the wake of his provocative appeal.

"You have been an unexpected friend to me tonight," he said. "All I want is to be with you a little longer."

I must control this situation, she thought. *I must influence his decisions.*

"I am glad you consider me a friend," she said, "even though I began as your enemy. If I had the chance, Nicholas, I would go back to that night and act very differently. You know that, don't you? I wish I had trusted you and confided in you at the outset."

"Do you trust me now?"

She hesitated slightly, then willed herself to nod.

"Then stay with me," he said. "I promise I will not take advantage." He paused. "It has been a difficult night, Véronique, and I have been captive in this room for days. Stay and have a glass of wine with me. We can talk about how to proceed from here. I still want to help you," he said, and she was immediately pulled in. "I haven't forgotten that you want your property back."

There they were—the words she needed to hear. But nothing was set in stone yet. D'Entremont still held the deed, and Nicholas was clearly torn over what to do.

She swallowed uneasily and bolstered her resolve to tread carefully and remain guarded, when what she really wanted to do was surrender herself completely to his safekeeping. Perhaps she could. He knew what she wanted.

"You indicated a moment ago that you trusted me." He rose to his feet and stood tall and handsome before her. "On my honor, I will not behave like the scoundrel that you and everyone else believe me to be. At least not tonight."

"I do not think you are a scoundrel," she told him. Then she narrowed her eyes at him accusingly, but with a hint of teasing. "Unless you say that to *all* the women . . ."

His lips curled into a small smile. "I confess, I *have* said it before, but I always keep the promise when I make it."

She sighed dramatically. "Now I don't feel special."

He chuckled, and his response thrilled her beyond comprehension as he held out his hand to escort her somewhere.

To the bed?

No, surely not. . . .

Nevertheless, taking a great risk, she slid her fingers across the warm flesh of his palm and allowed him to lead her to the table by the window, where a tray was set out with a decanter of wine and two glasses.

Chapter Nine

Véronique's eyes fluttered open at the sound of birds chirping outside and a heavy crashing thunder in her brain.

Grimacing at the explosive torment that seemed to stretch her skull and cheekbones outward, she pressed her palm to her forehead and slowly leaned up on one arm.

She glanced toward the window. It was not yet dawn. Only a faint hint of blue had touched the sky. Her gaze then shifted to the rest of the room, and she realized in a flash of panic that she was still in Prince Nicholas's bedchamber, and had spent the night there.

The panic shot a new frisson of pain into her skull.

Fighting through her discomfort, she turned her head on the pillow to look for Nicholas in the bed beside her, and discovered, with profound relief, that she was alone.

A swift scan of the chairs in front of the fire revealed the shadow of his form. He was slouched very low with his head resting on the back of the chair.

She squinted agonizingly at the empty wine decanter and realized what had occurred: The maids must have taken the decanter she had delivered to Pierre's room with the supper tray, and brought it here for Nicholas instead.

Véronique tried to remember what had taken place after he poured their drinks.

Nothing. She was quite sure of it. She had slept in her clothes and so had Nicholas. He had probably been in no condition to seduce anyone if he had consumed more of the wine than she had.

She should check on him, however, and make certain he was still breathing, for he appeared to be out cold. Then she would return to her own bedchamber as promptly as possible and prepare for what she must do first thing today: see Lord d'Entremont and demand that he pay her for her work. She had delivered what he wanted. He must therefore give her what he'd promised.

Carefully—so as not to cause another crash of thunder in her brain—she slid over the side of the mattress and touched her feet to the floor. She was not wearing her shoes and did not remember taking them off. Where were they?

A quick survey of the foot of the bed revealed them on the upholstered bench. She fetched them and slipped them on, then tiptoed lightly across the room to touch Nicholas's forehead. His temperature seemed normal, and he was breathing steadily.

She stood briefly in the pale dawn light, admiring the peaceful, handsome contours of his face and body, the way his massive form was sprawled so serenely in the chair. Images of the night before flashed in her brain, and she remembered talking to him about her home not far from here, and her mother's weakened condition over the past few months.

He had been sympathetic, but then the laudanum must

have taken effect. She remembered wanting to lie down.
He had taken her to the bed, sat on the edge of it. . . .

Véronique backed away as she recalled the weight
and feel of his body coming down upon hers, his hands
cupping her face, the whisper of his breath in her ear as
he brushed his lips across her cheek and down the side
of her neck.

What else had happened after that?

She remembered nothing, until the moment she woke
alone a short while ago.

Had he taken any further liberties? Had she been
willing?

Glancing around the room one last time, knowing
there was no answer to be found—and feeling unsettled by the lingering passion that still coursed through
her body—she moved to the door, and slipped out.

A moment later she was sneaking into her own
room—making an effort not to wake her sister—when
she discovered that bed to be empty as well.

Gabrielle's voice reached her from the floor beneath
the window. "Is that you, Véronique?"

"Good heavens, are you all right?" Véronique hurried around the foot of the bed.

Gabrielle slung an elbow onto the mattress. "This
must be some sort of moral punishment, for I have never
been so ill in all my life. I should mention that this is a
very fine chamber pot. There are butterflies on the inside, but now they are swimming."

Hooking her arms under Gabrielle's, Véronique
helped her sister to her feet and back onto the bed.
"Can I fetch you anything? Some dry toast perhaps?"

Gabrielle held up a hand in disgust. "Do not mention
food. I simply need to lie still for a while. It usually
passes by noon."

"Why didn't you tell me it was so bad?"

"You know I couldn't. And this is the worst day, by far."

Véronique tucked her sister back into bed and sat with her.

"Where were you last night?" Gabby asked with eyes closed. "I was worried. I went to listen at Prince Nicholas's door, but it was quiet inside."

Véronique let out a heavy sigh. "I am mortified to confess that we drank Pierre's wine with the laudanum, and both fell asleep."

Gabby's eyes flew open, and she smirked. "You cannot be serious."

"I am completely."

"Well, it appears I am not the only one being punished. To spend the night alone with a man like that, and to fall asleep at the outset?" She frowned up at her. "Is that all that happened?"

"Do not worry about me," Véronique replied. "I have a headache. That is all."

"I wasn't referring to your head. I am asking about your heart."

Véronique appreciated her sister's concern, but she really did not wish to discuss it. "My heart is fine, and my head will be fine in a few hours."

She rubbed Gabrielle's back until she appeared to be drifting back to sleep, then carefully slipped into bed beside her and did the same.

The sun was streaming brightly through the windows when Véronique woke for the second time that morning. She sat up and squinted at the clock on the mantel. It was past eleven.

At least the headache was gone. She felt only slightly groggy.

Looking around, she saw that Gabrielle was no longer in bed. "Gabby? Are you here?"

When no answer came, she assumed her sister had gone to the breakfast room, for they had been informed there would be no more meals delivered on trays now that the marquis had returned.

Thinking the same thing might be in order for herself, Veronique rose and washed and changed into a sea green muslin morning dress, something appropriate for her meeting with Lord d'Entremont—for she would think of nothing else until she had the deed to her father's property in her hands.

A short while later, she ventured downstairs to the breakfast room, where a single footman was in attendance, and served herself a plate of eggs and biscuits from the sideboard. She sat down at the white-clothed table, picked up her fork, and ate her breakfast while sipping a cup of hot coffee, which the footman refilled for her twice.

Afterwards, she wiped her mouth with the marquis's fine silk napkin, tossed the square onto the table, and departed from the room with resolve.

She went first to the library to seek out d'Entremont, but found no one there. On her way out, she nearly collided head-on with Monsieur Fournier, the butler.

"Good morning, mademoiselle. May I assist you with something?"

"Yes. I need to speak with Lord d'Entremont, and it is a matter of utmost urgency."

"I am afraid the marquis is unavailable at present."

She regarded him unwaveringly. "He is here, is he not? He spoke to Prince Nicholas last night. It is almost noon. Surely he can find time to see me for a few minutes. That is all I ask."

The butler shook his head. "Please accept the marquis's apologies, but he cannot see you now."

"Why not?" she demanded. "We had an agreement, and I have fulfilled my part of it. Now he must fulfill his."

The butler spoke with sympathy, which grated upon her nerves, for she did not want his pity. She wanted what belonged to her.

"I am sure he will be pleased to see you, mademoiselle, but you must wait until he sends for you."

"Why must everything occur according to *his* schedule?" she asked. "Perhaps I am in a hurry to leave."

The butler's eyes darkened with the first signs of his impatience. "May I remind you that his 'schedule' is very limited? He will not be long for this world, so pardon me if I do not consider your wishes this morning to be more important than his comforts."

She was taken aback by the butler's uncompromising reply, and found it impossible to argue or make further demands.

"When can I see him?" she asked, more gently this time.

"I will send for you when he indicates that he is ready to accept visitors."

He turned and walked away, but she followed. "Please remind him that he owes me something, and I must see him today."

The butler continued without looking back. "I will deliver your message."

Nicholas stood at the library window, looking out at the wide expanse of manicured gardens, rolling green hills, and the thick forest beyond. The windstorm the night before had left branches strewn about the lawn. A gardener was outside with a wheelbarrow, carefully raking around the shrubs and flowerbeds, gathering up the debris.

The activity outside distracted him only briefly, however, from his thoughts about what had occurred the night before. When Véronique had held out her arms to him and invited him to join her on the bed, he had acted too quickly and surrendered to his desires.

After the news he had received from Lord d'Entremont, he supposed he had wanted and needed a woman's comfort—which was odd, for *comfort* was not something he ever sought from women. And he had not yet forgiven Véronique for her deception when she lured him out of that Paris ballroom.

His bitterness toward her, however, had been shattered almost instantly by the scent of her soft skin, the sweet blush coloring her cheeks, and the breathlessness in her voice. The fact that she had kidnapped him a few nights ago seemed suddenly a thousand miles away.

"Let me kiss you." He had spoken the words across her lips as he settled his body on top of hers.

She'd had too much wine; he had known it was the source of her bold invitation, yet he could not bring himself to behave as a gentleman should and suggest that he escort her back to her own room.

No . . . that was the furthest thing from his mind when his gaze swept to her soft, lush breasts, and he found himself drawn in closer in a strangely emotional way that left him almost flustered—for it was a novel concept for Nicholas to feel anything outside of physical pleasure when in bed with a beautiful woman.

The door to the library opened, and Nicholas turned to see the butler enter with Monsieur Bellefontaine, the estate steward. Introductions were made, and the butler left them alone.

"You requested a private appointment with me," Nicholas said.

"Indeed, Your Highness. Lord d'Entremont has asked me to escort you on a tour of the grounds, if you would be so gracious as to accept his offer. I would like to take you to the village and show you the flour mill, which is part of the marquis's holdings. Then I will show you the tenant cottages. We could finish up with a brief drive past the vineyard and winery."

Nicholas clasped his hands behind his back and took a long, scrutinizing look at the man. The steward appeared to be in his late fifties, and while not very tall, he was slender and fit-looking. His ginger-colored hair receded only slightly at the temples. There was an obvious air of pride and confidence in his demeanor, for he held his head high.

"How long have you managed the estate?" Nicholas asked.

"Twenty-one years, sir. I inherited the position from my father who served the former marquis for thirty-one years . . . until the Terror. He died under the guillotine. The marquis fled to England until it was safe to return and reclaim his property. I quietly managed everything in his absence."

Nicholas considered all of this. "A loyal bunch, your family must be."

"Yes, sir."

Turning back to the window, Nicholas looked toward the horizon. "I presume you intend to impress me today with the marquis's possessions?"

"That is the goal."

"At least you are honest," Nicholas said.

Bellefontaine bowed his head slightly to answer in the affirmative.

Nicholas took time to consider his options. Part of

him wanted nothing to do with Lord d'Entremont or his impressive land holdings. He just wanted to leave here and forget any of this had ever happened. He wanted to return to the world he knew in Petersbourg, where he lived a life of superficial, hedonistic pleasures, always believing himself to be the legitimate son of King Frederick I. Never questioning the past. Never revisiting certain memories.

Now everything was turned upside down and he felt completely cut off from the man he thought he was.

"I will go with you on one condition," he said at last.

"What is it, sir?"

"You must extend the invitation to include Mademoiselle Véronique, who was my escort from Paris."

Bloody hell, he still didn't know her last name.

The steward remained silent. His Adam's apple bobbed as he swallowed over some obvious discomfort. "I would be pleased to extend the invitation," he replied nevertheless. "If you will give me a moment, sir, I will make the necessary arrangements with Fournier."

He left the room and returned a few minutes later.

"Fournier has gone to knock on the young lady's door. I have asked him to bring her out front to join us in the barouche. If you wish to accompany me now, we can wait for her there."

Disconcerted by how strongly he wanted Véronique at his side for this tour of the estate, Nicholas followed Monsieur Bellefontaine out of the library.

Chapter Ten

It was past noon when Véronique exited the house onto the shady step beneath the massive front portico of d'Entremont Manor. There was not a single cloud in the sky. The sun beamed hot and bright, forcing her to squint as she descended the wide stone steps.

The open barouche, drawn by a pair of handsome white horses, stood parked at the curb with the hood down, waiting for her. Nicholas and the steward, Monsieur Bellefontaine, were already seated inside. As soon as Nicholas spotted her, however, he alighted from the vehicle.

Her heart skipped a beat at the sight of his strong athletic form—which made her wonder if she would be able to keep her head and behave sensibly over the next few hours.

But she must. She absolutely must.

When at last she reached him, he held out a gloved hand to assist her up the iron step, which had been lowered by a footman.

"Good afternoon." His charming smile reached his

eyes, and fleeting images of the night before flashed in her mind. She couldn't help but smile in return.

"Good afternoon, Your Highness," she replied with a brief curtsy. "How good of you to invite me to join you."

"My pleasure entirely."

Was he, too, thinking of last night? And what exactly had happened beyond the first kiss? Did he remember everything? Should she ask him?

She stepped into the open carriage and took a seat across from the steward, who gave her a polite nod. "How nice to see you again, Mademoiselle Montagne."

"Greetings, Monsieur Bellefontaine. How is your family?"

"Very well, thank you," he replied.

It was a forced courtesy on both sides, for the last time they met, she had begged him to convince the marquis to show her father mercy and not take possession of the card table winnings from the night before.

Monsieur Bellefontaine had been contrary and uncooperative. They did not part on friendly terms. She had called him a swine.

She found herself clenching her jaw slightly at the memory of that morning meeting and the pretense of their easy familiarity just now, when she would have preferred to jab a hatpin into his knee.

Prince Nicholas slid onto the seat beside her and lounged back comfortably. "Mademoiselle Montagne . . . ," he said with eyes narrowing slightly, and she realized it was the first time he had heard her last name.

She felt a shiver of unease while he studied her face in the sunshine, for her identity was now out in the open. He would be fully within his rights to charge her with kidnapping, if he so desired. Which was why she must maintain a cordial friendship with him, at the very least.

He turned to the steward. "You wish to show me the grounds, Monsieur Bellefontaine?" he said, indicating that he was ready to begin.

Véronique wondered if he simply wanted to hurry things up and be done with it, or if he was genuinely curious about what could belong to him if he accepted the marquis as his father.

Would Nicholas be invited to tour *her* family home next? It was, after all, part of the marquis's legal holdings. Perhaps that was why she had been asked to join them.

The steward rested a hand on the ivory handle of his walking stick. "Do you have any preference about what you would like to see first?"

Nicholas turned to meet Véronique's gaze—as if he were seeking the wisdom of her opinion. "Tell me, mademoiselle, where should we go?"

"It makes no difference to me, sir."

He turned his attention back to the steward. "I should inform you that Mademoiselle Montagne has been fully apprised about the reason I was brought here. She knows the marquis has named me as his sole heir and that I am—according to him—his natural son. I have explained everything to the lady, including the marquis's claim that he and my mother were involved in an adulterous affair here in France many years ago. You may therefore speak openly this afternoon, Bellefontaine."

The steward shifted uncomfortably on the seat. "I see."

As the carriage rolled forward and started down the long tree-lined drive, Véronique raised a gratified eyebrow at Bellefontaine.

"In that case," he said, "we shall begin with the old oak tree on the hill. I believe, Your Highness, that you can see it from your guest chamber window."

Nicholas regarded him curiously. "Why there?"

Bellefontaine lifted his chin. "Because it provides the most spectacular view of the house and the Channel, but most important, there is something very particular that the marquis has asked me to show you today. Something that may help you to accept the truth about your mother's presence here."

The carriage suddenly picked up speed. Véronique was overwhelmingly aware of Nicholas's thigh bumping hers. She made no move to inch away from him, however. Nor did he move away from her.

Nicholas stared at the tree for a long moment, then approached it and ran his fingers over the letters carved into the ancient bark. There could be no denying that the words—and the heart that encircled them—had been carved many years ago. Decades, most likely.

ISABELLE
AND
JACQUES
FOREVER

Monsieur Bellefontaine approached and stood beside him. "It was your mother who carved this," he said, as if reminiscing. "I also have an engraved ring to show you, and dozens of letters if you wish to read them. Lord d'Entremont saved everything from the year they spent together."

A knot formed in Nicholas's stomach, for he had been clinging to the possibility that all this was a lie . . . or some sort of malicious scheme to smear his late father's reputation and topple the Sebastian monarchy from the throne of Petersbourg.

Nicholas, Randolph, and Rose had lived most of their lives under the threat of an overthrow. Their father, the king, had died from one such plot little more than a year ago, poisoned by enemies who hoped to seize his crown.

But *this*—a box of love letters, jewelry, names carved into trees—this was something else entirely, and all his instincts and intuitive powers told him that his mother had truly been here, and there were secrets that his father had never revealed.

As a child, he never felt as privileged, cherished, or loved as his older brother, Randolph, or even Rose, who had been spoiled rotten and doted upon by their father.

Nicholas had always assumed it was because he was not the heir to the throne, but merely the spare, but there was so much more to it than that. Perhaps he should have known. Why hadn't he? Had he consciously chosen not to look more deeply into the roots of things?

He had always assumed it was his fault that his father despised him—because he was badly behaved. Irresponsible. Wild. Perhaps he had simply been too young to see through the layers. . . .

"Boy, come in here."

Nicholas approached his father, who was seated at the giant desk in the Privy Council Chamber. He had never been summoned to this room before. Randolph had been, many times, but not Nicholas.

He was distracted briefly by the oversized portrait of his father that hung on the wall behind him. In it, his father sat on the throne like a proud and mighty conqueror on his coronation day. He was draped in heavy fur robes, and he gripped a golden scepter in his fist.

"Your mother is dead," his father said.

Wrenched out of his reverie, Nicholas sucked in a breath. His widening gaze met his father's.

"She died an hour ago, giving birth to your sister. I have named your sister Rose."

There was a ringing in Nicholas's ears . . . a weakness in his legs. . . .

No, not Mother. She cannot be dead.

"That is all," his father said, picking up his quill and returning his attention to the pile of papers on the desk. "Go now."

Burning panic shot into Nicholas's belly and overwhelmed him with its vigor. He took a step forward, closer to the desk, and pounded his fists upon it. "Where is she?"

His father's eyes lifted, and he glared at Nicholas impatiently. "She is with the angels."

"No!" Nicholas stared at his father with furious rage, then strove to bring his shock under control and speak in a calmer voice. "I mean . . . Can I see her?"

"No, you cannot. They have already removed her body."

Nicholas backed away from the desk. He felt dizzy and light-headed. He began to hyperventilate. "But I need to see her."

He needed to touch her hand, to feel her comforting arms around him, to bask one last time in the warmth of her embrace.

"She is gone now, boy. You won't ever see her again."

Later Nicholas learned that Randolph had been permitted inside the birthing chamber to see their mother shortly before she passed. Though she was weak, she had held Randolph in her arms and kissed him on the head. "You will be a good king," she had whispered to him. As far as Nicholas knew, they were her last words.

There had been no such words for *him*.

He found himself wondering what his father would have done if anything had happened to Randolph. Would he have allowed Nicholas to take the throne? Or would he have revealed the truth to the world? Would Rose have been crowned queen instead?

Nicholas felt a hand on his shoulder just then, and was startled by it. Turning, he looked into those deep green eyes that never failed to quicken his blood.

"Are you all right?" Véronique asked.

Nicholas took note of Monsieur Bellefontaine climbing back into the carriage, a short distance away on the lane.

"I told him to leave us alone for a moment," she explained.

"That wasn't necessary," Nicholas tersely replied.

"I disagree," she argued, "for you failed to answer him when he asked if you were ready to see the flour mill. He asked you twice, Nicholas, but you ignored him."

Nicholas glanced back at the carvings in the tree. "Did I indeed? I suppose I was recalling the past."

"I suspected as much." She touched his arm and stood quietly beside him, then lowered her hand to her side and cleared her throat. "I just realized that you are as much of a victim of d'Entremont's greed as I am."

He frowned. "I am not his victim." He turned toward her. "And our situations are not the same."

Too late he realized he had spoken rather harshly.

"No, of course not," Véronique replied while regarding him with a furrowed brow, as if she were disappointed by his response. "For you are about to inherit all of this. It is *your* choice to make, whether you accept it, or leave it all behind."

Nicholas took a moment to gather his thoughts. To think rationally. He was not the only person here with something to lose. "I apologize," he said. "You are correct. I do have choices, while you are waiting for *others* to choose their fates and determine your future, as if it were merely incidental to theirs."

Véronique looked down at the grass. He found himself staring at the top of her bonnet, realizing that she was indeed at everyone's mercy here. Today she was powerless, waiting for someone to be charitable enough to hand over her father's property, which was allegedly worth a great deal of money.

Nevertheless, only one thing was occupying his mind at present—and it was not the value of her father's property.

"I did not take advantage of you last night," he assured her. "I slept in the chair. You must have seen that when you woke, whenever that was."

She lifted her head. "I did see you there, but I do not remember what happened between us. It was the laudanum. We drank it by mistake. I do not even remember falling asleep. All I know is that when I woke—" There was a hint of anxiety in her eyes. "—I was not wearing my shoes."

Nicholas could have laughed at that, for he was the sort of man who woke naked in bed in the most unlikely places, and he couldn't tell you half the names of his naked bed partners, or their boorish husbands. When he remembered Véronique's brilliant performance as a seductress at the masked ball, and her tempting sensual allure in the perfume-scented coach, her charming innocence today touched something unfamiliar in him—*again*.

What was it? What did he *feel*? He didn't even know. He was confused, for he was standing under an ancient oak tree in France, where his mother had declared her eternal love for a man—a man she would be forced to give up and never see again. Not even after she gave birth to his child.

Nicholas found himself arrested on the spot. He felt disconnected from everything he knew. Everything except for Véronique. He could not take his eyes off her. She was impossibly beautiful, a golden silken flower in the dappled shade of the oak tree.

At least his physical desires were familiar.

"I did remove your shoes," he confessed at last. "But nothing more than that, my dear, and only so that you could sleep comfortably."

"We kissed," she asserted. "I remember that much."

It had been a passionate, tender kiss—one he would never forget.

"Yes," he replied. "Certain things were done, and you would be well within your rights to blame it all on the depraved scoundrel at hand, and the opium-laced wine."

Though it was *she* who had held out her arms and invited him to join her on the bed.

Véronique swallowed uneasily. "I would appreciate being able to do so, sir, if you do not object."

"Not at all." Instantly charmed by her answer, he looked away, back toward the house.

What the devil was happening here? Why did he care about what occurred, or how she felt about it? She was his kidnapper, for pity's sake. It was one night on the French coast with too much wine—nothing more—and no one would ever have to know about it. Her reputation was not at stake.

"Nothing happened," he nevertheless assured her again.

"You kept your promise, then." She gazed up at him with relief and a veiled message that was not yet clear to him until at last, she explained. "But there was another promise you made." He listened intently. "You said you would help me get my property back."

She was very tenacious. He admired that.

He also admired her full lips and rosy cheeks, and how her captivating long-lashed eyes shone dazzlingly as she looked up at him.

"You completed your task," Nicholas said. "Now d'Entremont owes you your property in return. Why do you need my help?"

"Because I don't trust him to keep his word," she quietly replied, glancing back at the carriage to ensure Bellefontaine was not eavesdropping. "He is putting me off, I can feel it. I tried to speak to him this morning, but he refused to see me."

Nicholas folded his arms across his chest. "And you believe I can influence him?"

"Of course you can. You're his son, not to mention a royal prince."

For the briefest moment, he considered saying yes and concluding the matter on the spot, but when she inhaled deeply in suspense, and her lovely, lavish bosom rose beguilingly to the occasion, he found himself bedazzled yet again by her beauty. He wanted her in the most ungentlemanly way a man could want a woman.

He thought about her virtuous concern over waking in his bed without her shoes, and tried to be a gentleman about this, but it was no use. Old habits were not easy to break. He *was* a scoundrel, and she had kidnapped him, tied him up with ropes, and locked him in a room for two days. In a way, she had it coming. . . .

"I will do what I can," he said, resting an open hand against the tree, "if you will do something for me in return."

Her moist pink lips pursed, and she placed her slender gloved hand on top of her bonnet as the wind gusted over the hilltop.

"What do you want?" she asked. "I am almost afraid to ask."

"Why? Do you believe I will try to seek revenge?"

"I am not sure. I've never been in a situation like this before, nor have I ever dealt with a man like *you*."

Taking that as a compliment, whether or not she'd intended it to be, he moved away from the tree so that his back was turned to the barouche and said, "I will talk to d'Entremont for you today—I will even try to negotiate on your behalf—if you will come to my room again tonight for another glass of wine."

She stared at him raptly, her eyes as green as a lush spring meadow, and lifted her face as if she wanted to be kissed.

He knew, however, that that was not what she wanted. It was something else on display here. Defiance, most likely, while he waited eagerly for her response.

A strong breeze hissed through the leafy treetops above and blew the pink ribbons of her bonnet in all directions.

"All right," she said, leaving him speechless with shock. "I will come to your room tonight, but not until you have spoken to d'Entremont. And I will expect good news."

Véronique turned toward the carriage. "Monsieur

Bellefontaine is waiting to show you the flour mill. We should leave now."

But he did not want to leave. He wanted to stay right here, shove her up against this thick, gnarled tree trunk, and kiss her senseless until she begged him to remove more than just her shoes.

Véronique started back to the barouche, while Nicholas lagged behind for a moment to wrestle with his desires, for it might be embarrassing for the others if he rejoined them in his current state of sexual arousal.

Oddly, the sensation of his physical desire for her eased his mind somewhat.

That part, at least, did not leave him confused.

Chapter Eleven

The tour of the estate lasted more than three hours, with a brief sojourn at the village inn for tea and a light lunch.

Nicholas listened with genuine interest to the steward's description of the land, the crops, and the industries that were all part of the marquis's holdings, while Véronique was quiet for most of it, making only polite conversation when the situation demanded it. She was a courteous, charming companion in the presence of Monsieur Bellefontaine, and did well at concealing her personal loathing for the marquis.

At the end of the day, as the open carriage rolled up the tree-lined drive toward the impressive mansion overlooking the English Channel, it seemed strangely familiar to him, as if he had spent his childhood here, which was not the case at all. He had never set foot in France until he was a young man, and was certain that he had never visited this part of the coast.

He could presume, however, that he had been conceived here, which was a jarring thought as the vehicle pulled to a halt in front of the wide steps.

Bellefontaine shook Nicholas's hand and said goodbye, for he would continue on alone in the barouche to attend to a few minor estate matters. A footman hurried to open the door and stand by as Nicholas assisted Véronique onto the gravel drive and escorted her up the steps.

When they entered the front hall of black and white marble and looked up at the frescoed ceiling, he stopped for a moment, feeling rather pensive. "I have not failed to recognize the fact that all this should go to a legitimate heir," he said. "D'Entremont had three children of his own, including a son who was evidently quite capable and responsible if he had been promoted to the level of commander in Napoléon's Imperial Guard. Now, to die childless . . . No wonder the marquis feels desperate."

Véronique strolled leisurely to the white statue of Adonis in the center of the hall. "It is, as you say, quite a legacy to leave behind. I had no idea it was so profitable. I wasn't aware that he owned the winery. He probably won it a card game." She sighed. "It makes me wonder why he felt it necessary to increase his holdings by taking my father's property as well. How much can one family possibly enjoy, when people are starving in the streets of Paris? Is it simply greed, do you think?"

Nicholas watched her run her hand over a smooth marble column and felt a stirring of arousal as he listened to her talk.

"I don't know the answer to that," he said, meandering around a bust perched on a heavy gilt chest. "I shall certainly ask him about it when I see him."

"Will you, really?" She faced Nicholas as she untied the ribbons of her bonnet and slid it off her head.

She was like some sort of golden goddess, fixated

upon the one thing she wanted, the thing she was determined to reclaim at all costs. He was in a position to help her and he felt a strong urge to do so—to become her hero and protector, though it hardly seemed she needed one. She was quite capable on her own.

"Yes. I will ask him because I am curious as well," he replied.

The butler entered the hall and approached to take Nicholas's hat and walking stick. "Welcome back, Your Highness. His Lordship has been waiting for you. He was pleased to hear that you had joined Bellefontaine for a tour today. I believe he was quite confident that you would find it to your liking."

Fournier almost seemed to puff out his chest as he spoke the words.

"No one could deny that it is a grand estate," Nicholas replied, "but do not assume I am prepared to accept it or recognize him as my father. I was brought here by force, not by choice. Nothing is yet set in stone. I still may decide to press charges against him."

The color drained from the butler's face. "I hope in the coming days that you will feel differently, sir. All this can be yours if you want it."

Nicholas had been raised in the royal palace of Petersbourg. He had enough money and property to serve ten lifetimes. He did not need this house or all the fine statues and works of art that it contained.

He glanced at Véronique just then and wondered what it was, exactly, that he *did* need. He had never felt truly happy, despite all his worldly blessings. Something had always been missing. He usually failed at most things. He even derived a perverse pleasure from stimulating the wagging tongues of the gossips and disappointing his father when he was alive.

"If you would like to speak with His Lordship now,"

the butler said, "he is in the library and has been there for the past few hours, awaiting your return."

Véronique raised an eyebrow at Nicholas. He approached her to hear what she had to say.

"He waits hours for *you*," she whispered, "but is far too busy to see *me*. Do you now understand why I need your help?"

He nodded and offered his arm. "I do. So why don't you come with me? I am sure the marquis will not argue."

Fournier cleared his throat.

"Is there a problem?" Nicholas challenged.

The man bowed his head in submission. "Not at all, sir. You are welcome, of course, to do as you please."

The butler sent a brief scowl in Véronique's direction before he pasted on a smile and escorted them both up the wide staircase.

Outside the door to the library, Véronique marveled at the fact that Nicholas had come to her rescue in this way. Surely the marquis would not betray his legal obligations to her in front of the prince he wished to impress. He would behave honorably and sign over the deed to her father's property right there.

Her pulse beat fast with excitement and anticipation. She had suffered terribly over the past few months, watching her mother grow ill while her father hid away in shame. But Prince Nicholas was about to change all that. She would walk into the marquis's library on the arm of his son, who had, by some miracle, become her champion today when she certainly did not deserve his charity. Not after what she'd done to him.

But of course, he would demand his own compensation later tonight. . . .

She realized with some chagrin that she would pay

any price to get her home back—even the price of her own virtue—and with this man, she would probably enjoy it tremendously. What did that make her?

The butler opened the double doors and announced them, then backed out of the room.

Véronique let go of Nicholas's arm but remained at his side.

The marquis was seated in a chair facing the window. He did not turn to greet them.

Suddenly a small bird flew into the glass, tricked by the reflections of the sky, and Véronique jumped with fright at the sound of the collision. The unfortunate bird fell to the ground, stunned or more likely killed dead.

"Did you see that?" she whispered to Nicholas while resisting the urge to run to the window and look down, for perhaps the bird would need rescuing.

The marquis, however, did not react and she wondered if he was sleeping.

"Yes, I saw it," Nicholas replied as he strode forward with concern and circled around the desk. He looked down at the marquis. "Dear God."

Véronique rushed to his side and halted at the sight of her mortal enemy lying back in his chair, his arms splayed out on either side of him, blood dripping steadily from both his wrists into two dark pools on the oak floor.

"Go and fetch Fournier," Nicholas commanded as he placed two fingers on d'Entremont's neck to search for a pulse.

Her stomach turned over with horror, but she reacted quickly and hurried out the door. She reached the top of the stairs and called out over the railing: "Monsieur Fournier! Come quickly! Something has happened to the marquis!"

She heard the sound of the butler's shoes pounding

across the marble floor in the hall, felt assured of his imminent arrival, and dashed back into the library.

"Is he all right?" she asked as she hurried to Nicholas, who was seated on the windowsill with his head buried in his hands.

"Bloody hell."

She laid a consoling hand on his shoulder and dared a closer look at the marquis. He was distressingly thin compared to the last time she had seen him. His face was stone gray. Dark circles underlined his eyes, which were closed, as if he were asleep.

"There's no hope," Nicholas said. "He has been dead for some time."

She stared in disbelief at Lord d'Entremont, then peered down in a daze at the two thick pools of blood on the floor.

The butler came barging in. "What has happened?"

Nicholas's eyes lifted. They were filled with torment. "He took a blade to his wrists."

Fournier ran to see for himself. He looked down at His Lordship and dropped to his knees. "Oh, God, I should have come to check on him, but he told me not to bother. He seemed well today."

Nicholas raked a hand through his hair. "Why would he do this?"

"He was in pain," Fournier explained. "There was a growth on his spine that pressed upon his nerves. You didn't see any of that. He didn't want you to."

"Yet he wanted me to see *this*?"

Véronique knew that Nicholas had recently buried the only father he'd ever known, King Frederick, who was poisoned by court enemies. Now he would have to bury a father he had known for less than a day.

She looked down at the marquis's legs, which were covered by a blanket, and could not imagine the agony that would drive a man to such desperate measures, but clearly it had been unbearable for him.

She'd had no idea he was so ill.

Moving closer, she laid a hand on his forehead and brushed his hair away from his face. "Poor man," she said. "No one deserves to suffer like that. No one."

She turned to meet Nicholas's tortured gaze. He reached for her hand and squeezed it. There seemed so much to say, but all she could do was move closer, wrap her arms around his shoulders, and pull him into the warmth of her embrace.

Chapter Twelve

"What will it mean for us?" Gabrielle asked as she hurried to follow Véronique across the back terrace of the mansion. Her shoes clicked rapidly across the sunbathed flagstones. "Does the marquis's will name Nicholas as his heir, or was that just something he was considering as a possibility? Is that why he brought Nicholas here? What if he has not yet altered the document? What if everything has been left to Pierre?"

Véronique reached the balustrade and paused there to look out over the back garden and the cherry orchard beyond. It was late in the afternoon and the wind had died down. The summer air was hot and humid, and she wiped a hand across the perspiration on her forehead.

"We will know very soon," she replied. "Nicholas is dining with the solicitor at seven o'clock."

"But what if it all goes to Pierre?" Gabrielle asked. "What will we do? Will Nicholas still help us?"

Véronique sighed heavily. "Why should he? We abducted him and dragged him here like a prisoner. If he learns he is not named in the will, I would not blame him for simply returning to his life in Petersbourg and forgetting any of this ever happened."

Gabrielle grabbed hold of her arm. "We cannot let him do that. Pierre cannot have that power over us. You and I have both rejected him more than once. Think of how he will enjoy tossing us out onto the street."

"That is not my worst fear," Véronique confessed. "I see how he looks at you, Gabby. I believe he would use that power to force you to become his wife, or serve him in some other way."

Gabrielle scoffed bitterly and dropped her arm to her side. "Wait until he finds out I am already carrying another man's child. Perhaps he wouldn't even want me then. Perhaps he would want you."

Véronique considered that. Could she sacrifice her own happiness, and accept Pierre as a husband, if it meant her parents could keep their home?

Please, God, do not let it be so. . . .

She turned and sat down on the balustrade. "We are getting ahead of ourselves. Perhaps the marquis has already changed his will, and Nicholas is the heir."

Gabrielle paced back and forth, chewing on a thumbnail. "If that is the case, then surely you can get our property back. There is something between you. It is obvious. He invited you on the tour today. He must find you appealing."

"What are you suggesting?" Véronique asked with a frown, as if she hadn't already thought about it a dozen times already. "That I seduce him into signing it over? That I offer my body in exchange?"

"It would be far preferable to offering your body to Pierre."

Overcome with disgust at the notion of any sort of intimacies with Pierre, Véronique stood abruptly. "That may be true, but surely I cannot possibly succeed in such a scheme. I am not a woman of experience. I am a virgin, and I have been nothing but prudish since that first night in the coach. Honestly, I was distraught because he had removed my shoes last night. My *shoes*! You should have seen the way he looked at me when I mentioned it today. He was quite amused."

"But you lured him out of the ball," Gabrielle reminded her. "Clearly you knew what you were doing that night."

Véronique raised her hands to bring a halt to this conversation. "Perhaps nothing like that will even be necessary. I believe we have established a certain friendship. He talks to me, confides in me." She stared across the garden pensively. "There is no one else he can talk to. I am sure he is close to his siblings in Petersbourg, but he is all alone here in France. . . ."

"Exactly," Gabrielle replied. "His siblings are not here to support him, so he needs *you*. He has just learned a shocking truth about his mother, and discovered that he is not the person he thought he was. Use all of that to become his private confidante. Perhaps then he will show some benevolence to our family—out of a genuine affection for you."

Véronique fanned her face with her hand, for she was overheated and perspiring. "Please understand, Gabrielle—I do not wish to use this connection to manipulate him. If I am being honest, I will admit to you, and to myself, that I want to be his true friend in every way. He needs one right now."

Gabby approached and clasped both her hands in hers. "You are the best person I know, Véronique. An absolute angel. He does indeed need a friend, so be that for him. Win his loyalty, for our situation is perilous. Mine especially." She lowered her gaze. "Oh, how I miss Robert. I must see him and tell him about the baby. I cannot bear another moment away from him."

Véronique pulled her sister into her arms. "I am sure he is missing you, too. Perhaps in the end he will be able to convince his father to allow you to marry." The words were optimistic, but in her heart, Véronique was not so confident.

Gabrielle sniffed. "I hope so, for I will die if I cannot be with him."

Her sister's pain was her own pain, and there were times Véronique wanted to sink into a chair and surrender to weeping, but she knew she must be strong and work toward some sort of positive outcome, whatever that turned out to be.

She stepped back and looked up at the house. "I wonder what is happening in there," she said. "The doctor arrived a short time ago. Nicholas greeted him at the door."

Gabrielle squeezed her hand. "And Nicholas will greet you at his own door later this evening, won't he? After his meeting with the solicitor?"

Their eyes met again, and Véronique realized it was not trepidation she felt at the notion of being alone with Prince Nicholas again tonight—but rather a very ardent anticipation.

With the humid fragrance of a rose-scented bath still heavy in the air, Véronique stood up from her chair in front of the fire. "It is eleven o'clock," she said. "He should have returned from dinner by now. Perhaps I should go to him. I hope this gown is all right. I have no idea what one wears to meet a prince alone in his bedchamber at this hour."

"Your gown is perfect," Gabrielle replied as she twirled a lock of Véronique's golden hair around her finger and set it back in place at her temple. "You look lovely. He will be very pleased to see you."

"But for what purpose?" Véronique wondered. "I am not sure what his expectations will be. If they are . . ." She paused to search for the right word. "If they are *improper,* I will have some difficulty with that, because I do not wish to surrender my honor in order to get what we want from him."

But would she even be able to resist? Standing there in the soft candlelight, she remembered the hypnotic sensation of his kiss the night before, when she was lying on his bed, drunk from the wine. . . .

Or had it really been the wine? She wasn't so sure. Even now, as she recalled the thrill of his hard, muscled form on top of hers, her body ached for his touch and she felt shamefully eager to pay any price he asked in exchange for the return of her home.

If he was now its owner, which he may not be . . .

"It's time to go," Gabby said. "Knock on his door, and scream if you need help."

Véronique raised an eyebrow. "I certainly hope it won't come to *that*."

By the time she reached his bedchamber, her blood was racing with exhilaration, which caused her some concern for the safekeeping of her virtue this evening.

When she knocked, those heavy footsteps across the floorboards made her breath catch. Then the knob turned and the door opened.

There he was—her splendid prince—tall, dark, and magnificently handsome in the dancing firelight.

"Véronique," he greeted. "I am pleased you came. Won't you come in?" He stepped aside and gestured for her to enter.

Slowly she crossed the threshold and realized that tonight was vastly different from the night in the coach, when she had played the part of a seductress. Tonight she was herself—her *true* self—and she was far more conscious of the attraction that existed between them. This was not an act, nor was it a game. It was real.

"How was your dinner with the solicitor?" she asked, for she was here to be his friend and confidante, not his lover. If she could remember that, she would be fine.

He motioned for her to take a seat before the fire, then went to pour her a glass of wine. He handed it to her and sat down across from her.

As she took the first delicious sip of the wine, she admired the muscles of Nicholas's thighs as he crossed one long leg over the other.

"The dinner was . . . explosive," he replied.

"How so?"

"Pierre was there."

Véronique sat forward. "Was he, indeed? What happened? Did the solicitor reveal the contents of the will?"

A surprising glimmer of satisfaction flashed in Nicholas's eyes. "Yes, he did, and it appears I am now full owner of d'Entremont Manor, though I cannot inherit the title, which unfortunately will die with the marquis. But I own all the surrounding lands, which includes close to three thousand acres of fertile farm country and tenant cottages, the flour mill in the village, the vineyard and winery, and another property to the south, less than a day's coach ride from here. You might be familiar with it." He inclined his head at her. "Care to hazard a guess at the address?"

Véronique cupped her wineglass in both hands and spoke shakily. "I am suddenly finding it difficult to breathe," she said as she comprehended the news she had so longed to hear—that Pierre had not inherited her father's home. Yet at the same time, Nicholas now held the key to her future, and she was not sure what to expect from him in the coming days.

"Why is that?" he asked.

"Because I am now entirely at your mercy."

"Does that distress you?" He raised his glass to his lips and watched her over the sparkling crystal rim. "I suppose it should, seeing as how you committed a crime against me."

A hot spark crackled and exploded in the fire, then floated up the chimney. Véronique strove to maintain her composure.

Leaning forward, Nicholas rested both elbows on his knees. "You needn't worry," he said. "I promise I will be easier to deal with than Lord d'Entremont. You and he were at an impasse, were you not?" He sat back again. "I promise not to ignore you, as he did."

She noticed the self-satisfied look on his face. "You mentioned Pierre was at the dinner," she said, clinging to the thread of the conversation, "and that it was explosive. Was he very upset?"

"Oh yes," Nicholas replied as he calmly sipped his wine. "He threw a tantrum and had to be physically restrained and dragged from the room."

"Good heavens."

"You should have seen it. He stood up from the table and swiped his full dinner plate onto the floor—cutlery, roast beef, gravy, and all. Everything smashed to pieces on the porcelain floor. Then he came at me like a charging bull, knocking chairs over as he circled the table."

"What did you do?"

"I broke his nose before he could quite . . . organize himself."

"You broke his nose?" Véronique exclaimed in

delight, for she had not forgotten what Pierre tried to do to Gabrielle in the garden. "So he received *nothing* in the will?"

Nicholas set down his glass. "He received a modest house and property outside of Paris. I suppose it did come as a blow, when one considers that he had served the marquis faithfully all of his life, and I barely knew the man."

There was a chill in his words, as if he cared nothing for the fact that his true father by blood had died that very day. Véronique knew it was a mask, however—a mask he wore to hide his true emotions. Nicholas *had* been affected by it, for she would never forget how he had stepped into her arms and clung to her in the library.

"Will you keep everything?" she asked. "Will you truly be master here?"

He leaned his temple on a finger and studied her, as if *she* somehow held the answer to that question.

"I haven't decided yet," he replied. "I could, I suppose, sell it off piece by piece. I'd be a very wealthy man. Not that I don't have enough already. As you said earlier today, how much can one man enjoy when there are people starving in Paris?"

She sighed, feeling slightly more relaxed. "I am pleased to hear you feel that way. Would you consider a charitable endeavor with the proceeds of such a sale?"

He regarded her rather slyly. "Perhaps."

Her blood skimmed through her veins as she sipped the wine again and felt very exposed beneath the intensity of his gaze. What was he thinking? she wondered as a number of possible scenarios danced around inside her head.

"What about my family's property?" she asked. "What will you do with it?"

"What would you *like* me to do with it?"

The question filled her with hope, and she waited until her pulse settled down before replying. "I daresay you are teasing me, sir."

"Yes, I am." He smiled, and his eyes burned with an irresistible sensuous flame.

"Do you really, *truly* own my father's property now?"

He nodded casually, as if it were nothing at all to take possession of a prosperous French estate, one that had been in another family's possession for generations, and wave it tauntingly before the previous owner's eyes.

"Then I suppose we have some negotiating to do," she said.

His mouth curved into a tantalizing smile. "Yes, we do, Véronique—which I believe calls for more wine."

Chapter Thirteen

Véronique watched Nicholas tip the decanter over her glass to refill it. As she listened to the sound of the dark liquid pouring into the crystal vessel, she found herself reclining back in the chair with a few improper ideas about how this negotiation would play out. Her uneasiness was gone. It had been replaced by something else. *What,* exactly?

Passion? Seduction? All at once, she felt like the woman she had become in the coach outside the ball, when she had lured him and teased him into wanting what she offered.

Nicholas returned to the fire and handed her the second glass of wine.

Before she accepted it, she said, "Is there any way to test this for laudanum, or must I simply trust that it's pure?"

A hint of amusement touched his rakish eyes. "Either way, you can trust *me,*" he said. "Didn't I prove that last night, when you were lying so prettily on my bed, stewed to the gills, and I only removed your shoes?"

She accepted the glass and again felt as if they were

back in the ballroom, flirting unreservedly with each other under the assumption that lovemaking would occur in the next few hours.

She had offered herself to him quite blatantly that night. Was she offering herself to him now as part of this negotiation? Is that what he thought?

"So tell me," he said as he sank into the chair across from her. "Why should I sign the property over to you, when your father was so quick to wager it in a card game? What if he does the same thing again? Perhaps you would be better off letting me keep it."

"But then you would be our landlord," she replied. "There is little security in that. How could we trust that you wouldn't sell the house out from under us one day?"

"There is that word again," he said. *"Trust."*

She sighed. "It is you who keeps putting a finger point on it, sir. Not I."

They both leaned forward in their chairs at the same time, and he chuckled. "Is this where we square off? Draw swords or muskets?"

Their faces were mere inches apart, and a shiver of excitement moved through her at the delicious proximity of those soft, full lips. The memory of their kiss was still imprinted on her brain.

His eyes roamed leisurely over all the contours of her face. "I suppose I should just sign the property over to your father," he said in resignation, "since you've earned it."

"If you were a gentleman of honor, that is exactly what you would do, because you know how badly I want it."

"I do," he replied, his gaze narrowing in on her mouth. "But we both know I am no gentleman. Therefore I feel I should claim some other form of compensation, since I certainly didn't enjoy being drugged, tied up, and locked in this room for two days. And whatever agreement you had with d'Entremont is not binding between you and me. This is a *new* agreement."

"A solicitor might argue that point," she said. "Since you have inherited all his assets, you have also inherited his debts."

"Hm, quite right, but I would also argue that since your contract with him involved criminal activity, it is not a *legal* contract, therefore not binding at all. If you don't believe me, go ahead and take your grievances to the authorities. See what they have to say about it."

She slouched back in the chair. "I thought we were going to be friends."

"We can be."

A long silence ensued while she sipped her wine and he sipped his.

"What do you want, then?" she asked.

He sat forward. "How about we start with a kiss?"

When she did not reply, he added, "Does it surprise you . . . that I would ask for such a thing?"

"Not at all. In fact, I am surprised to be getting off so lightly."

He grinned. "I said let us *start* with a kiss. I didn't say that would close the deal."

She shook her head at him. "You are very wicked, sir. But I suppose you know that already."

"Yes, I do." He smiled dazzlingly and her heart turned over in her chest as he inched forward even closer, set his glass down, and held her face in his hands. A captivating heat exploded in her belly as he pressed his lips to hers with an unexpected gentleness.

His mouth was soft and warm. As his tongue met

hers, she slid her hands up to rest on his broad shoulders.

Véronique was ashamed to admit it, but she was no longer thinking of the negotiation. Kissing Prince Nicholas had nothing to do with practicalities, and everything to do with her own wanton pleasures.

Ah, and he knew just how to make it last. . . . He kissed with slow lingering patience, and warm, teasing sensuality.

A heavy ache throbbed from within, and she feared she might surrender to him completely, right here and now. Her thoughts were floating in a haze. Surely it was not just the wine. It was him—*all him*. He aroused her masterfully with his lips and tongue, and the sublime touch of his hands.

"You taste heavenly," he whispered as his lips feathered across her cheek and he breathed hotly in her ear.

Tingling gooseflesh erupted all over her body, and all she wanted was more of this bliss.

"Is that enough of a payment?" she asked, the more sensible part of her brain hoping that he would say yes, and she would be removed from any further temptations.

Another part of her, however, wanted him to demand more and insist that she comply, for she was quickly melting into a soft ball of clay in his hands. She wanted to be stroked and kneaded.

"I hardly think so," he said, rising from his chair and holding out his hand. "I'll need at least an hour with you, Véronique. On the bed."

Her courage evaporated at once, and she blinked up at him.

His brow furrowed as he recognized the change in her mood. "Do not fret, darling. I won't do anything you don't want me to do. Trust that I will stop at any time if you wish it. I just want to lie with you. One hour," he said again, as if to punctuate their agreement with a firm deadline. "Then the property is yours."

Her heart leapt. "The property will be mine? I have your word?"

"Yes, you have it," he replied, and she rose to her feet with elation.

She had taken great risks for this one purpose. Now it appeared she had succeeded. Her family would not lose everything. Her parents would keep their home and Gabrielle might still have a chance to become Robert's wife, if she could win the approval of his father.

Véronique was overcome with gratitude. Could it be this simple? Could she spend the next hour enjoying the pleasures of Prince Nicholas's attentions, then be rewarded at the end of it? It seemed too good to be true.

If he could be trusted, that is . . .

She wanted to believe he could be. All her instincts insisted that he would not break his promise. One hour of kissing, and that would be enough to pay the price.

Consequently, she took his hand and followed him to the bed. He paused beside it and looked down at her feet. "May I remove your shoes again?" he asked, "so that you will be more comfortable?"

"Just my shoes, nothing more?" she asked.

"Nothing more." He knelt down on one knee before her.

Resting a hand on his shoulder to keep her balance, she lifted one foot and allowed him to slide his fingers up under her skirts and cup her calf while he slowly, gently removed her silk shoe and set it aside.

He looked up at her with a teasing smile as he took hold of her other ankle and she shifted her weight to the other leg. He removed the second shoe, then stroked the arch of her foot briefly before rising to his full height and pressing his lips to hers again in a light, intoxicating kiss that set her world on fire.

It all happened as if in a dream. He eased her onto the soft bed and covered her body with his own, while leaving a trail of romantic, openmouthed kisses down the side of her neck.

Throwing her head back on the pillow, she hugged him against her and wrapped her legs around his firm, muscular hips.

He began to thrust in a gentle but steady rhythm. If it were not for the barrier of their clothing, she was not sure what would be happening. All she knew was that it felt natural and irresistible to move her body beneath him and cling to him, as if he held her whole life in his hands.

He was going to give her back her home. He was nothing like d'Entremont. *Nothing.* And she did trust him to keep his promise tonight.

But no matter how tightly she held him, she could not seem to get close enough. He, too, embraced her with an almost suffocating fervor until he drew back and gazed down at her in the warm, golden firelight.

"I cannot believe how badly I want you," he said, frowning with confusion. "You're different from other women."

"Different? How?"

Was it her innocence? Her virginity? Or was it the fact that she had been his captor and his enemy?

"I'm not sure," he whispered. "You feel out of reach."

"I am right here," she replied, laying a hand on his cheek.

"But what I want from you, I cannot have."

Véronique lay very still. "Because of the promise you just made?"

"Partly."

It was sexual, then. He wanted to slake his lust, but she was not one of his easy lovers.

"Well, there is nothing to be done about that," she said, "for I do not wish to change my mind."

"I didn't think you would," he said, "which perhaps is what makes me so ravenous."

"You want what you cannot have."

He nodded.

Véronique lifted her head off the pillow and kissed him again, slow and deep. "Are you sure it's not because Pierre interrupted your supper?"

He stared at her, then began to laugh and rolled to his side.

She, too, rolled over, straddled him, and braced his wrists together over his head. "Now I have *you* pinned to the bed, Your Highness." There was a hint of bitterness in her tone, for she had not forgotten what occurred in this room when she first unlocked his door.

"You're still angry about our tussle," he said. "How, pray tell, do you intend to punish me?"

Véronique was breathing heavily. "Is that what this is about? An hour of revenge for both of us? Then you will pay me what you owe me, and we will never think of each other again?"

His eyes raked over her face and breasts. "I doubt I will ever forget you."

Still gripping his wrists, she tilted her head to the side. "I cannot imagine I will ever forget you either, Nicholas, or what has happened between us over the past few days."

Suddenly overwhelmed by a fierce desire that astonished her with its intensity, she leaned forward and kissed him hard on the mouth, her body ablaze with a shocking, tumultuous lust.

Véronique released his wrists and let out a gasp when his arms circled her waist and he flipped her over onto her back.

Chapter Fourteen

Nicholas stared down at Véronique and cursed himself for making that promise to her—for he wanted to do whatever it took to force her into a complete sexual surrender.

The desire was out of control, and he was bewildered by the ferocity of it, for he did not normally crave innocent young virgins. In fact, he avoided them like the plague . . . but there was something very unique about this luscious, golden-haired lady. He could not explain it. All he could do was press his mouth to hers again, and again, in the thick heat of the night.

He made love to her for at least an hour, maybe more—but it wasn't really lovemaking by definition, for he never raised her skirts or unfastened his breeches. Nevertheless, it was as passionate and sweaty as any full-blown fornication. Their bodies were locked together, intimately entwined in an amorous fever, thrusting violently. He stroked and kissed her breasts through the light fabric of her gown and ran his hands up and down her legs. It was enough to drive him mad with a lust that threatened to scar him forever.

At the end of the hour, he could no longer endure the torment, and it appeared that neither could she, for she began to recklessly hoist up her skirts until they were tangled about her waist. Then she began to tug at the fastenings of his trousers.

At last . . .

He braced himself above her on both arms, refusing to contribute to this forbidden turn of events, but not putting a stop to it either, as he looked down at her frantic, fumbling fingers.

When she tugged his breeches down over his hips and released his erection, he let out a breath of relief and dropped down onto one arm.

Her open mouth roughly collided with his and he could have swallowed her whole.

He tugged her skirts out of the way until their centers connected. He had promised he would not take it this far, but he was already thrusting his hips and pushing against her fragile maidenhead, while his body pulsated with painful, staggering need.

He couldn't think, couldn't find any more strength to resist, until he realized Véronique's eyes were open and her hands were pressing against his chest. It was a sobering moment, like a splash of cold water in the face, and he drew back instantly from the enticing wet heat of her virginity.

"You want to stop," he said shakily.

"I'm so sorry," she replied. "I don't know what came over me, but I cannot do this."

He paused to gain control over the abrupt routing of his desires. "Do not apologize."

Then he reached down and quickly pulled his breeches up as he rolled off her. Lying on his back, he fought to catch his breath.

She tugged her skirts down over her knees and covered her face with both hands, as if ashamed.

"You did nothing wrong," he said.

"I could have. I came very close, but I cannot be that sort of woman. My family has lost everything, and now that we are so close to regaining our dignity, I cannot disgrace them in this way. What if you and I conceived a child?"

He was always very careful about those things, but tonight had been unbridled and risky in every way.

Véronique looked apologetically into his eyes. "There are still things you do not know, Nicholas, things about my sister. I cannot repeat her mistakes."

He sat up and contemplated her words. "What are you saying? That Gabrielle has borne a man's child?"

Véronique's eyes were wet as she looked away to stare distantly toward the window. "She has not borne the child yet . . . but she will."

Nicholas laid a hand on hers, forcing her to look at him again. "Why did you not tell me this before?"

"I only just learned of it myself."

"Who is the man?" he asked. "Tell me his name. If it is Pierre, I swear, there will be hell to pay."

"No," she replied, sliding off the bed and rising to her feet. "It is not Pierre." She went to pour herself another glass of wine and raised it to her lips. Then she turned to face Nicholas as he, too, rose from the bed and began to retie his cravat.

"Do you remember when we were in the coach together," she said, "and I told you that I had a sister who was in love with a young man, but he could not marry her, because his father did not approve of the match?"

"Yes."

She sighed. "His name is Robert. They have been

sweethearts since she was fifteen, and they have been waiting a long time to marry. I believe he genuinely loves her, but since our father's disgrace—and with the loss of our property—Robert's father has threatened to disinherit him if he does not break their engagement."

Nicholas finished buttoning his waistcoat. "He cannot do that, not if there was a previous agreement between them, and certainly not if he had already claimed his husbandly rights."

"His father can do whatever he pleases," she said. "He is a wealthy viscount and Robert is his only male heir, and we have no power. It was an unlikely match to begin with, for we are not aristocrats and the viscount is ambitious. Robert is not like that," she added. "He is kindhearted and fair-minded. I do not believe he intended to put Gabrielle at such risk, but they are young and very much in love. I am quite sure he has not yet given up the possibility of marrying her, somehow."

"Does he know of the child she carries?"

"Not yet, and I cannot predict what Robert or Gabrielle will do. There is a great deal of money and property at stake. She does not want to be the cause of his downfall. I am sure he will take care of her, but it may not be a respectable situation." Véronique drained the rest of the wine from her glass and set it down. "So you see, I cannot allow the same thing to happen to me. I must be strong for my sister. She may need my help in the coming months. And years."

Nicholas felt rather flustered suddenly. It was a thorny situation to be sure, and now he understood her reservations about giving in to their passions just now, for she had the wisdom and experience to understand that sex—no matter how pleasurable—could be an extremely dangerous undertaking for an unmarried woman.

His mouth went dry, so he poured himself a glass of wine and took a sip, swallowing heavily while his concern for Véronique's welfare struck him like a punch in the stomach.

The sound of the clock ticking on the wall seemed thunderous in the silence of the room as he stared at her, wanting desperately to take her into his arms and promise that everything was going to be all right, that he would take care of her and make all her problems disappear.

He was going to return the property to her father. That had already been decided. But what about Gabrielle?

Véronique gazed at him with searching eyes. "Was it a full hour?" she asked. "Did I fulfill my obligation? Will that satisfy you?"

He could have sprayed his wine onto the floor. First of all, her question made him feel like a heel. And no, he was not satisfied. Far from it. She had left him throbbing and aching for more of her unfathomable sexual torture.

"Yes, it was a full hour," he said nevertheless, "and you may rest assured that in the morning, the deed to your father's property will be in your hands."

Her eyes filled with tears. "Thank you, Nicholas. I am so relieved. This will help us tremendously. Perhaps there is still hope for Gabrielle's marriage to Robert if we can become respectable again."

Her tousled hair was shimmering in the firelight. The flesh of her cheeks glowed like morning dew. Nicholas watched her shift uneasily on the spot, as if she wanted to leave his chamber now before any further licentious behavior could occur . . . for there was a definite note of danger and temptation in the air.

He should let it go at this, allow her to walk out with

a feeling of satisfaction and accomplishment, for she had achieved her goal, but something deep inside him could not allow that.

He wanted her with an urgency that shattered his understanding of himself as a man. He had never deemed to care about a lover's happiness beyond the pleasure of their sexual encounters. He prided himself upon satisfying his lovers in bed, but this was something else. He could not bear to think of Véronique's sorrow after she left here. He did not want her to feel ashamed of her desire for him, nor did he want her to spend another moment worrying about her sister. He wanted sunshine and happiness for Véronique, every day for the rest of her life. He wanted to provide for her in every possible manner, and offer whatever it took to bring her to the heights of ecstasy in his arms, without shame or inhibition.

His gaze came to rest feverishly on the soft pink heaving flesh of her bosom.

Then their eyes met.

She was distraught. He could see that she wanted to stay. She was still impassioned from their close brush with intercourse—which could very well have resulted in a pregnancy—and she feared the consequences.

"I must go," she quickly said, her cheeks flushed, her delicate eyebrows pulling together in dismay, as if she were nearly terror-struck.

"No, please . . ." He reached out to take hold of her arm, but she slipped from his grasp and hurried to the door.

Her hand wrapped around the knob and she pulled it open, but he crossed the room in a flash and shoved the door closed. *Hard.*

"Don't go," he whispered in her ear, his boot braced against the bottom of the door while the front of his body pressed up against the soft back of hers.

It was excruciating. He could smell the clean fragrance of her hair . . . feel its silken texture upon his lips.

Astounded by the blazing heat of his desires, he ran his fingers lightly over her nape and squeezed her shoulder. Her body shivered.

"Marry me," he said.

Good God. The words were out before he could pause to consider the lifelong ramifications of such a request, and what it would mean for his freedom. He had always lived for pleasure and could commit to nothing. He had never been faithful to one woman, nor did he ever imagine he would *want* to be. Nothing, however—no other woman from his past or present—existed for him in this moment, except for the delicious French creature before him, who was in need of a champion.

He wanted overwhelmingly to rescue her.

To possess her.

To conquer her.

Ah, God . . . She smelled of roses and made him feel light-headed. Inebriated. He brushed his nose down the back of her neck.

Slowly she turned to face him. He pinned her tightly up against the door as his hand stroked over her shoulder and settled upon her full breast.

"What did you say?" She looked up at him with those giant, shrewd green eyes, almost daring him to repeat it.

"I asked you to marry me," he replied.

She took a deep breath—which caused her breast to fill his whole hand—and wet her lips. "It wasn't a question if I recall," she said, "but rather a very arrogant command."

His body filled with a need that felt heavier than lead.

"Does it matter whether it was a question or a command? All you have to do is answer yes."

"But I do not believe you are truly asking," she said. "This is something else. You are just trying to entice me into staying."

He couldn't resist a devilish grin at the notion of spending the night with her. "Is it working? I hope so," he added, "because I would most certainly enjoy your company if you were so inclined."

"If I *did* stay," she replied, "would there be a marriage proposal in the morning? I think not."

He kissed her lightly on the cheek. Then he kissed her nose, eyelids, and forehead. "I suppose you think I propose to *all* the ladies who try to flee from my bed, before I've had a chance to pleasure them senseless?"

She made a sound that resembled a hiccup, and he smiled. "Have I shocked you, Véronique? Or did I tempt you?"

"Both," she replied, letting her eyes fall closed as he laid a trail of kisses across her neck. "I fear you are trying to seduce me."

"*Obviously,* that is the case."

They were both breathing hard as he ran his hands down the voluptuous curve of her hips.

Her eyes clouded over with desire as she gazed up at him. "This is madness."

"Without a doubt. But you must stay focused, darling, and answer the question."

"So it *was* a question, then?"

"If you insist." He dropped to one knee, slid his hands up under her skirts, and stroked her calves, her soft knees, and the inside of her luscious warm thighs. He wanted to go higher but refrained—at least for the moment.

"Will you marry me, Véronique?" he asked. "Be my wife and lover, and let me be husband and lover to you.

I vow that I will set everything to rights in your life. Especially in bed."

He ran his thumbs across her knees.

"But you are a prince," she argued. "I am your kidnapper, and a nobody. Surely your brother, the king, will wonder what folly came over you if you take me as your wife. I cannot possibly accept."

"Yes, you can, because you want to. Face it—you need me, Véronique, and you want to love me."

There it was—the word he never imagined he would ever say aloud to any woman.

Love.

But this wasn't love. He didn't know what it was, outside of something that resembled a drunken madness, surely brought on by rage, lust, and captivity.

She was right. He had lost his mind. But it was a delicious madness, and he wanted more of it. More of *her*—his fascinating captor, who affected him like no other woman ever had.

To his surprise, she urged him to his feet, rested her forehead on his chest, and placed her hands on his shoulders. "I am not sure I can believe this is happening," she said, her voice shaky and tremulous in the quiet of the room.

"Trust me, it is," he assured her as he lifted her chin with his finger to force her to look up at him. "I cannot explain it, but I feel a strong need to have you in my life. I cannot imagine leaving here and returning to Petersbourg without you, or abandoning you to any sort of peril. I want to help you, and I want to make love to you until you are ripped apart by pleasure and weeping with rapture beneath me."

Out of all that, she seemed to hear only one thing: "So we would return to Petersbourg? You would not stay here at d'Entremont Manor?"

He blinked down at her, pleased of course that she was making plans, but he was not so clearheaded at the moment. "Honestly . . . I haven't thought that far ahead," he replied. "I will need time to consider that."

But of course he had to return home. He could not stay away forever, or keep the news of these events from his brother, Randolph. He was Prince Nicholas of Petersbourg, and he had a duty to his family and his country.

But wait . . . no . . . he was not Prince Nicholas.

He was the half-French bastard son of a dead Bonapartist.

The realization struck him hard, and he found himself suddenly pulling Véronique into his arms and holding her tight. "I will need to ask your father's permission to marry you," he whispered in her ear. "We will leave tomorrow." That would give him time to decide what he would do with this place.

Véronique laid her hands on his chest. "Do you really mean this, Nicholas? You are not just trying to seduce me into your bed? You truly want me to be your wife, even though we barely know each other?"

"I know enough," he replied. "And though it defies all reason, I know that I must have you, and I cannot fathom the idea of leaving you behind. Never seeing you again."

"I would be a fool to say no."

"That's right, because I can make everything well for you—and for your sister."

She tipped her head back against the door and closed her eyes. "I must be dreaming. Someone needs to pinch me."

He gazed at her soft, moist lips and lightly kissed them. "There will be no pinching, for I do not wish to startle you."

Her eyes fluttered open and she gazed up at him with an unreadable emotion. "I am going to leave the room now, and give you time to reconsider what has just happened here. If you wake up in the morning and realize you were mistaken to have made such an offer, I will not hold you to the proposal."

He smiled at her. "*Never* will I feel this was a mistake. All I will do, after you walk out of here, is lie on my bed in agony, imagining the moment I will deflower you on our wedding night."

Her smile was as dazzling as the sun.

She reached for the doorknob, and he stepped back to permit her to leave—for she had given him the answer he wanted.

"Good night, Nicholas," she said with another smile as she slipped out and closed the door behind her.

For a long moment he stood motionless, transfixed, as he stared at the door and listened to the sound of her footsteps growing distant down the corridor. He wanted her back this instant, but fought the urge to follow. He must wait until the morning to see her again.

He realized that respectability such as this was a novel concept for him. It was an unnerving thought, to imagine how he was going to navigate in these waters, long into the future.

Eventually he backed away from the door and turned around to look at his empty bedchamber—in particular the rumpled bedcovers where he had lain with Véronique just now, and come very close to the conquest of her virginity.

He had never been so close to intercourse, then been forced to restrain his desires. The women he usually bedded were never virgins. They were always seasoned lovers, willing and eager. There was nothing to prevent them from enjoying themselves.

Véronique, however, was different. She was pure, and she needed him like no other woman had ever needed him before.

He had proposed marriage.

Marriage.

Something squeezed in his chest, and he sank down onto the chair in front of the fire, in shock. He slouched low, tipped his head back, and blinked up at the ceiling.

He would take her home to Petersbourg and introduce her as his bride.

There would have to be some sort of celebration.

Would they marry here, or wait until they reached Petersbourg?

What would the newspapers have to say about it?

He began to sort through all the logistics. Randolph would likely bestow a new title upon them as a couple—perhaps make them duke and duchess of something or other.

Certain women of his acquaintance would not be pleased. They would likely throw vases or other china knickknacks at the back of his head.

He sat forward, steepled his fingers together, and rested his forehead on them as if in prayer, while a slow wave of discomfort poured into his stomach.

A royal wedding. *His* royal wedding. Good God.

Had he really just proposed?

Chapter Fifteen

Gabrielle chattered exuberantly during the journey from d'Entremont Manor to their family home, farther inland to the south.

They did not depart until well after luncheon; otherwise, Gabby would have had her head in a bucket for the first ten or so miles. Perhaps that might have been preferable to this, Véronique thought, for she was well-nigh bouncing off the walls, eager to return home and see Robert.

Véronique was seated beside her, across from Nicholas, who listened to Gabby's chatter and seemed genuinely amused by her enthusiasm. He responded to her riddles and agreed with her opinions about the weather and the end of the war.

At least they shared the same political opinions about Emperor Napoléon and his voracious hunger for territory and power. That was over now, however. Napoléon was in the custody of the British, and with any luck, they would never see or hear from him again.

And so, the journey by coach continued with no lack of conversation, which was a blessing for Véronique, as she was nervous about reaching her home. In fact, she was almost sick with dread.

What would Nicholas think when he met her father? There would be no advance warning about their visit. A royal prince would stride up the Montagne steps carrying the deed to their home, and her mother would most certainly be caught off guard. Perhaps she would not even be dressed, and her father might be in his cups, weeping with shame under the stairs, or searching for coins in the sofa cushions so that he might join a card game somewhere in the village—or, heaven forbid, Paris—and turn his luck around.

Oh, God. Sitting forward, she peered out the window. It was nearly dusk, and she recognized this particular pasture. They would reach her home in less than an hour.

She jumped at the shock of Nicholas's hand upon her knee, and was aware of Gabby taking notice as well—then pretending *not* to notice by closing her eyes and resting her head on a pillow against the window glass.

"Are you all right?" Nicholas quietly asked. "You seem distracted. Are you anxious?"

She sat back and folded her hands on her lap. "I suppose I am. It's not every day a young lady brings a prince home to meet her parents."

"Nor is it every day a prince asks a man for permission to marry his daughter," Nicholas replied. "I am anxious as well. Will they approve of me, do you think?"

She could have laughed at that, but managed to refrain. "I believe you have no reason to be concerned, sir. I am quite certain you will be well received."

He smiled that slow, confident grin that sent flames of heat licking through her bloodstream.

"But what if they have heard about my notorious reputation?" he asked mischievously. "Perhaps they will wish to protect you from my clutches."

He slid a glance at Gabrielle, knowing of course that she was not asleep, but listening.

Véronique smirked at him and mouthed the words, *You are very wicked.*

He raised his eyebrows unapologetically, then leaned back in the seat, gazing at her with dark seduction in the early evening light.

They had not yet discussed a wedding date, and she wondered how long it would be before she could enjoy the pleasure of her deflowering, for he was a tempting and tantalizing man who was clearly well versed in the art of lovemaking.

But would he be faithful? she wondered uneasily as the coach rumbled along the lane. She wanted to believe that he would. She wanted very badly to believe in him in every way. Some might think her a silly fool to expect fidelity from a man like him, and perhaps they would turn out to be correct about that. Perhaps the Prince of Petersbourg would take her as a wife and live happily ever after with her for a few brief months at most—then return to his endless string of mistresses while she did her duty at the palace and turned a blind eye. That's how it was done in most royal courts, and this marriage was certainly no love match. She didn't know *what* it was.

Still . . . she couldn't help but believe that he was capable of more.

She looked at him carefully in the fading light. This marriage would solve all her family's problems without a doubt, and quite possibly rescue Gabrielle from disaster as well. Véronique wasn't sure exactly how Nicholas would accomplish such a feat, but he had implied as much, and he was a powerful man, so she would do what she must. She would become his bride and hope for the best.

Closing her eyes, she propped a pillow up against the glass to rest her head and tried to relax for the remainder of the journey—for surely when they arrived, the shock and upheaval in her father's household would be momentous.

It was just past dark when the coach pulled to a halt in front of Montagne Manor. Véronique waited for Nicholas to unlatch the door and push it open. He leaned out, looked up at the front of the Tudor-styled, ivy-covered structure—with only one light visible in an upstairs window—and turned to her. "No servants?"

She shook her head. "We had to let most of them go. It's a spare household now, but I am sure someone will be out shortly."

The front door opened and Gailliard, their devoted butler, appeared carrying a lamp to greet them. "Good evening, mademoiselle," he said as he approached. "We did not expect you."

She took Nicholas's hand and stepped onto the gravel drive. "Bonjour, Gailliard. My apologies for not sending word in advance, but our decision to return home was rather spontaneous. I hope that won't be a problem."

"Not at all," he replied with impressive composure as Nicholas assisted Gabrielle out of the vehicle.

Véronique gestured toward him. "As you can see, I have brought a guest." She turned and spoke to Nicholas. "Please allow me to present our butler, Gailliard."

Nicholas inclined his head at him.

She turned back to the butler. "And this is His Royal Highness, Prince Nicholas of Petersbourg."

Gailliard's eyes widened in shock. Then he bent at the waist and bowed with a deep, sweeping flourish. "Welcome, Your Highness, to Montagne Manor."

"Thank you," Nicholas casually replied.

Gailliard nearly stumbled backwards as he indicated the front entrance. Then he quickly hurried to speak to the coachman about guest room arrangements for the servants, and told him where to take the horses, for they had no groomsman to attend to such matters. Véronique glanced self-consciously at Nicholas, who politely ignored Gailliard's quiet explanations and apologetic tones as they made their way inside.

The front hall was shrouded in darkness, which came as no surprise, for her family had been conserving candles for quite some time. Nevertheless, a somber feeling settled into her heart, for this house had once been full of bright lights and laughter.

"Will you inform my parents that Gabrielle and I have returned?" she said to Gailliard as he entered behind them. "And please prepare a guest chamber for Prince Nicholas. Have my parents dined yet?"

"Not yet, mademoiselle. Dinner will be served at—" He paused uncomfortably. "—nine o'clock."

She knew of course that there was no dinner planned, and hoped that something reasonably palatable could be thrown together at the last minute, for she was famished, and they were, after all, about to entertain a prince.

"Lovely," she replied. "In the meantime, please bring a decanter of wine to the parlor. We shall make ourselves comfortable there until dinner."

Poor Gailliard. He looked completely flustered as he gathered Gabrielle's and Véronique's cloaks.

"I will send the maid to light a fire for you," he said. Again it came as no surprise to find the parlor shrouded in darkness as well. Gaillaird carried his lamp across the room to the pianoforte and lit all three wicks on the candelabra—a tremendous extravagance when the candles were already burned down to short stubs. She hoped he would return shortly to replace them.

They took seats in the dimly lit room to wait for her parents.

Nicholas sat leisurely at one end of the sofa, while Gabrielle sat forward on the edge of an upholstered Queen Anne chair, impatiently tapping her foot.

Véronique sat at the other end of the sofa, feeling an odd mixture of excitement and dread. She was about to deliver shocking news to her parents—that Lord d'Entremont was dead, but that she had secured the deed to their home, which Prince Nicholas had in his possession this very evening.

Not only that, but she would then reveal the fact that she was about to marry into a very prestigious European royal family.

She tapped her finger on her knee, only half-believing that the second part would ever come to pass, for everything had happened so quickly. It still seemed too outrageous to believe.

She glanced at Nicholas. He was watching her intently in the candlelight, his blue eyes gleaming almost broodingly. He spoke not a single word.

At last the maid arrived with a tray of wine and glasses, and set it down on the table. A short time later, the fire was blazing in the hearth and they were sipping her father's best cabernet. They chatted about a few light matters until the glow of a lamp appeared in the doorway, and her father and mother entered the parlor at last.

Nicholas stood. Véronique and Gabrielle followed

suit. Introductions were made and everyone took seats on the sofas and chairs around the fire.

While her parents asked politely about the weather, roads, and duration of the journey, Véronique took careful note of her mother's appearance. It was clear she had donned her best gown, combed and swept her hair up into a fresh knot, and had opened her jewelry box this evening—probably for the first time in months. She spoke courteously to Nicholas as if she were happy and well, but the dark circles beneath her eyes were still evident, and Véronique knew it was a struggle for her to be sociable, and she would be overcome by exhaustion later.

As for her father . . . he, too, had combed his hair, donned a freshly laundered pair of breeches and a clean jacket, but that woozy, sleepy look was ever present in his eyes. She wondered how long it would be before he nodded off.

Soon after they sat down, the polite conversation ground to an awkward halt. Véronique was about to bring up the death of Lord d'Entremont, and the reason for Nicholas's presence here, when he spoke first, to her father.

"I am sure you must be wondering, sir, why your daughters have brought me here to meet you. There is certainly much to discuss. Is there a place where we can speak in private?"

"We could go to my study," her father helpfully suggested.

Véronique experienced sudden heart palpitations and turned her body at an angle on the sofa to face Nicholas. "Perhaps I should join you."

She couldn't bear the thought of what might be expressed in her absence. Would Nicholas tell her father that she had abducted him from a masked ball where she'd had no chaperone? Would he allude to the physical intimacies that occurred in his bedroom?

Similarly, what if her father said the wrong things, or lied to Nicholas about his gambling? She must be there to ensure he did not make a fool of himself, or any of them.

"That won't be necessary," Nicholas firmly replied, leaving no room for argument, and suggesting, without ever saying so, that she must learn to trust him. He would take care of this, as he would take care of many things over the coming weeks and years.

She never found it easy to let others do the work, however. She preferred to make sure things were done right by doing them herself and never passing the reins to another. It was not easy for her to watch them rise from their chairs and leave the room alone together. But she weathered it. She would put her trust in Nicholas.

Chapter Sixteen

"We met at a ball in Paris," Nicholas explained, "where your daughter lured me into a coach, fed me enough laudanum to knock me unconscious for hours, then delivered me to d'Entremont Manor, where I eventually learned that my presence was urgently required by the marquis."

Montagne's head drew back in shock, and he laughed. "Surely you jest! She was visiting her aunt, sir. Why in the world would she do anything like that?"

"Because the marquis needed to ensure my prompt arrival at his home, and Véronique was willing to accept the task of delivering me there, for she wanted something from d'Entremont in return. I am sure you know what that is." He regarded Montagne with unwavering scrutiny and a look of warning, which encouraged him to speak truthfully.

"She did it in exchange for money?" the man asked.

"Not money," Nicholas replied. "She wanted the deed to this property, and I am pleased to inform you that she has acquired it. From me."

"From *you*." The chair creaked as Montagne shifted

uneasily. "Why would *you* have it? Did you purchase it from d'Entremont? Or perhaps you won it in a card game," he added bitterly.

"Neither is accurate, sir, for I have inherited all of the marquis's properties and assets, including d'Entremont Manor, which brings me to the unfortunate news that Lord d'Entremont passed away only yesterday. There is to be a funeral in a few days' time, and I shall be returning for that."

Montagne shook his head. "I do not understand. You said that Véronique acquired this property from *you*. Why would you give it to her? She has no money. She could not have purchased it." He slouched back in his chair and buried his forehead in a hand. "Oh, good Lord. Please do not tell me that she compromised her honor. I would never forgive myself."

Nicholas quickly leaned forward. "Not at all, sir. You have every reason to be proud of your daughter. Both your daughters. Despite our tumultuous beginnings, they were exceedingly helpful to me at d'Entremont Manor, and I wished to repay their kindness and fulfill the promises that d'Entremont had made to them. That is why I have signed the deed over to you. We will require a solicitor to witness the transaction, of course, and make sure everything is properly and legally transferred. But there is more," he added, charging forward with surprising vigor.

"What more could there possibly be?" Montagne asked, his lips parting in wonder.

Nicholas gave him time to prepare. "I wish to marry your daughter," he said at last.

Montagne covered his mouth with a hand. "Good God. Which one?"

"Your eldest. Véronique."

The man's jaw fell open and he stared blankly at

Nicholas, then looked around the study as if to ensure he was not dreaming, that all of this was really happening.

"Are you truly Prince Nicholas of Petersbourg?" he asked in disbelief. "The *country*? I do not understand how this can be real."

Nicholas found himself somehow charmed by the man's humility, and almost wanted to laugh and smack him firmly on the back to help him get the news down.

"It is very real, sir," he replied with a smile. "I am sure you know that your daughter is an extraordinary young woman. Not only is she charming and beautiful, but she is also intelligent, capable, and strong. Needless to say, this entire experience has been bizarre, but she was a steady, calm presence throughout, and I found myself depending on her, confiding in her, trusting her. I have never known another woman who could compare to her in all the qualities that would make a woman a fine wife. She is a remarkable person, and I believe she is destined to be my bride."

There. He had said all the right things—the words a father needed to hear when a man entered his home and asked permission to marry his daughter.

Were all those words true? Yes, Nicholas did believe Véronique was extraordinary, for no other woman had ever incited such impulsiveness in him before, or brought him even *close* to considering a life of matrimony.

He did not want to let her go, or lose her altogether. He had never felt that way about any other woman.

So this must be it, then, he thought. It had to be, for he felt somehow transformed.

"Well . . . of course my answer must be yes," Montagne said, "for clearly you are an extraordinary man yourself, and what father does not want the very best for his daughter? If you love and respect Véronique as much as you claim, how could I possibly object?"

He had never said *love*.

Or had he?

Montagne rose to his feet and offered his hand. "I am most pleased, sir. Most pleased indeed!"

"As am I," Nicholas replied. "I thank you for your generosity, monsieur."

Montagne's eyebrows flew up with laughter. "You are thanking *me*? Good heavens, man! You have it backwards! You have brought my daughters home to me, along with the deed to this property. I hardly know what to say. I cannot believe my luck!"

A sudden dark cloud rolled over Nicholas's optimism. He waited for Montagne to sit down again.

With some concern, he took a seat himself and said, "It is not luck, sir. It is a direct result of your daughter's personal sacrifice and devotion to you. Therefore, you must make a pledge to me when you accept this deed. You will give up the card table and never again take part in any sort of wager. You mustn't lose everything to this dangerous vice of yours—which has very nearly ruined all of you. There will never be a second chance like this, and I assure you, if you repeat such a blunder, I will wash my hands of you."

Montagne's whole face seemed to crumple and sink like a mound of melting wax. His eyes lowered slightly and he stared at Nicholas's chest.

Not entirely sure what was going through the man's mind, Nicholas leaned forward. "Are you feeling unwell, sir?"

When Monsieur Montagne's eyes lifted, they were gleaming pools of wetness. "I apologize. You are right, and I cannot possibly convey my gratitude and my shame to you. I have been a weak and irresponsible husband and father. I know it. I have known it for a long time, while I watched my family suffer. My wife, especially. I do not wish to continue down that path or repeat my mistakes. I feel that today God has offered me a chance to redeem myself. I do not wish to squander it. I shall not take this gift lightly, sir. I promise you. I love my family dearly, and I regret the pain I have caused them." Montagne lowered his head into his hands and wept.

Nicholas sat quietly until his future father-in-law recovered, then laid a hand on his shoulder. "I know you are a good man," he said. "Otherwise, you would not have raised such a lovely daughter, and for that I congratulate you."

Montagne looked up. "You are a kind and generous soul," he said. "I am in awe of your charity and your compassion, your integrity as a great man of honor. I feel truly blessed on this day."

Suddenly speechless, Nicholas sat back. No one had ever praised him in such grand terms before—not since before his mother died. He was always the black sheep, the cad, the scoundrel, the selfish, irresponsible rake who seduced women for his own pleasures without a single care for their hearts or virtues.

Kind and generous soul?

"Perhaps we should return to the parlor now," Nicholas suggested, "and raise our glasses to celebrate your daughter's engagement."

Montagne's eyes filled with tears again. He pressed a fist to his mouth, as if he could not contain his emotions. "Yes, that sounds like a fine idea."

As they stood to leave the room, Nicholas clasped his hands behind his back. "Since we are on the topic of marriage," he said, "I understand your other daughter, Gabrielle, is in love with a viscount's son who lives nearby?"

"Yes," Montagne replied. "They have been sweethearts for years, but the boy's father is uppity. He doesn't approve of us, for we are merely country bumpkins in his eyes. We don't move about in Parisian society as he does. I have nothing against Robert, of course. He is a decent young fellow, nothing at all like his father. He prefers country living to all the trappings of Paris."

"I should like to meet the viscount," Nicholas said as they crossed the front hall. "Perhaps Véronique and I could pay a call tomorrow to inform them of our good news. They are your neighbors, after all."

They reached the parlor just then, and when Nicholas set eyes on his future bride, he experienced an unfamiliar mix of pride and desire.

She would soon be his—he could not wait for the moment he would bed her—but he also wondered what he had done to deserve a woman like her. Pure, intelligent, steady as a rock, and beautiful. Then he heard his dead father's voice in his ears. . . .

You are a wild, irresponsible, degenerate young buck. I hope you never marry, for you will be a worthless adulterer. I pity the woman who becomes your wife.

With a sharp pang of agitation, Nicholas glanced around at the others in the room, his future family by marriage, and felt suddenly adrift in uncharted territory—with people who actually thought highly of him.

Véronique tossed and turned for hours in her bed that night, for her body was wide awake.

Before dinner, Nicholas had received her father's permission to marry her and had informed him of the return of their property. He'd called it a groom's gift to his future in-laws.

Nicholas had no parents of his own to bestow gifts

upon—he mentioned it after the toast was made—and Véronique had fallen a little more in love with him at that moment, for what a hero he had become in all their eyes. Until now, she had been working hard to resist such feelings, and remain practical about this marriage arrangement, but suddenly she felt like a romantic fool, and since climbing into bed, a storm of lust had taken over her body.

By two o'clock in the morning, she gave up the fight. She tossed the covers aside, reached for her dressing gown, lit a candle, and carried it into the dark corridor.

She padded down the hall to the green guest chamber where Nicholas was sleeping, and knocked gently. She waited a moment or two.

Perhaps that knock was not loud enough. Véronique rapped a second time and pressed her ear to the door.

The sound of the mattress creaking and a husky groan from inside were evidence of Nicholas's awakening, and just the image of him turning over in his bed rekindled the fires of her passions.

He stirred from within and she stepped back, candle in hand, as he walked across the floor. At last the doorknob turned, and she found herself standing before him on the threshold—staring at her gorgeous fiancé in the flesh, his nightshirt open at his chest, his hair tousled from sleep.

"I needed to see you," she explained.

"Why?" But his gaze simmered with an expert awareness of her desires, like a wolf scenting blood on the wind.

"May I come in?" she asked.

He opened the door wider and stepped aside.

"So it is official now," she said as she set her candle down on a table and shrugged out of her robe. "We are engaged."

"Yes, we are," he replied, moving closer. "Your father gave us his blessing. Now there is only the small matter of a licence and a wedding, and vows spoken before God. Then we will be man and wife."

"Sharing the same bed," she boldly added.

He stopped and slid a suspicious look at her. "Is that why you are here, darling? To pull the trigger before the powder has been loaded?"

She smiled. "An interesting metaphor, but I am not the one who will fire the musket. That is man's work."

He chuckled. "Now you are being facetious. You and I both know you are quite capable of firing a musket. You are the one, after all, who just charged into *my* bedchamber uninvited in the dead of night."

"Perhaps." She slowly approached him and laid her open palms on his muscular chest. Sliding her hands up to his shoulders, she wet her lips as a passionate infatuation for him sparked in her blood. She wanted him with impossible yearning, and didn't care that they were not yet married, or that her parents were asleep in their beds—she hoped—a few doors down.

"You shouldn't have come in here," he warned, the words sensible and responsible, but contradicting the blatant seduction she saw in his luminous blue eyes. "I should send you back to your room without supper."

"And with a spanking as well?" she asked, not knowing from where that improper allusion had come.

"Only if you ask nicely."

Then his mouth covered hers in a forceful kiss that made the room spin in circles. His mouth was hot, wet, and demanding, and she felt completely swept away.

Smoothly, he pushed her toward the bed, eased her down, and settled his heavy muscled body on top of hers. "How else would you like me to punish you to-night," he asked, "now that you are here?"

It was too much for her innocent mind to comprehend. She was shocked by the intensity of her desires, for putting herself in the position of being ravished by a masterful libertine who was no doubt accustomed to women knocking on his door at all hours of the night, their bodies blazing with need. And he knew just how to satisfy, how to flirt, how to draw a woman into his delicious sensual world, and make her do things she never imagined she would do.

Such as offering her body to him before the marriage certificate was signed.

Nicholas began to slide her nightdress up over her knees, then stroked her thigh. She parted her legs for him and knew that this time, she would not stop him from claiming her as his bride, for she wanted him with an urgency she could not suppress.

He found the damp center of her womanhood, and she arched her back at the pleasure of his touch. He stroked the tingling outer flesh—slick with the moisture of her arousal—and gently fingered the sensitive bud until she gasped with delight and surrendered to the sweet floating sensations that carried her into some sort of fantasy world.

Before long, the pleasure rose to a peak, exploded, and trembled through her in an unexpected climax, which left her panting on the bed. Only when she opened her eyes did she realize that Nicholas was watching her intently in the silvery moonlight streaming in through the windows.

"Are you going to make love to me now?" she asked.

The seduction was gone from his eyes, however. She almost did not recognize him as he shook his head.

"No, darling, I am going to do something else— something completely out of character for me."

"What is that?" She rose up on her elbows while he lowered her nightdress to cover her knees.

"I am going to do the gentlemanly thing," he replied, "and send you back to your room, because I intend to wait until our wedding night to take your virginity."

Véronique frowned. "Don't you want me?" She felt utterly bereft as he stood and offered his hand to her.

"Of course I do," he assured her. "You are everything to me."

She recognized the practised delivery of the response—the way he flattered her in order to dodge a bullet, so that he would not have to engage in an honest conversation.

"Why, then, do you want to wait?" she pressed. "I am surprised, Nicholas. I thought you never turned a lady away."

Now on her feet, she faced him.

"You are not just any lady," he told her, as he took her chin in his hand. "You are my future wife, and if I had any sense in my head, I would have rejected you at the door when you first arrived."

She was hurt by the sudden chill in his voice. "Why?"

"Because you do not appreciate the concessions I am making for you."

"I don't understand."

He looked away coldly. "If we were back in my own world, I would have deprived you of your innocence tonight without a second thought. But I do not want to be that man. Not with you."

She saw the torment in his eyes and laid a hand on his cheek, but he removed it.

"Do you know what my father used to call me?" he asked.

Shaking her head, she waited apprehensively for him to explain.

"I am not sure where to begin, actually, for there was always an endless string of nasty words put together. Wastrel. Sinner. Worthless degenerate. Future adulterer. I could go on."

The mood in the room turned suddenly dark and somber.

"I do not believe any of those things," she firmly told him. "For even after what I did to you, and how I deceived you, you have behaved honorably and kindly toward me and my family."

He pinched the bridge of his nose and sighed in defeat. "Ah, I fear you are mistaken in your opinions of me, Véronique. You don't know me at all. And you have done nothing but wreak havoc on my existence since the first moment we met. On that night you took away my freedom, yet for some reason I have agreed to a lifetime of it. I should hate you for all this. So count your blessings that I am choosing a path of restraint tonight. Go now, before I change my mind and throw you back on the bed."

She had come here wanting just that, to be ravished by her future husband who had been her hero tonight, but the harsh tone of his voice and the anger in his eyes forced her to take a step back, away from him. "You haven't forgiven me," she said.

His chest heaved while he seemed to weigh his emotions. "Perhaps I should be grateful to you for lifting the veil on my true heritage, but I believe, in the process, you have snapped me in two. I now feel like a broken bone that must be wrenched back into place, and I need something to bite on to keep from screaming my lungs out."

He was referring to his parentage. Before now he had revealed very little angst about that revelation. He seemed almost indifferent to it, but clearly it had affected him more than he let on.

"It will take some time to adjust to everything," she said, "and understand who you really are."

"Yes," he replied, though he said it through clenched teeth.

She decided it would be best to respect his wishes and leave. She started for the door. "I won't come to you again until we are married," she told him, "for I do not wish to cause any further . . . havoc."

She wrapped her hand around the doorknob and opened it a crack, only to be startled by his sudden rush to push it closed.

He had done this when he proposed, and she reveled in the familiar sensation of his tall, hard body brushing up against the back of hers, preventing her from leaving his bedchamber.

She felt his breath on her neck. "Thank you," he whispered.

For what? For leaving? For promising not to return any time soon?

Or for disagreeing with your father's cruel words?

She closed her eyes and knew in that moment that this man needed her, that no one else in the world could understand what he'd been through, or give him what she could.

He stepped back and she felt the cool air on her shoulder blades as he withdrew. Then she pulled the door open and returned to her own bedchamber.

Chapter Seventeen

The following day dawned with an idyllic pink sunrise over the mist-shrouded forest to the east, and sparkling drops of dew that gleamed on the southern meadows. By noon, the sun had risen high in the sky and a steady breeze was blowing over the treetops.

"It is so good of you to pay a call to our neighbors," Gabrielle said as they sat together in the coach, traveling through the thick forest and crossing the border onto Richelieu land. "They will be thrilled to meet you. Don't you agree, Véronique?"

"Yes," she said with a smile. "I am sure they will be very pleased to meet Nicholas." For they were shameless social climbers, and he was a shiny royal prince.

It galled her to think that Lord Richelieu and his wife deserved such a boon when they had treated Gabrielle so deplorably all these years. She had never been good enough for their beloved eldest son.

Véronique would not bother with any of this if it were not for Robert, who was nothing like his father. He was friendly and forthcoming, and he paid calls often when he was out riding, simply to ask after her parents, or to help her father with estate errands and chores. He had even chopped wood once, for the mere pleasure of it.

He loved Gabrielle. Véronique was certain of it. Unfortunately, recent events had sparked some doubt in her, for what if he had never intended to marry Gabby, but wanted only to sow his youthful wild oats until it was time to choose a "real" wife?

They had just emerged from the forest and begun the short drive up the steep hill to Richelieu House when Gabby peered out the window and called, "Stop! I see Robert! Look, there! He is riding this way!"

Véronique leaned to see Robert trotting up alongside the moving vehicle. She lowered the window glass to say hello, while Gabby thrust her head out.

"Robert! We were just on our way to see you and pay a call to your parents. Are they at home?"

He smiled brightly in the afternoon sunshine and thumbed the brim of his hat. "Good afternoon, ladies. It is wonderful to see you. I thought you would never return." His eyes were trained on Gabrielle's, and his cheeks were flushed from a vigorous noonday ride. "Yes, my parents are at home," he added. "Perhaps, Gabrielle, you would do me the honor of walking the rest of the way with me? It is such a glorious afternoon."

"I would be delighted." She turned to Nicholas, who had remained in the shadows during the exchange. "Can we stop, please?"

Without a word, he thumped his walking stick on the roof and signaled the coachman to pull to a halt.

The pair of horses shook in the harness as Gabrielle flung the door open and spilled out of the vehicle while Robert dismounted. She dashed into his arms, nearly knocking him over. "I missed you," she said.

"I missed you, too," he replied. "I have been positively useless here without you."

The young lovers had no eyes for anyone but each other, so Nicholas pulled the door closed and tapped his stick again on the roof of the coach.

They lurched forward and Véronique watched her sister from the window, then sat back, feeling more at ease now, after seeing that Robert's affections still burned as ardently as ever.

"He seemed pleased to see Gabrielle," she said.

Nicholas nodded. "Yes, but being pleased to see an affectionate young lady on a sunny afternoon in the country is not the same thing as making her an offer of marriage. Is he an honorable man? Is he worthy of her?"

"Honorable and worthy, yes," she replied. "But he is in a difficult predicament. He does not wish to disappoint his father."

Nicholas lounged back in the seat and gazed out the window. "Perhaps we can do something to make his predicament a little less difficult."

"There . . . *do you see*?" she said. "You are a good man, Nicholas. Anyone who thinks otherwise is a blind fool."

For a long time he did not respond or turn his gaze in her direction, and she wondered if he was even listening. Then his hand slid across the seat and clasped hers. "That is very kind of you to say, but be careful with your expectations," he said. "Or you might end up getting hurt."

The warning was more than a little disconcerting, but Véronique could say no more about it as they reached the house and a footman hurried down the steps to open the door for them.

* * *

Véronique should not have been surprised when she and Nicholas were immediately shown upstairs to the Richelieu drawing room, where their host and hostess greeted them with welcoming smiles and flourishing bows and curtsies—directed at Nicholas, of course.

She stood beside him in the spacious lime green and gilt room, looking up at the sparkling crystal chandelier overhead, and feeling rather blinded by the multitude of floral upholstery fabrics and window coverings, and the thick patterned carpets on the floor—all so very fashionable.

She had not set foot in this room since she was a young girl, and the Richelieus had not yet discovered the threat that her younger sister would later present when she claimed their eldest son's heart. Véronique honestly did not believe they had even contemplated the possibility that the two country girls from the bordering property would ever amount to anything other than scanty marriages to clerks or cabinet makers.

Now here she stood on the arm of a prince, while her younger sister was outside walking with their son—and carrying their first grandchild.

"What a pleasure to see you again, Mademoiselle Montagne," Lady Richelieu said as she stepped closer with hands outstretched, and kissed Véronique on both cheeks as if they were the closest, dearest of friends. "Please sit down. Allow me to pour you a cup of tea."

Nicholas escorted her around the back of the sofa, where they sat beside each other, facing the viscount and viscountess.

"What brings you to Richelieu House on this fine day, Your Highness?" Richelieu asked as he sat back and crossed one short pudgy booted leg over the other. "I heard you were in Paris with Wellington and Castlereagh, dealing with the aftermath of Waterloo."

Richelieu squinted suspiciously at Véronique, as if he could smell some sort of impossible plot. If he only knew the half of it.

"Yes, I was taking part in the discussions," Nicholas replied. "I presume you heard that Napoléon has surrendered to the British."

"Yes. What good news," he said.

"It will certainly narrow down the squabbling," Nicholas added, "though there are still many issues to be settled now that the king is back on the throne."

"Indeed. Will you be in France for a while, then?"

Nicholas reached for Véronique's hand. "As it happens, we shall be returning to Petersbourg very soon, for I wish to present Mademoiselle Montagne to my brother, the king, and eventually show her off to the people."

He turned his gaze toward her and smiled with charming appeal, as if they were alone together and he was out to flatter and seduce. She found herself smiling in return, briefly forgetting that the viscount and his wife were seated not far in facing chairs, watching them with painful curiosity.

Nicholas turned his smile in their direction and said cheerfully, "We are to be married, you see."

Véronique's neighbors stared in stunned silence for one of the most satisfying moments of Véronique's life. Then they quickly reacted.

The viscountess covered her cheeks with her hands. "How wonderful! We could not be happier for you both!"

Lord Richelieu cleared his throat and stood to pump Nicholas's hand and pat him on the shoulder. "Well done, sir! Now, you must tell us, how did you two meet?"

"At a masked ball in Paris," Nicholas replied. "She quite literally stole me away from my duties as ambassador to my country and completely captured my heart."

Their hosts laughed at the analogy while Véronique's own heart swelled with happiness.

At that precise moment, Robert burst into the room, holding Gabrielle's hand, almost dragging her behind him while she appeared quite thrilled to be making such a dramatic entrance.

"Father, I must speak with you," Robert firmly said, "and it cannot wait."

The viscount gave his son a stern look and turned to Nicholas. "Please pardon the intrusion, Your Highness. Allow me to present my son, Lord Robert. I presume you are already acquainted with Mademoiselle Gabrielle."

Nicholas inclined his head at Robert, who bowed properly. "I, too, apologize for the intrusion," Robert said, seeming suddenly shaken by his introduction to a prince. "But I have an important announcement to make."

"By all means," Nicholas said with a welcoming gesture, as if this were his home, not the viscount's.

Robert cleared his throat and lifted his chin. "I have just asked Gabrielle Montagne to become my wife, and she has done me the great honor of accepting. We do not wish to endure a long engagement, because we are very much in love, and have waited long enough. We have therefore decided upon a quiet ceremony here at Richelieu House to take place in three weeks. Are you happy for us, Father?" he asked with challenge in his eyes.

Véronique was quite certain that if Richelieu said no, Robert would have drawn a pistol.

A muscle clenched at the viscount's jaw. No doubt he was unaccustomed to hearing his son dictate terms concerning his own future. Nevertheless, the game had changed since Nicholas's announcement, and so, naturally, would the viscount's response.

"Why, of course I am delighted to hear this happy

news! I presume you are aware that your fiancée's sister, Véronique, is pledged to marry Prince Nicholas?"

Robert blinked a few times, as if confused. "No, I was not aware. . . . Good heavens, did I intrude upon your announcement? If so, I do apologize, sir. How uncouth of me."

Nicholas smiled and circled around the sofa to shake Robert's hand. "No apologies are necessary. Congratulations to you. You are a very lucky man. I wish you every happiness."

Robert's eyes widened in astonishment, as if he'd realized only then that he was shaking the hand of a prince, who would soon be his brother-in-law.

Nicholas turned to the viscount. "I had intended to present Gabrielle at court in Petersbourg. I do hope you will send your son to escort her there after they are married. The king will be most pleased to meet them both."

"Oh, yes!" the viscountess replied, rushing forward to embrace Robert. "We are so proud of you, dearest!" She turned to Gabrielle. "And oh, you are the most darling and beautiful creature. We could not be happier. I hope you will think of me as a second mother. In that regard, I should like to invite Mrs. Montagne for dinner soon. We can discuss wedding plans and flowers and . . . I shall also introduce you to my modiste. She comes all the way from Paris to bring the most delectable fabrics and show me the latest fashion designs. What fun we shall have. Oh, my word, but you are such a pretty young thing!"

Véronique wasn't sure if she wanted to jump for joy or expel her lunch onto the Richelieus' expensive Persian carpets—for the viscountess had never been anything but condescending and rude to both her and Gabrielle since they outgrew their little-girl dresses and blossomed into handsome young women.

Véronique decided, however, that it would be best *not* to expel her lunch presently, for this was what Gabrielle wanted, and Robert was well worth every moment of agonizing hypocrisy from his social-climbing parents.

For the next half hour they sipped tea and talked mostly about Petersbourg, until it was time to take their leave.

Their hosts walked them to the coach and showered them with French cheek kisses and a string of open invitations for future visits.

When the door of the coach was finally closed and they began the short drive home, Gabrielle buried her face in her hands and began to weep. "I am so happy," she cried, "and so very proud of Robert for standing up to his father."

Nicholas handed her a clean folded handkerchief.

"What happened between you?" Véronique asked. "Did you tell him the truth about your condition?"

Gabby lifted her face and dabbed at the corners of her eyes. "Yes, I told him as we were walking back to the house. I didn't know how he would react at first, but he took me into his arms and told me I had made him the happiest man alive. Then he got down on one knee and proposed. He said the most romantic things to me. I barely had a chance to say anything beyond a laughing yes before he grabbed me by the hand and dragged me into the house and upstairs to the drawing room. I never even told him about you and Nicholas, or that the two of you were engaged."

Véronique embraced her sister. "So he stood up to his father without knowing you were about to become sister-in-law to a prince. I am so happy for you, Gabby. He is everything you deserve."

Gabby snorted as she nodded in agreement, then she

turned to Nicholas on the opposite facing seat. "This is all *your* doing, you know. I believe you are an angel sent from heaven to rescue us all."

His eyes lifted. "An angel? Me? I hardly think so, but I appreciate the compliment, and I am pleased to be of service."

She smiled broadly at him, then blew her nose like a trumpet. "Have you two set a date for *your* wedding?"

Véronique looked to Nicholas, for she felt it was he who should decide. Perhaps he would choose a very long engagement to give them each a chance to come to their senses.

"I would like to be married immediately at d'Entremont Manor," he said, surprising her with his reply. "We must return for the funeral in a few days. Will your parents be willing to join us?"

Véronique was speechless at first, then managed to regain control of her senses. "Yes, I am sure they would be delighted to attend."

"Good," he replied as he slouched lower in the seat and folded his arms across his chest. Then he closed his eyes and dozed for the rest of the journey.

Chapter Eighteen

The Marquis of d'Entremont was entombed in the mausoleum overlooking the English Channel. It was also conveniently within view of the giant oak tree that dominated the hill on the northeast corner of the estate, which did not go unnoticed by Véronique as the carriages made their way to his final resting place.

Nicholas had instructed the vicar to refrain from mentioning his relation to the marquis during the service, for he did not want the world to know of it—at least not yet. Perhaps he would never want anyone to know.

The steward and butler each agreed to respect his wishes, but that did not stop the inquiries. During the funeral, there was much speculation about how the property would be divided and bequeathed, for everyone knew the title had already died with the marquis.

It was a massive and invaluable piece of land. Whom had he named as his heir? the guests wondered insistently, and why was Prince Nicholas of Petersbourg in attendance? D'Entremont was a well-known Bonapartist. Was there some political connection?

And where in the world was Pierre Cuvier, the

illegitimate but devoted son of the marquis's dead sister? Why was he not present?

All those questions remained unanswered as the guests drove off after the final good-bye.

Véronique was equally curious about Pierre's whereabouts, for he had left the premises the night the solicitor revealed the contents of the will at dinner, and had not yet returned.

Perhaps he had traveled to take possession of his property outside of Paris, and would never set foot here again. She would not be sorry if that were the case.

She hoped he could start a new life for himself there, and appreciate the bounty he had been given.

That evening as Véronique was dressing for dinner, a knock sounded at her door. Her maid hurried to answer it.

"Good evening," Véronique's mother said as she entered the room. "You look lovely. Remember when I used to do your hair when you were younger? You always liked it when I brushed it before bed."

Véronique, seated at the dressing table, smiled at her mother's reflection in the mirror, for she was standing behind her, looking radiant in a royal blue gown of Indian silk.

"Would you like to help me with the combs tonight?" Véronique asked. "I am sure Marie has better things to do," she added, speaking to her maid with a smile. "You can go now and see to Gabrielle."

The young maid curtsied and left the room. Véronique's mother took over the task of placing the adornments in her hair.

Véronique watched her mother in the mirror, taking note of the renewed color in her cheeks and the light of contentment in her eyes as she tucked the decorative combs into her thick upswept hair. "You look well, Mama," she said. "May I dare to presume you are happy for your daughters?"

Her mother smiled. "Happy is too small a word. I have known for years that Gabrielle was in love with Robert, but I was never certain that a marriage would be possible. And you . . . You have taken us all by surprise with your handsome fiancé. I see the way you look at each other. How can I help but be overjoyed? And to have our home back . . . It is like God has granted many miracles all at once. My heart was heavy before, but now my girls are happy and in love. It is everything a mother could wish for."

Véronique reached over her shoulder to clasp her mother's hand. "I am pleased you are feeling better."

Her mother nodded as she slipped another comb into place. "Nicholas is a true prince in every way," she continued. "Not only is he exceptionally handsome, but he is so very chivalrous. But I cannot help but ask . . . and I hope you do not resent me for prying . . . but why was he named as d'Entremont's heir? People were curious today, and there was much speculation about political dealings and such. Everyone knows Nicholas has a voice in any peace treaties that may be negotiated. Some were saying this property was some sort of bribe. Others suggested it was Nicholas's winnings in a card game. All sorts of rumors were flying about, and I must admit I am curious. I only hope that it is not something shady. Do *you* at least know the truth?"

Having set the last comb in place, her mother stepped back. Véronique stood and turned to face her. "Yes, I know the truth, but I cannot reveal it, for I have promised Nicholas my discretion. He trusts me to keep that knowledge to myself, and I must not betray his trust, not even to you. I am sorry."

"Do not be sorry," she replied. "I am proud of you for keeping your word to him, for he is your future husband. Trust between you is paramount."

Véronique rolled her shoulders in an attempt to relax and ease the tension that suddenly flooded to the forefront of her mind.

Trust, at least on Nicholas's part, seemed a great distance away at present, considering the grand deception under which they had begun, and his own misgivings about his future fidelity. But she could not unload that emotional burden on her mother, who was finally smiling again for the first time in months.

"You are quite right," Véronique said. "Nicholas has shared everything with me, because he trusts me."

"So I have nothing to worry about, then," her mother replied with cautious relief. "This inheritance has nothing to do with Bonaparte, and it will not cause some horrendous scandal in the future?"

Véronique placed her hands on her mother's shoulders. "I assure you it has nothing to do with Bonaparte." At least she was telling the truth about *that.* "And he didn't win the house in a card game either."

But was there something shady or scandalous about the inheritance? Yes, there most definitely was, but she was not at liberty to say so. Not even to her own mother. So she simply smiled cheerfully and went in search of earbobs.

For the first time since his arrival at d'Entremont Manor, Nicholas sat at the head of the dining table, which was only proper since he was now master of the house.

On the night of the funeral, Véronique, Gabrielle, and the Montagnes joined him for a sumptuous meal of roast pork with spiced gravy, and fresh garden vegetables. Dinner was a somber affair, however, for the funeral service was not far from anyone's thoughts, Nicholas's especially.

He had buried another father today—one with whom he had spent a single hour. He did not know him at all, yet over the past few days he had at least read his private love letters, and had learned all there was to know about his business holdings and family history.

The steward, Monsieur Bellefontaine, had been indispensable and forthcoming in every way. He had held nothing back, even when Nicholas asked the most personal questions.

Bellefontaine revealed his admiration for Lord d'Entremont and considered him an honorable man, except when he gambled, for he lost more often than he won.

"With regards to his taking ownership of the Montagnes' property," Bellefontaine had said as they talked late into the night upon Nicholas's return from Véronique's home, "I considered it a fair winning, and while I sympathized with the ladies of the house who had lost their home, I could not feel sorry for Monsieur Montagne, who had been very foolish to wager everything he owned." Bellefontaine slowly sipped his brandy and reflected upon recent events. "I believe it was good of Lord d'Entremont to offer Véronique a chance to earn it back. Why did she not see that? Why did she continue to despise him?"

Nicholas sighed heavily that night. "She is loyal and protective of her family," he explained, "and felt that d'Entremont had taken advantage of a man who was clearly in his cups and in a weakened position. You cannot blame her for resenting the marquis for that. He could have refused the wager and sent Montagne home."

Tonight—as Nicholas pondered that conversation and watched Véronique converse with her parents at the table—he was glad he had defended her to the steward, for she would be mistress of this house one day. She would require everyone's respect.

If he decided to keep the property, that is.

Then he found himself watching the Montagnes, admiring how they seemed so at ease with one another. There were no pretentions here. They were a close-knit family.

"So tell me, Nicholas," Madame Montagne said pleasantly as she set down her fork, "will you and Véronique be able to attend Gabrielle's wedding to Lord Robert, or will you be traveling back to Petersbourg immediately after your own wedding?"

The mere mention of his wedding day should have put him in a foul mood, for he had never imagined himself capable of becoming a husband. In fact, he had always considered marriage a form of prison with iron shackles. This evening, however, he found himself imagining the pleasures of a wedding night to a woman he found completely irresistible as she gazed at him alluringly from across the polished mahogany table. Her cheeks were flushed in the candlelight, and her lush full bosom in that lavender gown made it impossible for him to remain focused on the question at hand.

Just as he was about to form an answer, however, the dining room doors flew open and his gaze shot toward the unexpected intruder.

Pierre Cuvier shoved a footman out of the way as he staggered the length of the room behind Madame and Monsieur Montagne.

"And here he is!" Pierre bellowed, spreading his arms wide. "The notorious Prince of Petersbourg! Eating off a dead man's dishes as if he were lord and master here."

Nicholas stood. "I *am* master here, and you, sir, were not invited to dine this evening." Two larger footmen hurried into the room. "Show him out," Nicholas commanded.

They moved to surround Pierre, but he swung his arms clumsily about and dropped to his knees in a fit of sobbing. "You don't deserve any of this!" he cried. "It should have been mine!"

Véronique's father stood up as well. "Who is this man?"

Pierre fell onto his backside on the floor, still flailing his arms about at the servants who tried to restrain him and pull him to his feet. He was a large, bullish man, however, and it was an impossible task.

"I am Pierre Cuvier. The marquis was my uncle, and I loved him like a true father all my life—which is more than this privileged royal pirate can say. *You* never loved him. You didn't even know him. Why you, and not me? You are as much a bastard as I am!" Pierre was now rolling on the floor and kicking his legs at anyone who tried to touch him.

Nicholas left his place at the table to approach. "Step aside, everyone. Leave him be," he said to the footmen. He stood over Pierre, looking down at him in such a pathetic drunken state. "Pull yourself together, man," he firmly said. "You're making a spectacle of yourself." He offered his hand to help Pierre rise.

For a long moment his half cousin stared up at him with bloodshot, tear-filled eyes and mud-stained clothing. Nicholas suspected he had walked here from the mausoleum.

"I don't need any help from you," Pierre said as he struggled to his feet and swayed ominously. He tried to grab hold of the back of a chair to keep his balance, but fell against the table, causing the china to rattle. One glass of wine tipped over and spilled.

"You're drunk, sir," Nicholas said. "Allow us to show

you to your room, where you can recover and collect yourself."

Pierre sobbed wretchedly. "It's not *my* room anymore. Everything belongs to *you* now. It's not fair. It's not fair."

Véronique stood up and slowly circled around the table. Without saying a word, she carefully approached Pierre from behind and laid a hand on his shoulder.

He jumped, as if startled, and every nerve in Nicholas's body sparked to high alert, for he would knock Pierre flat on his back again if he was foolish enough in his flummoxed state to mistreat Véronique.

"There, there, now," she gently said.

Pierre took one look at the compassion in her eyes and steadied himself. "It's not fair," he sobbed again.

Véronique clasped his elbow. "You are quite right about that. Sometimes life is not fair. Perhaps we can talk about all this in the morning."

He continued to sway while his foggy gaze perused the others in the room. They were all staring at him with concern and fear.

"Please show Monsieur Cuvier to his room," Véronique said to a footman. "Would you like a hot supper sent up as well?" she asked Pierre directly.

"Yes, that would be very good," he replied, seeming calmer now as he cooperated at last, and accompanied the footman out of the dining room.

Nicholas regarded his future wife with admiration, for she had set her prejudices aside and taken pity on a man who once tried to assault her sister.

Their gazes found each other's. She lifted her chin. "He was a danger to us, and to himself, tonight. I hope he can regain his composure."

"Well done, darling," her mother said.

Nicholas nodded in agreement. "Yes, well done. Shall we resume our dinner, then?"

Everyone sat down in awkward silence while one footman quickly wiped up the spilled wine and another brought a fresh glass to the table to replace it.

The plates were cleared away and dessert was ushered in. They were each served chocolate mousse with raspberry sauce in sparkling crystal cups.

Feeling oddly as if everyone were staring at him, Nicholas looked up from his dessert to discover that that was not the case at all. Everyone at the table had their eyes fixed on the chocolate mousse before them. Nevertheless their silence was somehow thunderous in its intensity.

"How is your dessert, Monsieur Montagne?" Nicholas asked, needing to break the tension.

Véronique's father looked up. "It's very good, sir."

Setting down his spoon, Nicholas decided to fire the first cannon shot across the field. "Is there something you wish to ask me?"

He was very aware of Véronique clearing her throat.

"About what, sir?" his future father-in-law asked uneasily.

"About what just happened here."

Are you suddenly rethinking your first impression of me? Do you see now that I am not the hero you thought I was? Are you worried about your daughter's future happiness?

Monsieur Montagne also set down his spoon. "Indeed, I am curious about that man's emotional state. Clearly he was distraught and . . . I am sure you are aware that many of the guests at the funeral today were curious about why d'Entremont left all this to you. What did Pierre mean when he said that you were as much a bastard as he?"

The temperature in the room seemed to rise. Nicholas picked up his linen napkin and dabbed at the perspiration on his forehead while his blood pumped heavily in his veins.

Tossing the napkin on the table and tugging at his cravat, he said in a cold and rather threatening tone, "You have a theory, I suppose."

His future father-in-law shifted nervously in his chair. "No, sir."

Véronique also set down her spoon. "This is ridiculous," she said. "We are all going to be family soon. Nicholas, may I speak to you in private, please?"

He forced himself to respond courteously. "If you will excuse us," he said as he rose from his chair and escorted his betrothed into the sitting room beyond.

She walked to the sofa, sat down, and patted the seat cushion beside her to invite him closer. He found himself instantly drawn toward her, as if she had all the answers to every question in the cosmos.

"I could see that you were uneasy," she said as he sat down. "You haven't decided yet what you want people to know, have you?"

He did not answer right away.

"I am sure that Gabrielle can be trusted," Véronique continued, "but unfortunately Pierre is a blabbermouth, which may present a bit of a challenge."

It struck Nicholas suddenly that he was fascinated with her, for she had come to his aid just now. She had intervened before he was forced to reveal the truth to her father. As her scent washed over him, he felt the calming effects of her presence in his life.

Nicholas laid his arm along the back of the sofa. "Pierre may be a blabbermouth, but he is also a drunk with very few respectable friends. No one will believe him over me, and I trust Bellefontaine and Fournier to keep the secret, at least for now."

"You'll probably have to offer them some sort of compensation for their silence."

Feeling tired all of a sudden, Nicholas ran a hand through his hair. "It won't be the first time I've had to pay to cover up a scandal. But what about your parents? Do they not have a right to know the truth about their daughter's husband?"

"And the bloodline of their future grandchildren," she added.

The mere mention of children—of Véronique giving birth to sons and daughters—caused him to stiffen. He thought of his mother suddenly, and the image he had of her in his mind—of the day they took her body away before he could say good-bye. Why hadn't they let him see her? Was it so very bad? Was there a lot of blood? Or had his father simply wished to punish him for being a reminder of his wife's extramarital affair?

"I don't want your father to know," he found himself saying firmly as he leaned forward to rest his elbows on his knees. "I don't want *anyone* to know."

She touched his arm. "They won't think any less of you. My parents judge a man by his actions, not his lineage."

"They should judge me very poorly, then," he replied, "for you know my reputation. Perhaps they are better off believing me to be some sort of mythical knight in shining armor." He paused and thought about it. "And the scandal it would evoke in Petersbourg . . . God help us all. My brother has been sitting on the throne for less than a year, and has had to fight tooth and nail against the enemy Royalists, who do not believe our family deserves the crown. They'll use anything to create scandals and smear our names. This could destroy the Sebastian monarchy."

"Then you must do as you see fit," Véronique replied. "I will support you in your decision, whatever it is, but allow me to say that my family would never betray you, not after all you have done for us. No matter what happens, you will always be a hero to them. My father will love you like a son, if only you will let him."

Perhaps, Nicholas realized, this woman was to be the greatest challenge of his life, for she was almost too perfect. Not only had she turned the tables on him and become the seducer while he had become the prey, but she was sensible and loving and far too good for him. How would he ever live up to such standards? He could not go back to his old ways and treat her shabbily. He did not want to disappoint her family, not when—for the first time in his life—someone actually thought well of him.

For that reason, he could not reveal himself to the world as the bastard son from his mother's adulterous affair. . . . If he wanted to make a change, that was not a good way to begin.

Nicholas stood. "Please make my apologies to your family," he said. "I have business to attend to, and must bid you all good night."

"Will we see you tomorrow?" Véronique asked, rising to her feet as well.

"I will be spending the day with Bellefontaine and the solicitor," he said, "going over the estate books and records. Surely you will have plenty to do on your own to prepare for our upcoming nuptials. That is, of course, if you haven't changed your mind."

A part of him *wanted* her to change it.

He wanted to go home to Petersbourg and forget any of this had ever happened.

Another part of him would tear this house apart if he lost her.

"No, I have not changed my mind," she replied, and he nodded with relief. "I can think of little else but our wedding night," she added with a teasing smile, which was meant to put him at ease, for she understood that his sexual desire for her was the only thing that felt the least bit familiar to him.

So he did what he knew best. He responded by taking her into his arms and pressing his mouth to hers. It was a deep kiss that resulted in a return trip to the sofa and many more moments of kissing, groping, and other sensual pleasures while the rest of her family finished their desserts.

Véronique's cheeks were flushed when she returned to the table, and Nicholas was on fire with lust as he departed from the room.

He knew then that there would be no turning back. He wanted Véronique, he needed her, and he would have her. All the rest would simply have to fall into place around them. Somehow, he would do what was required to make their problems disappear.

In that regard, when they woke the following morning, Pierre was long gone—as if he had vanished into thin air and Nicholas wondered if God was somehow playing a part in all of this. Perhaps there was another destiny waiting to be laid out for Nicholas, now that everything he once knew was no longer his reality.

His world, and his life, had been turned completely upside down, but he still had no idea which way was up.

Chapter Nineteen

Three days later, Nicholas did the unthinkable. He stood next to a woman at the altar, slipped a ring on her finger, and declared his devoted love and fidelity until death parted them.

If not for the imminent pleasures of the marriage bed, he might very well have hesitated before saying "I do," but as they spoke their vows, he was overwhelmingly aware of his desires—further aroused by the scent of Véronique's perfume, the soft creamy ethereal glow of her complexion in the colored light streaming in through the stained glass windows, and the heat of her body next to him.

She was dressed in a simple gown of white silk with antique lace trimmings, and sprinklings of baby's breath in her hair. She looked like an angel.

When she entered the chapel on her father's arm, any thoughts Nicholas had entertained about changing his mind and bolting back to his home country—and his former life as a libertine—evaporated like a drop of water under the full glare of the sun. His libido was pulsing with anticipation throughout the ceremony, and when at last the vicar pronounced them man and wife, he grew ever more impatient for the sun to set, for candles to be lit, and for everyone else to bloody well leave them alone for the important task of consummating their marriage.

If not for the promise of that . . . he might very well have bolted, because this was too bloody much for a man like him to comprehend.

The master's chambers at d'Entremont Manor bore no resemblance whatsoever to the room where Nicholas had been held captive. That room was in essence a prison cell with comfortable pillows, luxurious fabrics, and plenty of books.

The marquis's bedchamber, however, was located at the opposite end of the house, with breathtaking views of the English Channel as well as the stately oak tree on the hill.

The room was very grand, filled with polished, gleaming mahogany furniture that stood upon thick crimson carpets. The walls were papered bloodred and adorned with gilt-framed oil paintings of landscapes and seascapes. Tall white candles in gold-plated candelabras illuminated every corner.

The bed was cloaked in a red velvet canopy and curtains. It provided privacy and warmth in the winter months, but since it was summer—and because Nicholas's body was already blazing with passion as he led his virgin bride into the room—he expected to be flinging the windows wide open in short order to let in a cool breeze off the water, lest the whole room burst into flames.

"Clearly this is the finest room in the house," Véronique said as she followed him inside. "Yours now to enjoy."

Her green eyes met his in the flickering glow of the candlelight, and he found himself enraptured by thoughts of what they would enjoy here together in the coming hours.

"Yes, it is the finest room," he casually replied, "now that *you* are here."

Their eyes met once more with a shared look of desire, their pent-up urges screaming for release.

"I suppose this is rather profound," she said, "for not long ago, Lord d'Entremont had taken possession of my home and everything I held dear. Now I have taken possession of *his* home, so to speak, for I am now mistress here."

"Yes," Nicholas replied, moving closer. "All that I possess is now yours. Would you like to explore the bed? I am sure you will find it more than adequate to meet your needs."

"*Our* needs," she countered with a mischievous grin that sent a shiver of lust through his body.

For a moment he stood before her and drank in the intoxicating essence of her beauty and innocence in the firelight—knowing that after tonight, he would forever be the possessor of her virginity.

Aroused by that thought, he turned her around and slowly began to unhook her gown, until it fell loose over the creamy curve of her shoulders.

He kissed the back of her neck and felt her body tremble beneath his touch. "Are you afraid?" he whispered.

She tilted her head back. "No."

Slowly, he undressed her, piece by piece, letting each article fall to the floor in heaps of light fabric, until she stood naked before him, as radiant as a burst of firelight before his eyes.

He folded her into his arms and held her for a rapturous moment before covering her mouth with a deep open kiss that blazed through his senses and thrust him into this marriage with the full force of a cavalry charge.

He had been waiting too long for this. The need to feed his hunger for her was immense. Perhaps he should have moved more slowly, for it was her first time, but his desires were out of control. He simply had to have her, and could not wait another moment.

Sweeping her into his arms, he carried her to the bed and set her down. He marveled at her splendor as she lay before him like a lush golden goddess, exquisite in her nudity. He tugged roughly at his cravat and ripped it from his throat. After tossing it carelessly aside, he unbuttoned his brocade waistcoat, shrugged out of it in a mad rush to rid himself of his clothes, pulled his shirt off over his head, and stepped out of his breeches.

The warm summer air touched his flesh and heightened his senses. He clenched his hands into fists as he beheld his bride on the bed. She was watching him with burning eyes. Her gaze traveled down the length of his form, pausing to stare in fascination at his large, rigid erection.

"I'll try to be gentle," he said in a strained voice, though he wasn't entirely sure he could be, for he wanted her like a raging, bucking stallion after a monthlong confinement in the stalls.

As he climbed onto the bed and settled his weight upon her, he reveled in the softness of her breasts and the flavor of her tongue, like sweet candy in his mouth. A wave of sensual pleasure flooded to his groin and filled him with fierce carnal urges that were violent in their intensity.

He stroked a hand down the luscious curve of her hip and the top of her soft warm thigh, hooked his arm under her knee to allow his body to fit snugly into the warm valley of her legs, parted just for him.

"I apologize in advance," he said, "for my artless lack of foreplay, but I am impatient."

"No need to apologize," she replied in a rush of desire that matched his own in its impetuosity. "All I want is to be yours, and give myself to you fully—body and soul."

They were romantic words—too romantic for a man like him, who was accustomed to licentious talk more suitable to endless nights of debauchery in unfamiliar rooms with nameless strangers.

This was something else. Her heartfelt words touched his emotions and stirred his passions in a way that was rare and new and completely foreign to him. He didn't know what to make of it.

Véronique sucked in a breath as Nicholas pushed into her, breaking at last through the tight barrier of her virginity.

The pain was sharp and instant, unlike any other sensation. She did not possess the experience to understand why she welcomed it, and was therefore amazed at the pleasure that pulsed through her body, filling her with an urgent need for more. The pain did not matter. To the contrary, she was enchanted by its intensity.

Nicholas let out a groan of profound satisfaction when he thrust as far as he could into the feminine depths of her body. Véronique dug her fingernails into his back and realized she was panting like an animal, wanting more.

He remained still, as if allowing her to become accustomed to the feel of him inside her. Then slowly he began to move. He slid almost all the way out, then pushed in again, filling her with sweet pulsating ecstasy for a second glorious moment.

Each time he withdrew, she clung to him and arched her back in sizzling anticipation, knowing he would plunge into her again, and shoot an even hotter bolt of pleasure into her core.

Then he rose above her, both arms braced on either side of her on the bed, and watched her face as he perfected the rhythm of their coupling. Her eyes were open, but she felt lost in a fog of sensual delight, all her attention focused on this sweet, hot, pounding friction.

She let out a moan and writhed like a woman possessed.

Soon Nicholas's movements quickened, and he shut his eyes as his mouth found hers, wet and open in the fever of the night. She drank in the delicious taste of him as their bodies pounded together in a rhythm that was both violent and graceful.

Their orgasms came quickly—hers first, as a trembling wave poured through her like wine. She cried out while he continued to pump into her, prolonging the duration of her climax until her body could throb no more. Then he released his own passions, ejaculating into her with a hot rush of his seed.

Nearly delirious with exhaustion, Véronique let her arms fall to the sides while he collapsed on top of her, his body heavy and damp with perspiration.

"Can you breathe?" he asked, his face buried in the crook of her neck.

"No," she answered honestly, for he was built of hard sinewy muscle and fine thick bones. The weight of him upon her slender frame was crushing.

He gently withdrew from her sweltering depths and rolled to lie beside her on the bed. She welcomed the cool air upon her damp flesh, but regretted the loss of their physical connection.

Lying on her back, she turned her head to look at him. With a slight frown, he was staring up at the crimson velvet canopy over their heads. She worried that she had not performed as well as others in his past.

He seemed to sense her eyes on him, and rolled to face her. "What did you do to me?" he asked, his expression curious and bewildered.

"What do you mean?" she replied. "I thought it was you who did something to *me* tonight."

His eyes searched all the corners of her face as if hoping to find answers; then he searched lower, pausing at her breasts and taking in all the curves of her body in the warm glow of the firelight. "I don't want to go back," he said. "Not yet."

She leaned up on one elbow. "You mean to Petersbourg?"

He nodded and slid an arm around her waist to pull her closer. "We were married just today. Don't you think we deserve a honeymoon?"

She could not suppress a grin. "So we can do more of *this*?" She wiggled her hips to rub up against him. "I think it is a brilliant idea, because I still have so much to learn."

"And I intend to teach you everything. Besides that, we can attend your sister's wedding." He flipped her over onto her back again and pressed his mouth to hers. He kissed her firmly, as if staking one more claim upon her; then he drew back and rose up on all fours above her. His hair fell forward over his temples.

With a sudden burst of energy, he leaped off the bed and strode naked to the desk. "I will write to my brother tonight and convey our happy news." He searched around for paper and quill, flipped open the lid of the ink jar, and immediately dipped his writing utensil into it.

Véronique sat up and hugged the silk sheet to her breast. "How will you ever explain any of this?" she said with a laugh.

"I'm not sure yet," her husband replied. "I only hope he survives the shock of it."

Petersbourg Palace, one week later . . .

King Randolph's breathing was suspended momentarily as he blinked a few times and struggled to refocus his vision on the words he could not possibly have read correctly.

He rose from his chair at the large table in the Privy Council Chamber and walked to the window to hold the letter up to the light.

"What is it?" his wife, Alexandra, asked with concern as she set down her quill. She had joined him at the table in the chamber a short while ago to answer her own correspondence, and had obviously taken note of his surprise.

"It's a letter from Nicholas," he told her as he continued to read the rest of it.

"What does it say?"

Randolph laughed and lowered the letter to his side. "You will not believe it. He is married!"

"I beg your pardon?" Alexandra held out a hand. "Let me see it for myself."

Rand circled around the table and handed it to her. She read it quickly and looked up. "It cannot be possible. This must be a hoax."

"I don't believe so," Randolph replied. "I know my brother. He would never joke about something like that. I assure you, he would find no humor in it." He took the letter back from her and reread some of the details. "It says he plans to stay in France for a month to enjoy his newlywed status, but asks that we do not alert the newspapers just yet, for he wants to present his bride properly upon his return."

Alexandra shook her head in disbelief. "Who in God's name is this unlikely bride? She must be quite a woman to have succeeded where every other woman has failed before. *Nicholas! Married!*"

Randolph laughed in agreement. "It is a miracle, isn't it?" He stared at his beloved queen and smiled before referring back to the letter. "According to Nicholas, she is of French descent, and he met her at a masked ball. He will explain everything when he arrives at the end of the month. Until then, he intends to remain at d'Entremont Manor, which he says is on the coast, near Dieppe."

"I wonder if that is her family's estate?" Alexandra asked.

Randolph flipped the letter over to look at the back. "He doesn't say. He hasn't even told us her name. That is so like Nicholas."

Alexandra's eyebrows lifted. "I just hope he doesn't find a way to turn this happy event into another scandal—for that, too, would be so like Nicholas."

Randolph sat down, tipped his head back to look up at the ceiling, and squeezed the chair arms. "My God, you're right. What if she's a barmaid?"

"Or a widow with six children."

He sighed as he regarded his wife in the fading light. "I suppose we should brace ourselves for anything."

PART II

A Prince's Homecoming

Chapter Twenty

"Is something wrong, Nicholas?" Véronique asked as she sat forward in the coach and laid a hand on her husband's thigh. "You've seemed irritable since we crossed the border."

Not just irritable, she thought. *Distant*. All those leisurely days of sensual enchantment at d'Entremont Manor had been magical. They had gone riding together each morning at dawn, and had dined privately by candlelight in his bedchamber each night. He had loved her unreservedly and been a perfect husband, but now it all seemed a lifetime away—as if it had been a mere dream, but it was time to wake up. Soon they would return to *his* world, which would be strange and unfamiliar to her.

He propped an elbow on the windowsill of the coach while resting his temple on a finger. Eventually he turned to look at her. "Have I?"

"Yes. You've hardly spoken to me. You seem lost in thought. I hope—now that we are returning to your home—that you are not suddenly steeped in regret."

She had known when she entered into this that it was a stretch to imagine he would be a faithful husband. Even Nicholas had warned her against believing such a thing. But she couldn't help herself. She would not give up on him.

He angled his body on the seat to face her. "I suppose I don't enjoy endless coach rides over bumpy roads, but you are mad if you think I could have any regrets. How many times must I tell you? You are my obsession." He pressed his lips to hers, and she was immediately pulled into the intoxicating fire of his allure.

He was her husband now, and their month together in France had been the most pleasurable of her life. Surely she had nothing to fret about, for later today, they would reach Petersbourg Palace and she would meet his brother, the king.

She had married a handsome prince, and she was the luckiest woman on earth. It was time to embrace her new life.

There was some talk of having Véronique formally presented to Randolph and Alexandra in the throne room, but Nicholas quashed that idea when he barged into his brother's private apartments and found him dozing on the bed at four o'clock in the afternoon.

"I roll into the courtyard after two months in France, and you cannot be bothered to get out of bed and welcome me home?"

Randolph sat up. "Nicholas!" He leaped off the bed, strode quickly across the room, and pulled Nicholas into his arms. He slapped him heartily on the back. "Welcome home! We didn't expect you until next week."

Nicholas collapsed into a chair before the unlit fireplace. "The weather was good. We made excellent time."

"The weather was good? That's all you have to say?" Randolph chuckled as he uncorked a decanter and poured a couple of brandies.

"Should there be more?" Nicholas responded with teasing mischief.

"Bloody well right there should be. Your letter nearly knocked me unconscious when I read it." He handed the drink to Nicholas and sat down in the facing chair. "And poor Alexandra . . . The next day she thought she had been hallucinating."

Nicholas contemplated the amber liquid in the crystal glass and swirled it around. "I thought the same thing myself when I woke up to find myself in bed with a wife. Good God."

Randolph laughed and shook his head in disbelief. "What the devil happened? Did the woman put some sort of spell on you?"

"Not exactly. She drugged me with laudanum, though," he casually added as he tipped up his glass and poured the entire contents down his throat.

Randolph threw his head back and laughed. "I'm sure she did. Then she tied you up like a prize sow and dragged your drunken ass to the altar, no doubt."

Nicholas leaned forward. "We both know I am no sow."

"Indeed." Randolph raised his glass as if to toast to Nicholas's gentlemanly charms and renowned good looks. He took a drink, then lounged back in his chair again. "Damn, it's good to have you back. And I might as well tell you now. I've already bestowed a new royal title on you. You are the Duke and Duchess of Walbrydge. It comes with a property, of course. Now, tell me, really—how did you two meet, and how in God's name did she convince you to propose? No doubt she is a beauty, but did she have any idea what she was getting into when she said yes?"

"Probably not," Nicholas replied, "and she is indeed a beauty. You will see for yourself when you meet her, but I warn you, the French accent is somewhat . . . inebriating." He raised the empty brandy glass to reference the effect.

"I don't doubt it." They clinked their glasses together; then Randolph reached for the decanter and refilled Nicholas's drink. They sat back in easy companionship and sighed heavily.

"How is Rose?" Nicholas asked about his sister, who had recently married the future emperor of Austria.

"She is very well," Randolph replied. "She writes often and tells me that Joseph is recovering from the wounds he suffered at Waterloo. She is eager to put the past behind her, and seems content with the choices she has made."

Rose had nearly married another man entirely, but came to her senses when that man turned out to be a secret Royalist and an enemy of the Sebastian monarchy. Leopold Hunt was rotting away in prison when she finally walked down the aisle in Austria . . . though Hunt was a free man now, after commanding the Petersbourg cavalry at Waterloo.

"I hope she can be happy," Nicholas said, though he was not entirely confident, for Rose had been quite passionate about Hunt.

But he mustn't think of that now. He had his own wife to present to the country and a great deal of explaining to do in regards to his inheritance of d'Entremont Manor.

Setting the brandy aside, he rested his elbows on his knees. "We've been laughing and joking," he said to his brother, "but I do have something to tell you, which you may not find quite so amusing."

Randolph's brow furrowed with concern. "I had a feeling there was going to be something."

"Yes . . . well . . . Remember when I said my new wife drugged me with laudanum?"

Randolph regarded him with narrowed eyes. "Yes?"

"That's not the worst of it," Nicholas continued. "I wasn't joking, you see, and she *did* tie me up and drag me out of Paris like a piece of cargo."

There was a pause.

"Why?"

"She was hired to lure me out of the ball . . . to kidnap me."

The hands on the clock ticked a full five seconds before Randolph voiced any response.

"*Kidnap* you!"

"Yes," Nicholas replied. "And she performed this task for reasons I must now explain to you, Randolph. But I warn you . . . it will not be easy for you to hear. For it concerns our mother."

Randolph frowned. "It sounds like we might need more brandy."

"Most definitely. Perhaps you should send for a rather large bottle."

"What in the world is he going to do?" Alexandra asked later that afternoon as she rocked young Frederick to sleep in her arms. "First of all, does he believe it's true? Is there any proof?"

Randolph paced back and forth in front of the fire. "He said he saw enough to be convinced, and he has brought much of the evidence with him."

"What sort of evidence?"

"Love letters," Randolph replied. "And engraved jewelry. He says our mother spent a whole year in France with Lord d'Entremont, while our father was working to build the new government and put out the fires of the Revolution."

Alexandra stopped rocking in the chair, for the babe—their precious son and heir to the throne—was now sleeping soundly. "Had you ever suspected anything like this?" she asked. "Do you remember her absence?"

Randolph stopped pacing and thought about his childhood with the mother he adored. "No. I do recall being told she had traveled to France to visit her family when I was very young—too young to remember. Then she came home, and I had a new brother, and life went on."

Alexandra carefully stood up, laid their child in the golden cradle, and pulled the organza curtains closed around him. She then crossed to Randolph and pulled him into her arms. "It changes nothing," she said. "Your mother loved you both, and Nicholas is still your blood brother in all ways."

"I am surprised," Randolph said, "and pleased to hear you support him, when not so long ago you and he were enemies."

Alexandra had come to Petersbourg from England, and was the secret lost princess from the House of Tremaine—the very monarchy their father had toppled during the Revolution. Nicholas had suspected that Alexandra intended to seize back the throne through unscrupulous means.

"That was before he realized that my love for you was true," she replied. "We have made our peace, Nicholas and I." She drew back and went to pour a cup of tea. "What will you do? Will you reveal this information to the world, or will you leave it in the past?"

"Nicholas is torn," Randolph said. "He felt some connection to d'Entremont Manor, and to our mother who has been dead for many years. He told me there was a part of him that did not want to come home. He felt somehow . . . transformed after being there."

Alexandra's eyebrows lifted. "I am shocked."

"So was I. Now that he is home, however, he is remembering what is more familiar to him. He said he was beginning to feel more like his old self, except for the wife, of course." He raised an eyebrow.

"Oh dear," Alexandra said. "You don't suppose he regrets it."

Randolph went to look at his infant son, sleeping soundly in his cradle. "For the present moment, I believe he is quite infatuated with his new bride, which might have something to do with the fact that she was his captor, and then his rescuer. I fear, however, that his life is about to become very complicated, for if he decides to reveal the truth about his ancestry, all hell will break loose."

"If *he* decides? It cannot be his decision alone," Alexandra said. "She was your mother, too, and you are king. Nicholas must consider your wishes as well, and you must do what is best for the country."

Randolph reached into his son's cradle and adjusted the coverlet. "At least now we have an heir. We are protected from a Royalist overthrow, for our child is a direct descendant of the Tremaine dynasty, thanks to you. For that reason, I don't believe another scandal involving Nicholas will topple us." He faced his wife. "Yet I don't see what good could come of it, for Nicholas has always been tortured by the press. He has a wife now, which should put him in everyone's good graces, as long as he behaves himself."

Alexandra raised a skeptical brow, for she knew Nicholas's lifestyle.

"If he reveals the truth, however," Rand continued,

"he will be forever branded as a bastard, and the traditionalists will no doubt criticize and resent his life of privilege here at Court. He will become a subject of gossip. There will be no escaping it."

"Will he care about the gossip?" she asked. "He never has before."

"No, but he has a wife now, and he seems to regard her very highly. He may see things differently."

"So you think we should all let bygones be bygones and keep quiet about it?" Alex asked. "Will you be able to convince him of this?"

Randolph moved to the bed and lay down. "I have never issued an order to Nicholas before. We have always been brothers first."

"But you are his king. He is your subject. He must respect and obey your wishes."

Randolph exhaled heavily. "I wouldn't want it to come to that."

She joined him on the bed and lay on her side, facing him. "I am sure it won't. I cannot imagine he would wish to tarnish your mother's memory in the eyes of the people. They worshipped her."

"You're probably right."

They were quiet for a moment while they enjoyed the sweet, blissful peace of their infant slumbering softly.

"When will we meet his new bride?" Alexandra asked as she snuggled closer and rested her cheek on Randolph's shoulder.

"Privately, before the banquet this evening," he told her. "Then we have the perfect opportunity to present her to a few important people. The prime minister and his wife will be in attendance, as well as the usual courtiers and Privy Council members."

Alex lifted her head. "Is that not a bit cruel? Shouldn't

we give her a chance to get her bearings first, before we throw her to the wolves?"

Randolph chuckled. "She must have known what would be expected of her when she agreed to marry Nicholas. It's not as if she didn't know he was a prince, and from what I gather, she is no shrinking violet. Let us not forget that she kidnapped him out of a masked ball, tied him up, and dragged him all the way to the French coast. Then after all that, convinced him to marry her."

Alex leaned up on an elbow. "Perhaps the real question is whether or not *Nicholas* knew what he was getting into, marrying a woman like that. I cannot wait to meet her."

He smiled. "I confess, I feel the same."

Chapter Twenty-one

Nicholas escorted Véronique into the private family drawing room an hour before the banquet reception was scheduled to begin. It was to be his wife's formal presentation to the king and queen, though Nicholas assured her there would be nothing formal about it, for Randolph and Alexandra were brother and sister to her now.

Nevertheless, she dipped into a deep curtsy upon meeting them.

Randolph smiled warmly as he offered a hand to help her rise. "So this is the lady who captured my brother's heart. It is an honor to meet you, Your Royal Highness."

"The honor is mine, Your Majesty."

Alexandra came closer as well. "You weren't lying, Nicholas. She is lovely. Allow me to welcome you to our family."

Véronique smiled. "Thank you, Your Majesty."

Nicholas led his bride to the sofa.

"We heard the story of how you two met," Alexandra said with a smile, "but I fear that if the gossipmongers get wind of it, they will have far too good of a time."

"Well, we mustn't let *that* happen," Nicholas replied lightheartedly.

A footman served them sherry in small stemmed glasses, and they spoke of other matters—like Véronique's first impressions of the city and palace—while getting better acquainted.

Véronique described her parents' home and the weather in France while Nicholas sat back and listened with pleasure to the charming cadence of her voice. Tantalizing memories of their intense conversations through a locked door reminded him of the passion that had knocked him off his feet at d'Entremont Manor, and how he simply had to have this woman. He had to take her for his own.

When he glanced at the clock on the wall, however, and saw that it would soon be time to meet the guests in the banqueting hall, he realized he would have preferred not to share her with the rest of the world. He wished he could leave her in her bedchamber for the evening and simply return to her afterwards.

He hadn't felt that way at d'Entremont Manor—he had enjoyed moving about local society with her, spending every waking moment in her presence—but everything had seemed so out of place there. Disjointed, as if it were not part of his life, but rather a temporary, parallel existence. He soon found himself withdrawing from the conversation.

When it was time to enter the banqueting hall, he wrenched himself back to the present reality, stood up, and offered his arm to Véronique.

By some miracle, Véronique survived her first function at the palace, which included her formal presentation to a stunned crowd of onlookers in the marble and gold banqueting hall. Though she tried to hide it, her heart pounded like a drum when Nicholas led her into the hall, and the majordomo shouted boomingly, "The Royal Highnesses, the Duke and Duchess of Walbrydge!" over the heads of all the guests.

Dead silence followed while Véronique stared into a vista of wide eyes and slack jaws, until the hum of conversation finally resumed.

Dinner at the head table was relatively painless after that. It was not until much later, when everyone was mingling about after dessert, that she experienced her first wave of doubt.

She stood chatting with the palace master-at-arms when she noticed that his wife appeared distracted. The woman was glancing repeatedly at something over Véronique's shoulder.

When Véronique turned around, she saw Nicholas talking to a strikingly beautiful dark-haired woman in an amethyst gown. They stood just outside the banquet hall, beyond the doors, arguing heatedly about something. Then they each stormed off in opposite directions.

Véronique locked gazes with Queen Alexandra on the far side of the room. She, too, had noticed the scene, but shook her head at Véronique, as if to say, *It's nothing*.

Later that night when Nicholas slipped into her bed, settled his naked body upon hers, and began to kiss her neck with sweet erotic tenderness, she couldn't help herself. She had to ask. . . .

"Who was that woman you were conversing with this evening? The one with the dark hair?"

He went still, then drew back to peer down at her. "Why do you ask?"

"Is there a reason I *shouldn't* be asking?"

For an intense moment of deliberation, he remained braced above her until he rolled to the side, shut his eyes, and rubbed at his forehead with the heel of his hand.

"She is a former lover. She didn't expect me to bring a wife home from France. I am sorry you had to see that, Véronique. She was upset that she hadn't been informed."

"You only just arrived in the city this afternoon," Véronique replied in his defense. "Did she expect you to pay her a call immediately upon your return, and apprise her of all your activities?"

"Evidently, she did." He turned his head on the pillow to look her in the eye. "But I *didn't* pay her a call."

"No, you did not, and for that, I am grateful."

Not wanting to spend their first night at the palace arguing about his irate former lovers, Véronique sat up, straddled her husband, and wiggled her hips enticingly. He grew stiff and hard, and his expression warmed with intrigue. Grabbing hold of her hips with his big hands, he rolled his pelvis beneath her.

"How am I possibly going to manage my jealousy now that we are back among all your former lovers?" she playfully asked.

The corner of his mouth curved up slightly. "Perhaps you'll have to lock me up again, darling. Hold me captive until every last one of them gets the message that I am no longer available."

"Can't I simply make them disappear? Perhaps I should hire a thug to do the dirty work for me."

He chuckled, then groaned with pleasure as she reached down, took hold of his erection, and guided it to the center of her ardent desires.

He thrust his hips slowly until he entered her, pushing very deep, stretching her . . . filling her with everything he was as a sexual being. Véronique quivered with pleasure as she stirred her hips in tiny circles, sliding up and down the glorious length of his shaft.

"If my rivals know what's good for them," she said, "they will give up any hopes for your attentions in the future, and accept the fact that you belong to *me* now."

"You're a devil," he growled with a smile. Then he flipped her over onto her back without ever breaking their intimate connection.

A wave of erotic bliss rose up within her. Véronique threw herself into its mercies and forgot about the dark-haired woman from the banquet—and all the others who would surely, in the coming months, appear unexpectedly and express their discontent over losing their handsome and gifted lover.

She and Nicholas made love three times that night and did not speak of other women again—at least not until a week later, when they attended a private dinner at the home of the prime minister.

Chapter Twenty-two

Véronique had just handed her opera cloak over to the butler and was walking with Nicholas into the drawing room at Carlton House when her shoe caught in the hem of her gown and she stumbled.

Nicholas stopped in the doorway and steadied her. "Are you all right?"

"I'm fine," she replied. "Just a little clumsy this evening, that's all."

He leaned close and whispered in her ear. "If you're going to end up on your back, darling, I would prefer that you wait until we are at home, so I can join you."

She grinned mischievously. "I'll keep that in mind, sir. When we reach the palace, I will try not to trip again, at least not until your bed is in sight."

She looked up to discover all the guests in the room were staring at them. A few leaned their heads together and whispered. One guest in particular, however, caught Véronique's eye, for she was glaring at them with piercing venom. Véronique knew immediately that she was another one of Nicholas's former lovers. This one had flaxen hair and a freckled complexion.

She stood abruptly and left the room conspicuously through the door on the opposite side as Véronique and Nicholas entered.

The prime minister was quick—almost too quick—to approach and greet them as they were formally announced.

"Welcome, Your Royal Highnesses," he said. "Did you enjoy the opera?"

The usual pleasantries were exchanged, and Nicholas and Véronique soon joined the other guests in conversation. The flaxen-haired woman never returned.

Later, during the coach ride back to the palace, Véronique again could not supress her curiosity. "Who was that one?" she asked. "And why did she feel it necessary to leave the party?"

"Who knows?" he replied. "I have never been able to fathom the minds of most women—present company excepted."

She linked her arm through his. "You still haven't told me who she was. The prime minister seemed noticeably shaken. Was there some horrendous scandal involving the two of you?"

Nicholas pulled his gaze from the passing cityscape outside the window and looked down at her. "She is Mrs. Kennedy, but her friends call her Lizzie. She is the prime minister's niece."

"His niece!" Véronique sat back. "You had an affair with the prime minister's niece?"

Nicholas raised a finger to his lips. "Shh, darling. You'll frighten the horses. Before you get too excited, permit me to explain that she is not some innocent young virgin I seduced and left brokenhearted by the side of the road."

"Is she a widow, then?"

He turned away from her briefly and tugged at the

cuffs of his shirtsleeves beneath his jacket. "Not exactly."

"How . . . not exactly?" Véronique pressed. "Her husband is either dead or alive. He cannot be both."

Nicholas sighed impatiently. "She is married to a navy captain who is at sea most of the time. Is that enough information for you?"

"So it was an adulterous affair?"

Nicholas rested his arm along the back of the dark velvet upholstery and stared intently into her eyes. "Are we going to argue about basic morality now?" he asked. "If so, I forfeit. You win. Adultery is very bad."

Realizing at once that she was picking a fight with her husband when he had done nothing wrong at least not this evening—she fought to withhold her judgments, for he was right. He did not need to explain his past affairs, as if he had been unfaithful to her.

"I am sorry," she said, laying her hand on his thigh. "I don't mean to be possessive."

He took hold of her gloved hand, raised it to his lips, and kissed it. "Do not apologize for being possessive, darling. If you weren't, I would think you did not care."

Her body warmed at his touch. "Oh, I care, Nicholas." And when his mouth met hers, she leaned into the kiss to prove exactly how much—with both passion and exuberance.

The following week, on the way home from an appointment at the office of the Dutch foreign minister, Nicholas realized he had not set foot in his club since before he left for France, shortly after the defeat of Napoléon. Leaning out the window, he called to his driver to take the next left turn.

Had it really been over two months? he wondered as he walked through the front door of Carroway's, looked around at the familiar dark paneled walls and floor-to-ceiling bookcases, and removed his hat and coat.

In short order he was seated in one of four upholstered chairs with three other married gentlemen—good friends he knew well from the old days when his father was alive and Randolph was not yet king.

Life had been different then, for they had all been unruly bachelors, sought after by every single young lady in the city. Married ladies, too, he supposed.

Over the past year, all four of them had taken wives. It seemed almost preposterous that he could be sitting with them now, talking politics while keeping an eye on the clock on the wall.

He was expected home later this evening. Neither he nor Véronique had made firm arrangements, of course, but in the six weeks since their wedding, he had gone to her bed every night and made love to her numerous times, so it had become both a habit and an unspoken promise that he would knock on her door at some point.

Tonight, however, he felt restless. He had been looking out the window to watch the carriages roll up and down the street. He wondered where everyone was headed.

"What do you say we all take a drive over to Wolcott's and see what's what?" the Earl of Rutherford suggested. "We could play some cards."

Nicholas leisurely sat back, waiting for the other men to respond.

"That sounds like a capital idea," Danforth replied. "Though the wives won't appreciate it." He turned his attention to Nicholas. "Yours, especially."

Nicholas frowned. Did they consider it an inevitable outcome of his marriage—that his wife would be continually disgruntled? His gaze lifted and he regarded Danforth with a hint of displeasure. "How do you mean?"

Danforth cleared his throat awkwardly. "Nothing . . . I only meant to imply that you are newlyweds. I doubt she's ready to give you up yet. The fires of nuptial bliss are still burning brightly, surely?"

"I certainly hope *she* thinks so," Nicholas coolly replied, and the others chuckled uneasily.

Lord Rutherford set down his glass. "Well, then? Who's in?"

Nicholas finished his drink and looked out at the shadowy movement of the traffic rolling by.

Was it midnight yet? he wondered. Perhaps there was time for one quick game. Then he immediately resented his awareness of the hour, for he hadn't had a curfew since he was fourteen years old. Just because he had taken a wife did not mean he must live like a recluse.

"I'm in," he said decisively as he set down his glass and rose to his feet.

Véronique woke late the next morning and realized with disappointment that it was the first night she had slept alone since speaking her wedding vows in the chapel at d'Entremont Manor.

Immediately she began to explore the possibilities. Perhaps Nicholas had fallen asleep, for they were both in need of rest. She had not slept a full night—uninterrupted—since before the abduction in Paris.

She rose from bed, rang for her maid, and enjoyed a light breakfast of honey ham, eggs, and toast with elderberry preserves. Just as she was finishing the last of her tea, however, she heard a ruckus in the courtyard outside the window, and rose from her chair to look below.

A carriage had just pulled up. A groomsman was running to take hold of the team, while a footman lowered the iron step and opened the door.

To her horror, out stepped her husband—looking

quite decidedly disheveled. He climbed the palace steps and entered through the front door. Véronique immediately rang for a maid to collect her breakfast tray.

So. He had not come home at all last night.

Where in the world had he been?

Fighting against an instinctive wave of feminine suspicion, she forced herself to sit down and remain calm. She must not presume the worst. She promised herself that when she saw Nicholas, she would not accuse him of anything, and she would certainly not behave like those other women, who threw jealous fits and tantrums, and stormed out of rooms.

But where had he been?

Since it was her usual habit to stroll in the back garden with Alexandra in the mornings, she decided she would not alter that routine. She made her way to the family drawing room to meet her sister-in-law, but found it empty. Perhaps Véronique was too late, and Alexandra had already left the palace without her.

Véronique was on her way to the back terrace when she encountered her husband descending the stairs. He stopped halfway and said, "I was just looking for you."

"Were you indeed?" she cheerfully replied.

He inclined his head as if he were suspicious of her overly decorous response, then continued down the steps in a relaxed fashion.

She noticed with some discontent the dark shadow of stubble at his jaw, and the fact that he wore the same clothes he'd had on the night before. Had he removed them at any point and dressed himself again this morning? Where had he slept? A wild assortment of images whirled about in her brain, and she found it increasingly difficult to convey a casual cheer.

"All right, let's have it," he said, bracing both feet on

the floor and folding his arms. "You're angry with me." He spoke as if he *wanted* it to be so.

"No. I am not."

"Are you trying to tell me that you failed to notice my absence last night?" he asked. "That you are oblivious of the fact that I didn't come to your bed?"

She let out a huff. "*Fine*, Nicholas. I noticed, all right? If you wish to torture me with it, you have achieved your goal. Are you satisfied?"

"Not really, because torturing you was not my intention."

Véronique hesitated, and ran her hands over her skirts. "Where were you last night?" she asked. "I waited and waited . . . then I couldn't stay awake any longer."

His eyebrows lifted and his eyes smiled at her, as if all the problems in the world had just been resolved. "I apologize for keeping you waiting," he said. "I did think of you last night, my love. Might I mention you look splendid today?" His gaze dipped to her breasts and the full length of her gown. "That color becomes you."

What a perfectly charming and evasive answer, Véronique thought.

When he offered no more explanation about his whereabouts the night before, she resisted the urge to question him further, turned away, and crossed the hall to the back doors. "If you will excuse me, darling, I must meet Alexandra for our daily walk."

"Very well, then," he replied as he, too, turned to walk in the opposite direction. "I shall see you later."

Chapter
Twenty-three

"He didn't come home last night," Véronique said to Alexandra as they strolled together across the wide expanse of green lawn beyond the cedars.

Alexandra twirled her lace-trimmed sunshade. "Well . . . it's not the first time he's stayed out until dawn, though he hasn't done that since he brought you home." She paused, then spoke carefully. "If it makes any difference, you should know that he is not the same man he was before you entered his life. The fact that he wanted marriage at all is a miracle in itself. So you have caused a transformation in him, Véronique. Randolph and I are quite astounded by it. We almost do not recognize him."

Véronique contemplated the rhythm of their matched footsteps as they spoke openly in the warm autumn sunshine. "I am happy you are pleased about our marriage, but I don't want to be the sort of wife who tries to change the man she married, and honestly, I am not even sure I know who that man is, now that we are here. Our honeymoon was lovely, but everything is very different in Petersbourg."

Alexandra considered that. "You believe he was not himself in France?"

"Honestly, I do not know. I always knew he had a reputation, but I saw something more in him. I *still* see something more. I believe he is ten times the man his father made him out to be. I just hope Nicholas believes it, too."

They continued to walk at a steady pace. "Are you worried about other women?" Alexandra asked.

Véronique squinted up at the sky. "They do have me a bit unhinged, I'm afraid. I see how they look at him, and who can blame them? I am working hard to keep my head on straight, however. I just wish I knew where he was last night."

Alexandra linked her arm through Véronique's. "Oh, my dear sister. The first year of marriage is often the most difficult, especially when you don't know each other very well, but you will both soon settle in. Give it time."

Véronique thought of her home in France and her sister, Gabrielle, now married to the great love of her life and living happily in the country with a child on the way. Perhaps Robert was carving their names into a tree at this very moment and circling them with a heart.

For the first time since her arrival here, a wave of homesickness washed over Véronique, but she did her best to send it back out to sea.

Véronique took her time dressing for dinner, for she required some peace and solitude after a full afternoon at the hospital with Alexandra.

It had been her first official function as a royal, and though she took great pride in the work they had accomplished in addressing the need for a new hospital, she had not relished the crowd's intense and probing fascination with her as a person.

Eyes were trained on her constantly. Ladies whispered to one another while openly judging her hairstyle and choice of gown, even the set of her shoulders and the length of her strides.

Though she did her best to smile and shake hands with everyone, it had been an exhausting experience, and she was relieved when it came time to return to the coach and drive away.

This evening, as she stood before the cheval glass watching her maid fasten the pearl buttons at the back of her gown, she took a moment to be grateful for her situation. She had made a spectacular marriage and had wedded a handsome prince, and was now a duchess living in a royal palace. In addition to all that, her husband was a wonderful lover—

A knock sounded at her door, and Nicholas walked in. He was clean-shaven and impeccably dressed, which was a stark contrast to his appearance earlier that morning.

"Leave us, please," he said to the maid, who immediately scurried out.

As soon as they were alone, Véronique faced him. "What are you doing here?" Her tone was less intimate than she'd intended.

But why? Was she worried that his warnings were coming to pass, that he could not live up to her lofty expectations and be the faithful husband she believed he could be?

"I wanted to see you," he replied, striding closer and reminding her how easily she could tumble into the tempting splendor of his good looks and impossible charm, for he was wielding both with full force this evening.

He stood before her and held up a blue velvet draw-string bag, which he dangled before her eyes.

"What's this?" she asked, making no move to touch it.

"A gift."

"What for?"

He continued to hold it suspended between them. "Can a husband not present a gift to his wife, for no reason at all?"

Still, she did not reach for it. "Perhaps."

His shoulders slumped in disappointment, and he lowered the velvet bag to his side. "What is wrong, Véronique?"

"Nothing. I just—" She swallowed. "—I would like to know where you slept last night."

There. She'd said it. She'd laid it all out.

"I didn't sleep anywhere," he explained as he watched her sit down on an upholstered stool and slip on a pair of shoes. "Did you think I was with someone?"

"No, of course not," she replied.

"But you're lying to me," he said. "I can hear it in your voice . . . see it in your eyes. You are not sure. You think I may have betrayed you last night."

She did her best to maintain an aura of faith in him. "No, Nicholas, that is not true."

"I have nothing to hide," he assured her. "If you want to know every detail, I was with a few old friends at Wolcott's playing cards until dawn—and winning, I might add. Ask them if you want. They will vouch for me, though I would prefer it if you would take me at my word."

"Cards?" She faced him.

"Yes." He seemed very disappointed in her, and she wanted to sink through the floor. Then he slipped his fingers into the velvet bag and withdrew a diamond necklace. "This is what I purchased with my winnings this morning. Do you like it?"

She stared numbly at the exquisite adornment, which was worth more than anything she'd ever worn in her lifetime. The diamonds sparkled like exploding stars. "It's beautiful," she said.

"May I put it on you?"

She laid her hand on her bare throat and let out a small laugh, for she was determined to lighten the mood and put that disagreeable—and regrettable—conversation behind them. "A man who offers diamonds to a lady may do anything he likes."

With a somewhat subdued smile, her husband moved around her to fasten the chain behind her neck. Véronique walked to the looking glass. "It's too much," she said.

Was it possible for a woman to be blinded by such dazzling extravagance?

"Not for you," he replied as he laid both hands on her shoulders.

His touch sent a wave of heat into her depths. He had been playing cards with old friends, and he had spent his winnings on *her*.

Véronique turned to face him. "I am sorry for doubting you," she said. "You did not deserve that, and it was wrong of me."

His gaze fixed upon her lips, and desire sizzled through her body as he pressed his mouth to hers. Seconds later he swept her into his arms and carried her to the bed.

"Did you see the paper today?" Randolph asked Nicholas when he entered the sunlit breakfast room.

Nicholas poured himself a cup of coffee and sat down at the table. "No. Is there a headline worth reading?"

He already knew by the tone of his brother's voice that it was something out of the ordinary, perhaps even shocking. It would not be the first time Randolph had thrown a newspaper at him over the breakfast table, for Nicholas had been the subject of many colorful headlines over the past decade. Usually they required clever maneuvering to control the damage.

This morning, however, Randolph slid the paper across the white tablecloth and sat back looking pleased.

Nicholas picked it up.

DUKE AND DUCHESS OF WALBRYDGE
WIN HEARTS AT LOCAL ORPHANAGE

The article went on to praise Nicholas and Véronique for their recent visit to Gibson House, where they inspected the grounds, played ball with the children, then Nicholas gave a speech to encourage donations to the city's oldest orphanage.

"How does it feel to be the subject of adoration for a change?" Randolph asked when Nicholas set the paper down.

"It feels better than being the subject of scorn," he replied, "but I don't trust the editors to keep it up. I've been a target long enough to know they can adjust their aim in a heartbeat."

Randolph sipped his coffee. "You are too jaded. Enjoy it for once, will you? And thank your wife for charming everyone within a twenty-mile radius. I don't believe she realizes how lovely she is, and how popular she has become. They are quite fascinated by her."

"Because she has captured and tamed the wild dog," Nicholas finished for him.

"Yes, I suppose that is part of it, but what does it

matter? The people are taken with her, and they admire your new respectability."

Nicholas looked up. "So I shouldn't disappoint them, then."

It was a loaded question, but he wanted to hear his brother's opinion on a matter they had not discussed since the day he arrived in Petersbourg.

"You are referring to your inheritance in France," Randolph said.

"Yes. I need to know what you think about it. The way I see it, there are two choices: I could quietly dispose of the property and bury the scandal, and continue to shock the world by being faithful to my wife. Or I could confess my illegitimacy and prove to everyone that I am—and always will be—a permanent disaster."

"Does it matter to you what they think?" Randolph asked.

"Six months ago, I would have said no, it doesn't matter a damn—but that was before Véronique. Now, I find I do not want to disappoint her."

It was an unusual concern for him—to care what a woman thought of him outside the bedroom, long after the initial seduction and conquest had taken place. But Véronique was different. She saw something in him—something worthwhile—and she had helped him when he needed her. He owed her a great debt.

And he craved her body every waking moment of the day.

He suddenly felt like a man on a ledge, teetering at the mercy of the wind, which could blow him over at any moment. He, who'd never wanted a wife, was terrified that she would eventually discover the truth and find him lacking in all qualities that made a man worthy of being a husband.

He was afraid he would take a wrong step and prove

himself unfit for a life of matrimony. In truth, he felt almost destined to disappoint her.

"I believe it should be your decision," Randolph said. "So what will you do? Will you keep d'Entremont Manor, or wash your hands of what happened in France, so that no one ever knows?"

Nicholas experienced a flash memory of swimming naked in the lake at d'Entremont Manor with Véronique one night at dusk. He also recalled lying beneath the stars on the lawn overlooking the Channel the night before they departed for Petersbourg. They had been happy there, near to her family.

The memories continued. . . .

He thought of the afternoon he spent with her father patching up a hole in the plaster ceiling of Véronique's childhood bedchamber, which Mrs. Montagne wanted to convert into a sewing room, so that she could make little shirts and dresses for her future grandchildren.

How could Nicholas wash his hands of such a life? It was a very different world, and he did not wish to let it go.

"I do not know what I will do," he replied, "but I am certain of one thing. I would die before I dragged Véronique into a scandal. She doesn't deserve it, nor does her family. They believe I rescued them from the very depths of dishonor and despair, and I suppose I did. I do not wish to drag them back down again."

Randolph considered all of that. "You asked me what I thought, and I will tell you now. I believe it is the right decision to keep Mother's infidelity a secret. I don't see what good could come of revealing it now, after all these years. Lord d'Entremont is gone—therefore, he has no hold over you, nor can he be a true father to you. Your life is here in Petersbourg. You are my brother. Nothing will ever change that."

Nicholas stood up and paced around the room. He stopped to look up at the portrait of his parents over the mantel, and wished there were a way to understand the decisions his mother had made.

His father, King Frederick, had been an intimidating man, and it was not surprising that she had obeyed his command and returned to her post as his queen. At the same time, Nicholas suspected she would have returned regardless, out of a sense of duty and a love for Randolph.

His brother was right. What good could come of smearing all their names and endangering the future stability of the country, when it had taken so long to achieve peace and see people satisfied with their new monarchy?

He turned to his brother. "Let us not speak of this again. We will continue to move forward, and I will do my best to stay out of trouble."

With that, he took his leave.

Chapter
Twenty-four

For a full month, Nicholas was as devoted as any husband could be. He spent the majority of his evenings at home, dining either privately with his wife by the fire, or with the king and queen in the formal dining room.

If there were no official functions at the palace, he and Véronique went out to the theater or attended political assemblies and private parties with friends, who were generous in helping Véronique settle into her new role as Duchess of Walbrydge.

The Walbrydge property, located near the western border of Petersbourg, was undergoing substantial renovations and was scheduled to be ready in time for Christmas. Nicholas and Véronique traveled there regularly to inspect the changes and make decisions about paint colors and fabrics. They happily anticipated the moment they could inhabit the premises at last, and turn it into a real home.

Thankfully, Véronique was less anxious about certain outside influences. There were blessedly few incidents with other women. Perhaps, she thought, all the lovers from Nicholas's past had been reading the newspapers and had finally accepted the fact that all hope was lost, for the prince was now a changed man. Everyone who saw him in the presence of his wife commented on it incessantly and on one particular night, she overheard the following conversation while sipping claret behind a tall potted tree fern:

"I always knew he'd grow into his responsibilities one day," the Earl of Mulgrave said at the Autumn Ball for Charity.

"Indeed," Bishop Canfield replied. "I daresay he'd make as good a king as his older brother. We are fortunate to have such fine family men in the palace representing our postwar interests."

"A child should be on the way soon," the Countess of Mulgrave added. "Do you see the way Nicholas obsesses over his wife? He is very protective, and cannot take his eyes off her."

"One can hardly blame him," the earl said. "She is as beautiful, charming, and hospitable as they come. She would make a fine queen, too."

"Pity she's French, though," the countess mentioned. "It would have been nice for the prince to marry a local girl."

"Perhaps that was part of the duchess's allure," the earl said. "It's a fresh start for him, and Lord knows he needed it. From what I've heard, her family despised Bonaparte. They are devout Royalists in every way and they support King Louis."

"That is excellent news," the bishop commented.

The headline in the paper the following day was as flattering as the gossip in the private parlors and ballrooms.

DUKE AND DUCHESS OF WALBRYDGE PLAN TRADITIONAL FAMILY CHRISTMAS DINNER AT NEW HOME. KING, QUEEN, AND TOP MEMBERS OF PARLIAMENT EXPECTED TO ATTEND.

And so the holiday season began on a very high note.

Though Nicholas did his best most nights to remain at home with his wife in the evenings, occasionally he kissed her on the cheek and ventured out to Carroway's for an evening of cards and cognac. She did not begrudge him for it, and he was thankful that they had settled into a comfortable routine. She had not expressed any discontent or mistrust since the night he stayed out until dawn and bought her the diamond necklace with his winnings.

As Christmas was fast approaching, Carroway's was uncharacteristically quiet one particular night when he found himself sitting alone. It was not an unwelcome circumstance. There had been much attention paid to him lately—most of it complimentary—but he was pleased, for once, to be spared the backslapping congratulations.

It was past midnight when he decided to return home to the palace, forgoing the usual trip to Wolcott's for cards.

As he placed his hat on his head and walked out the door, he looked up at the sky. It had just begun to snow. Nicholas paused to breathe in the fresh winter scents and blinked up at the giant snowflakes falling lightly through the mist. They landed on his cheeks, and he reveled in their coolness as they melted onto his skin.

Approaching the curb, he waved to his driver, who

was parked a few doors down. The coach pulled up and Nicholas greeted his driver. "Straight home tonight, Jenkins. Not much going on."

"As you wish, sir."

Nicholas opened the door of the coach and stepped inside, taking note of the fact that the lamp was not lit. It mattered not. He would simply close his eyes for the ride home.

He was just brushing the snowflakes from his shoulders when he became aware of a shadowy presence on the opposite seat, facing him.

The coach lurched forward and Nicholas squinted through the darkness. "Since it's Christmas," he said, "and a time for goodwill toward men, I will give you ten seconds to identify yourself, then I will have my driver stop here while I politely allow you to vacate my vehicle. No questions asked."

A throat cleared, and he knew at once that it was a woman.

A few months ago, he would have lounged back comfortably in his seat and awaited his traveling companion's next move, but tonight he found himself unnerved and irritated by this person's presumptuousness, for he was no longer available for such games, and had certainly not extended any invitations to anyone.

"Please do not make him stop," the lady said as she lowered the hood of her cloak.

"Ah . . ." He recognized the voice. It was Elizabeth, the prime minister's niece. *Lizzie,* to him. One of his former, more regular lovers. "Good evening, Mrs. Kennedy."

She stared at him. "Is *that* how it's going to be now, Nicholas? You are going to address me as Mrs. Kennedy and forget what we were to each other?"

He shifted uncomfortably on the seat. "I shall never

forget it," he courteously replied, "but what we were is no longer relevant."

She was quiet while the coach wheels rolled over the snow-covered cobblestones. "You are telling me that I must accept it—because you are respectable now."

"I am a married man," he reminded her.

She sighed as she removed her gloves and set them on her lap. "I suppose your wife would not appreciate knowing the nature of our acquaintance."

"Véronique knows who you are," he informed her. "You attracted her attention when you walked out of your uncle's dinner party so abruptly last month."

"I see." She rolled her shoulders with a clear show of discontent. "Well, I apologize for that. It was impolite of me, but I was still in shock over your unexpected marriage. I wasn't up to meeting your wife just then."

He gave her a moment to recover her composure.

"You would like her, I believe," he said.

Elizabeth let out a small *hmph*. "Of course I would."

They traveled in silence for a few minutes. Nicholas looked out the window, wondering how much time he had before they reached the palace. He couldn't very well drive through the front gates with his former lover in tow.

The level of his impatience escalated. "What do you want, Elizabeth?" he bluntly asked.

She, too, gazed out the window. When she spoke, her voice was casual and composed, as if she were in no hurry at all. "Your driver doesn't know I am here," she explained. "I sneaked in, because I needed to speak with you alone. I didn't know how else to arrange it. You haven't answered my letters." Her eyes met his with concern. "Are they keeping them from you?"

"No," he replied. "They are not keeping anything from me. I received all of them."

He had burned each one without reading a single word.

Suddenly, Lizzie slid across the dark space to sit beside him. "Forgive me, Nicholas, but I cannot continue to watch you play this charade. Please tell me that you will not live this life forever."

"To what charade—what *life*—are you referring?" he asked with a frown, knowing, of course, where she was headed with this line of questioning.

"The life of a proper, faithful husband," she answered heatedly. "It is all very inspiring, but I know you too well. Surely you are growing bored. I cannot imagine how you are coping."

"I am coping very well, thank you," he replied, recognizing the familiar fragrance of her perfume and taking note of the rapid pace of her breathing.

She scoffed. "Nicholas, this is *me* you are talking to. When will you come back?" she asked. "How much longer must I wait?"

His chest tightened as he comprehended the risks of being alone with this woman in his coach . . . this woman, with whom he had been sexually intimate—as intimate as a man and a woman can be. They had done wicked things together—depraved things—that would shock most married couples. They had spent countless hours in bed—in hotel rooms, in her home, outdoors. In public places, even. The depth and extent of her sexual knowledge of his body would astonish anyone. Véronique, especially.

"You shouldn't be here," he said. "My driver will take you home."

And pray God Jenkins wouldn't blab about it.

"No, Nicholas, not yet. . . ." She inched closer, pressing her leg up against his thigh. He couldn't help but recall the lushness of her bosom, and how she had always been so . . . *accommodating.*

This was dangerous.

"I know you and your sexual appetites," she said. "You will go mad under the glare of everyone's expectations. Please know that I will be here waiting for you when you feel the need to . . . spread your wings."

Her lips were now mere inches from his own, and he could smell brandy on her breath.

She laid a hand on his leg and stroked him. A fierce arousal stirred in his loins, but he fought to suppress it.

"I appreciate your kind offer," he said as he grabbed hold of her wrist and pushed her hand away, "but I am a happily married man now, Lizzie. Go home to your husband."

Sensing that she was enjoying his vicelike grip on her wrist a little more than she should, he released her.

With another blatant move to entice him, she pulled open the collar of her cloak to expose her deep cleavage. She wiggled her hips. Her ample breasts strained against the fabric of her low décolletage.

"How I've missed you," she softly cooed. "You can have me now if you like, right here in the coach, as many times as you wish."

Her soft, open mouth was close enough to taste. His heart pounded in his ears. She was a woman of vast sexual experience, always eager to please, willing to try anything, and he found himself tensing beneath her feminine offerings.

"Don't," he said in low voice that was full of grave warnings.

She stared at him fixedly. A small breath escaped her. He could feel her desire like an inferno inside the coach.

"Are you afraid I will get you into trouble?" she asked. "Because I can be very discreet. We can find a way to meet secretly. No one has to know." She wiggled closer, and he felt a surge of dirty, degenerate lust.

"Go home," he repeated firmly, then pounded a fist against the side wall of the coach to signal his driver.

Lizzie gasped with delight as he grabbed her around the waist and lifted her onto the opposite seat, plunking her down like a misbehaving child.

Disappointed, she slumped back. "I see you're not ready yet."

He practically fell back into his own corner and swallowed uneasily as he straightened his cravat with trembling hands. "No, madam, and I would not hold my breath if I were you. Stay away from me, do you understand?" He shouted at Jenkins. "Dammit, man! Let me out!"

The coach jostled to a sudden halt a few blocks from the palace. Nicholas flung open the door and spilled out, as if the inside were on fire. "My driver will take you home," he gruffly said, "and if you tell anyone about this, Lizzie, I swear to God I will deny everything and ruin you for it."

He did not wait for her reply. He slammed the door shut in her face and explained the situation to Jenkins, demanded his complete and utter discretion, and gave him Mrs. Kennedy's address.

A disconcerting moment later he was standing at the curb, watching the coach grow distant while rage pounded inside his skull. He shut his eyes, breathed in the cool air, and waited for his erection to diminish.

Dammit. Nausea rolled in his guts. He had not wanted this tonight. He wanted to be faithful to Véronique, and he certainly did not wish to fall backwards into a torrid affair with Elizabeth Kennedy. She was a beautiful but lonely woman with an uncommonly overactive sexual libido. He had enjoyed her tremendously at one time, and was not proud of the fact that he had taken advantage of her willingness for his own pleasures on more than one occasion, but that was another life. He had a wife now. A wife who waited for him at home.

Should he tell her about this?

Nicholas turned to walk through the gently falling snow. When he finally walked through the palace doors, he did not stop to remove his coat and hat. He went straight to Véronique's bedchamber, unfastened his breeches, and made love to her on top of the covers, while still wearing his shirt and boots.

It was over too quickly, and he felt guilty about that. Yet he did not want to make love again. He just wanted to sleep.

So he apologized, said good night, and left her room.

When he reached his own bed, he lay on his back for a long time, staring up at the canopy, feeling unsettled by what had occurred in the coach with his former lover. He worked hard to push their encounter from his mind, but it continued to torment him long into the night.

Chapter Twenty-five

When Nicholas finally walked into the breakfast room the following morning, Véronique waited anxiously for him to sit down with his coffee before she turned in her chair and spoke to the servant, who stood against the wall behind her. "Will you excuse us, please?"

The footman left the room while her husband watched her in the late-morning sunlight streaming in through the large bank of windows. The snow was melting fast. Drops of silvery water were dripping from the eaves.

"Is something wrong?" he asked, setting down his cup.

Véronique cleared her throat. "I am not sure. Maybe that is a question you should answer."

His eyes were hooded, unreadable, and when he gave no reply, she took a moment to gather her thoughts.

"What happened last night?" she asked. "You weren't yourself when you came home."

He had walked into her room and exercised his husbandly rights without the slightest show of seduction or foreplay, which was not like him at all. Then he'd left without a word, leaving Véronique both baffled and sexually frustrated.

Nicholas sat back. "What makes you think something happened?"

"You were different."

"How so?"

"I don't know. It felt . . . *rushed.*"

His hand, which was resting on the table, curled into a fist, then straightened and flexed. Véronique fought an acute sense of dread.

"If you must know . . . ," he said at last, but stopped at that.

She braced herself. "Yes?"

He tapped his forefinger on the table, as if contemplating whether or not he should explain, and if so, how best to phrase it. Her stomach, by this time, was in knots.

"A woman sneaked into my coach last night," he told her. "She was waiting for me when I left the club."

Véronique tried to ease the tension that suddenly gripped her shoulders. "Who was she?"

"What difference does it make? Nothing happened. I had Jenkins take her straight home."

"But I want to know," Véronique insisted.

Again, he paused. "Fine. If you must . . . It was Mrs. Kennedy. You saw her once, very briefly, at Carlton House. Remember?"

"The prime minister's niece?" Véronique made every effort to speak in a calm voice. "What did she want?"

"Do you really need me to answer that?"

Having suddenly lost her appetite, she pushed her plate away. "You said nothing happened. Is that not the truth?"

Nicholas gazed at her intently. "Mrs. Kennedy made

me an offer. I declined. Then I got out of the coach and sent her home."

"What kind of offer?" Véronique asked with a frown.

"Trust me, you do not need to hear those details."

"Yes, I most certainly do. I want to hear exactly what she said. Let there be no secrets between us."

Recognizing the stubborn tenacity in her voice, her husband stared long and hard at her. A muscle twitched at his jaw. "She said I could have her in the coach if I wanted her. As many times as I liked."

Véronique swallowed over the bitter tasting bile that rose up in her throat.

"You see?" he added. "You did not need to hear that."

Perhaps he was right. Perhaps she would have been better off not knowing. But she would have gone mad in the process, wondering about it.

"What did you say in reply?" she asked.

"I told you, I declined."

"Did you kiss her?"

"No."

Véronique's chest was heaving. Despite the fact that he swore nothing had happened, she still wanted to break something. "Did you touch her?"

"Of course not. How could you even ask that?" Her husband regarded her steadily with a frown from across the table. "All right . . . I put my hands on her to lift her off my seat and place her on the opposite one. Then I told her to stay away from me in the future, or I would ruin her. Are you satisfied with that, darling, or do you have more questions?" His eyes were cold. He spoke with a knifelike edge.

Véronique labored to remain calm. "No, I do not have any more questions. Did you really say that?"

"Yes."

They both sat in silence, while she thought about the manner in which he had made love to her the night before.

Perhaps he knew she was thinking of it, for he sat forward. "You *do* have one more question," he said.

The footman appeared in the doorway, but Nicholas held up his hand. "Not yet." The footman quickly made himself scarce.

Véronique leaned forward. "Why did you make love to me when you came home?"

"Because you are my wife, and I desire you."

Desire, not love.

She slowly shook her head. "Your desire for me last night was different."

"Different . . ." His eyes narrowed. "I am not sure I understand."

Véronique simply couldn't bring herself to say that she believed he only wanted to slake his lust, which had nothing to do with her, and everything to do with Mrs. Kennedy's provocative offerings.

Instead she lowered her gaze. He tapped his finger on the table, while she turned her wedding ring around on hers.

When at last he spoke, his voice was gentle. "She put me in a foul mood," he explained. "That is all."

Véronique sighed heavily. "I see."

"Would you have preferred I didn't come to your bed at all?" he asked.

She looked up. "No, I am glad you came, but I wish you had told me the truth last night."

He pondered her request. "I will remember that next time."

"Do you expect there to be a next time?" she asked, lifting her eyebrows.

Her husband sat back in his chair with a hint of a

smile and a touch of his famous, irresistible charm. "I cannot promise anything," he replied. "I am very popular, you know."

Véronique picked up her napkin, crumpled it into a ball, and pitched it at him.

Later that night, he made up for his uncharacteristic haste in the bedroom by taking his time undressing her—and showing tremendous patience and endurance as he pleasured her generously until dawn.

She did her best to forget about Mrs. Kennedy and place her trust in her husband.

For the next fortnight, all was well. Nicholas was not accosted by any more former lovers, nor did he take part in any card games that lasted from midnight until dawn. Everything seemed rather perfect, in fact, and Véronique was just beginning to believe that their success as a married couple in Petersbourg was achievable, when an unexpected visitor arrived and upset all her hopes and wishes.

Two weeks before Christmas, Véronique ventured into the city proper with Alexandra to attend an early-morning outdoor performance by Saint Peter's Cathedral Choir.

As they drove past the shops on Lewis Avenue, she deliberated over the right gift for Nicholas, for it was to be their first holiday season together as a married couple. She wanted to choose something lasting and memorable.

Since they would be moving into their new home in a few days' time, she considered giving him a strong young Thoroughbred, for they would be living in the country and he would likely be doing a lot of riding.

"What about a shotgun?" Alexandra suggested as the palace coach approached the concert stage in the park. "For the spring and fall hunting parties."

"A shotgun . . ." Véronique tried to imagine it. Perhaps she could learn to use it herself. It might come in handy to frighten away all the ex-lovers. "Does he like to hunt?" She was embarrassed to admit she did not know the answer to that question.

"Very much so."

The coach reached the entrance to the park and rolled to a halt in front of the ornate stone archway and iron gate, where a crowd had gathered to shake hands with Alex and Véronique on a brief walkabout.

Véronique took one side of the square while Alexandra moved along the other. She greeted the people, shook hands with mothers and children, and wished everyone a happy Christmas. The mood was relaxed and cheerful until she reached the gate and clasped hands with someone she recognized, someone she did not wish to see . . . *Pierre Cuvier.*

"Monsieur . . ." She forced a smile, so as not to appear flustered. "What brings you to Petersbourg?"

She tried to pull her hand away, but he would not let go. He smiled that crooked sneer she remembered all too well, and said, "I've been here for a fortnight, Your Royal Highness. I came to pay my respects to my dear cousin."

Swallowing uneasily, Véronique managed to pull her hand from his grip. "Does he know you are here?"

"Not yet, but I am sure you will relay the information for me." He reached into his pocket and withdrew a sealed letter. "Happy Christmas," he said as he held it out.

She glanced over her shoulder at the guards who were looking on. "Thank you." Slipping it into her fur muff, she quickly moved along.

The concert was a joyous affair that lasted a full hour, but Véronique felt anything but joyous. Her unexpected encounter with Pierre had left her shaken. She found it difficult to keep her eyes on the choir, for her gaze was constantly sweeping the audience, searching for his face.

What did he want? She was desperate to read the letter, but it was addressed to her husband and she did not wish to betray his confidence.

She would therefore wait until she returned to the palace, and would say nothing to anyone until then. Not even the queen.

"He was there in the crowd?" Nicholas asked with a frown. "Were your guards nearby?"

"Yes," she replied, "but I did not wish to arouse suspicion, so I was polite and moved on as quickly as I could. I said nothing about it to anyone, not even Alexandra."

Her husband beckoned for her to sit on the sofa while he broke the seal and proceeded to read the letter.

"Good God."

"What does it say?" Véronique sat forward on the edge of the cushion. "Please tell me. I cannot bear the suspense."

He finished reading and lowered the letter to his side. "He wants to be invited to our Christmas celebrations at Walbrydge. He wants to come and stay."

She shifted uneasily. "Is that all he wants?"

He raised an eyebrow. "I highly doubt it. The problem is, he goes on and on about how we are family now. . . ."

"But the king and queen will be there for Christmas, and he is . . ."

"A nobody?" he finished for her.

"What I was going to say," she added, "is that he knows your secret, and if he wishes to be presented as your cousin, he is, at heart, threatening to reveal it."

"Yes. I believe that is the point of this," Nicholas replied.

"You don't think he truly is lonely, do you?" she asked. "It's his first Christmas without the marquis."

He studied her countenance. "Do *you* believe that?"

She sat back. "I don't know. I've always seen something sinister in his eyes, and I will never forget how he tried to mistreat Gabrielle. If he is lonely, I will find it very difficult to feel sorry for him."

"He may very well be lonely," Nicholas said, "but if he has been here for a fortnight, he knows that my connection to d'Entremont has not been revealed publicly. He should know better than to ask to be presented as my cousin. For God's sake—"

"What are you going to do?" she asked.

He looked at the letter again. "It says here that he is staying at the Wild Rose Hotel. I believe I shall pay him a visit."

"Not alone, surely," she said.

"You don't think I can handle him?" Nicholas asked. "I broke his nose once before, remember?"

She gave him a look. "I do remember. But what if he has a pistol? You must be careful, Nicholas. Take a guard with you."

Thankfully, he agreed, and nodded before leaving the room to make the necessary arrangements.

Chapter Twenty-six

The Wild Rose Hotel was located in the east end of the city, past the park and theater district.

An unmarked palace coach took the long way around to avoid passing through Green Street, which was known for its prostitutes and cutthroats. How the cousin of a prince could take up residence in such a place reminded Nicholas that he was venturing into another world outside his own.

Though he was not truly a part of his own world—for he was a bastard son, just like Pierre. The only difference was that no one knew it.

He waited for the coach to come to a full stop before he pulled on his gloves and straightened his cravat. The guard who had accompanied him opened the door, waited for him to step out, then followed him into the hotel.

Nicholas had requested that his guard wear plain clothes that afternoon, and he, too, had dressed casually so as not to arouse attention.

He tossed a few coins onto the innkeeper's desk and asked about Monsieur Cuvier. A few minutes later he was climbing the creaky staircase, venturing down the dark narrow corridor, and tapping a knuckle on the door of room 6.

The noisy creak of the bed inside and the heavy tap of footsteps across the floor alerted the guard, who stood behind Nicholas. The man reached for his pistol, but Nicholas raised a hand to calm him. "Let us keep our cards close to our chest for the time being."

The door opened, and Nicholas locked eyes with the man who had been his kidnapper and his jailer. The man who was eventually revealed to be his half cousin by blood.

Pierre blinked a few times in surprise, then peered at the guard and bowed with a flourish as he stepped aside. "Welcome, Your Highness. Won't you come in?"

Nicholas spoke quietly to the guard. "Wait downstairs." Then he followed Pierre into the room and looked around.

Pierre spread his arms wide. "As you can see, it's not a room fit for a king or a prince, but I am neither, so I apologize for the lack of luxury. I am sure it's not what you are accustomed to."

"It matters not." Nicholas kept his eyes fixed on Pierre's. "I read your letter."

"Excellent!" he replied. "So we will enjoy a happy family Christmas together, then? I shall look forward to it. In fact, I have already been to your new home. I drove past it last week and stopped to compliment the builders on their impressive work. Just between you and me, however, I don't think it compares to d'Entremont Manor. It doesn't have the same . . . regal style. It's rather dark and depressing. Too much heavy stone. What is *your* opinion?"

Nicholas breathed deeply and counted to ten. "What do you want, Pierre? Why are you here?"

Pierre's eyebrows lifted innocently. "I thought I made it clear. I want to spend Christmas with my family. Unless that is a problem for you and the duchess."

"You know very well it is a problem."

Pierre sighed. "Ah, yes, because your countrymen are not yet aware of your mother's . . . *holiday* in France all those years ago."

A flashing spark burned in Nicholas's retinas, and before he could consider a more diplomatic response, his feet carried him fast across the room. He wrapped his hand around Pierre's throat and pinned him up against the wall. "I will ask you one more time, Cuvier. What do you want?"

The whites of Pierre's eyes flared as he gasped for air and kicked his heel against the wall in protest. "D'Entremont Manor," he rasped.

Nicholas frowned. "What are you saying?"

"I want the manor house and all the property that goes with it," he explained while the veins at his forehead bulged repulsively and his cheeks turned red.

Nicholas released him and backed away. Pierre dropped to his knees, panting.

"What are your terms?" Nicholas demanded.

Raising a hand to beg for a few seconds' reprieve, Pierre eventually rose to his feet. "I want what should have been mine from the beginning. Give me back my home, and I will never breathe a word of our association to anyone. I won't reveal how your duchess committed a crime by drugging and kidnapping you, nor will I expose your mother as the whore that she was."

Nicholas clenched his hands into fists to resist knocking Pierre's head off, and backed away. "If I refuse?"

"Then I will spill everything to the newspapers, which would be a terrible shame for you and your pretty wife, who are so beloved by the people." He paused.

"Do you really need d'Entremont Manor? Surely you have enough. You have *everything*. Must you be so greedy?"

Greed was the last thing on Nicholas's mind at the moment. His chest constricted when he imagined the truth about his mother reaching the newspapers, not to mention the scandalous circumstances of how he and Véronique came to be married. What would the world say if they knew about the laudanum, the captivity, her pregnant sister, and all the rest of it? Some might call for Véronique's arrest. Their reputations would be ruined.

He wanted overwhelmingly to barrel all his weight into Pierre and beat the man senseless.

"Are you forgetting that you, too, were involved in my kidnapping?" he said. "You committed a crime against me, sir, and I could have you arrested, or worse."

Pierre glared at him with malice. "And condemn your wife at the same time? Because if I find myself in Briggin's Prison, I will most assuredly be forced to talk. Naturally, I would wish to cooperate. I would have no choice but to confess everything."

Nicholas rubbed the back of his neck while his blood pulsed feverishly through his veins. "I will need time to consider this," he replied as he imagined all the worst possible scenarios.

"I will give you three days," Pierre said. "All I require is that you bring me the deed to d'Entremont Manor, sign it over, and all this will go away. No one will ever know. You can continue to enjoy your respectable new life with your lovely bride, and I will have what is owed to me. It will be a happy ending for everyone all around. Otherwise, I will go to the papers."

"And confess your own guilt," Nicholas reminded him.

Pierre shook his head. "It won't matter, because by the time the news becomes public—if it comes to that—I will be long gone. Without Lord d'Entremont, I have no more ties to France. Who knows where I might choose to live?"

"Have you forgotten the property he willed to you?" Nicholas asked.

Pierre's mouth pulled into a thin-lipped smile. "I have already sold it."

Nicholas stood before his half cousin in a state of blind rage, cracking his knuckles while he contemplated the disastrous state of his life. He had faced scandal before and never broken a sweat, but everything was different now. He had a wife. He couldn't let this get out.

All at once, he felt almost murderous. He wanted to shove Pierre's head into a bucket of water and watch him drown. He'd keep the secret then, wouldn't he?

It was the first time Nicholas had ever felt such a strong desire to kill a man. The urge was vile and carnal, like a disease in his blood.

Véronique said she saw something sinister in Pierre. Perhaps they were more alike than he realized. Cut from the same cloth, so to speak. The thought made him shudder.

"I will meet you in this room in three days," Nicholas said as he turned and headed for the door. "Be here at this hour."

"Oh, I will," Pierre replied with a chuckle that caused all Nicholas's muscles to strain against his skin as he forced himself to walk out and shut the door behind him.

Nicholas's hands shook uncontrollably when the coach pulled away from the hotel. He felt dangerously on edge, and had to crack his neck from side to side to release some of the pent-up tension in his shoulders.

"Is everything all right, Your Highness?" the guard asked, sounding concerned.

Nicholas merely nodded as he stared out the window, for he could not discuss what had just happened.

He would discuss it with Randolph, however, and together they would decide how best to proceed. Just the thought of that conversation gave Nicholas a headache, for he'd foolishly begun to imagine that all the scandals were behind him.

Then he began to envision what would happen if he wrapped a cord around Pierre's neck and pulled it tight. But what would he do about the body?

No, he couldn't think that way.

Growing more agitated by the second, he ripped his hat off his head and set it on the seat beside him, then pounded a fist hard against the side wall of the coach. "Let me out!" he shouted. "I need air!"

"But, Your Highness," the guard argued. "We're in the Green District."

"I bloody well know where we are. I've been here before." Many times, in fact, when he was living a life of debauchery, outside the courtly realms of Petersbourg Palace. Perhaps this part of town was a more suitable outlet for a man like him—a bastard son who contemplated murder and had no business calling himself a prince.

The coach pulled to a halt and he got out. He was not surprised when his guard followed and walked a short distance behind while the coach rolled along beside them.

Bloody hell.

He stopped abruptly and looked up at a wooden sign that said simply: ALEHOUSE.

Perfect. He strode through the door and down the steps to a damp, musty, dimly lit cellar with low ceilings. The floors were wet under his feet. The place reeked of stale liquor.

It was blessedly quiet, however, except for a few hard-looking patrons who sat alone on benches at the long tables.

Nicholas went to the bar, ordered a tankard of ale, then found a small private table in the shadows at the back. He sat down and kicked his booted legs up onto a second chair.

His guard also ordered a tankard and took a seat at one of the long tables near the door, where he could keep an eye on things.

Where was this obsessive sentry on the night Nicholas attended a masked ball in Paris and was abducted by a beautiful Frenchwoman? A woman who had been working secretly with the man who now threatened to destroy him and everything he cared for?

Nicholas took another swig of ale. A part of him wanted to blame Véronique for all this, but how could he, when it was *he* who suggested marriage and allowed her to turn him into a gentleman hero for the first time in his life—at least in the eyes of the people.

But he was no gentleman. He was the same bastard he'd always been, and he doubted he could ever truly become what she expected him to be.

Could he really be faithful to one woman for the rest of his life? A few short months ago, the answer would have been a resounding no, but somehow Véronique had made him believe it was possible. He wanted it to be, but there was so much water under the bridge of his miserable life. He couldn't erase all the women, nor could he erase the fact that he was the product of his mother's secret adultery, and the proof had finally come back to haunt him. And he wanted to murder it with a thin rope.

The barkeep arrived with a second tankard of ale and set it down on the table. Nicholas fished in his pockets for coins and dropped them into the man's open palm.

A few minutes later he was waving at the barkeep for something stronger—a bottle of whiskey—and feeling grateful for its numbing effects, for it took some of the edge off his murderous inclinations. Though the self-loathing was becoming rather more profound as he took in his surroundings and wondered what the hell he was doing here in this abominable place on the worst side of town.

A hand came to rest on his shoulder just then. He tipped his head back on the chair to look up through clouded vision at the upside-down image of a woman's face.

She was leaning over him.

Golden-haired. She wore a pale blue gown.

Her hand slid across his chest as she bent forward to whisper in his ear. "Would you like some company?"

Nicholas was drunk, but not that drunk. He knew better than to invite this woman to join him, for she was a whore, and he was Prince Nicholas of Petersbourg, recently married and teetering too close to the edge of a terrible fall from grace.

"I appreciate the offer," he said, "but I'll be on my way shortly."

Her eyes warmed with a smile. She moved around him to push his legs off the facing chair. "Then I'll just sit with you for a little while until it's time for you to go. What's your name? I'm Jennie."

"It's a pleasure to meet you, Jennie," he replied with seductive charm—for old habits died hard, especially when one was soused. "What brings you out on this fine afternoon?" he asked.

She leaned forward in her chair and slid her hands up his thighs. "The chance that I might meet a man like you. But clearly, the more pertinent question at hand is what brought *you* out on this fine afternoon? I've never seen you here before, and you don't look like you belong in this part of town."

Her hand continued to massage his thighs, and he found himself wondering if she knew who he was.

He also wondered if he would ever be capable of forgetting the wife who waited for him at home. Would he ever wish to return to this perverted existence, where he could flirt unreservedly with willing women, and give them what they wanted? Take what he wanted?

"I should go," he said, blinking slowly through the heavy haze of his inebriation.

She slid onto his lap. He sat back in the chair, wanting to get up, but he couldn't seem to make his body move.

"One kiss," she said with another tempting smile that reminded him of his old self when he could charm a kiss—and a great deal more—out of any woman he desired.

"No," he gently replied, so as not to reject her too cruelly.

Seconds later, however, he regretted not using a firmer tone, for her moist lips found his in the cold shadows of the alehouse—and he allowed it, at least for a few seconds before he shoved her away.

"I said *no*."

She slid her hand into his coat and stroked his chest. "I don't think you mean that. I think you want to come upstairs and let me open your breeches. This mouth of mine likes to do more than just kiss."

His head nodded back. He was drunker than he realized, but not so incapacitated that he couldn't lift this woman off his lap and place her on the opposite chair. After doing so, he rose unsteadily to his feet. She glared up at him with seething anger.

Tossing a few coins onto the table, he walked out of the shadows, past his guard. "If you tell anyone about this," he said, "I swear to God you'll rue the day you were born."

Chapter
Twenty-seven

By the time Nicholas reached the king's royal court chamber, he was sober again—at least sober enough to speak clearly and make some sense out of the situation. He explained everything to his brother and showed him the letter Pierre had handed to Véronique at the outdoor concert.

Randolph stared at him, incredulous. "He is blackmailing you?"

"Yes. He wants d'Entremont Manor." Nicholas sat down. "Perhaps I should just give it to him."

Randolph scoffed. "Or he could conveniently meet with some sort of unfortunate accident."

"Believe me, I've thought about it," Nicholas replied. "In far more detail than I should have. But he has left instructions with someone in France to send the incriminating information to the Petersbourg newspapers if he does not return in person by a certain date. So if anything happens to him, the truth will be revealed, regardless."

Randolph paced about the room. "He will not get away with this. You will give him nothing. We will take him into custody and force him to confess who has this information."

"As I suggested before," Nicholas said, "wouldn't it be easier to simply give him the manor house? Do I really need it?"

Randolph stopped pacing. "That is for you to answer, not me."

Nicholas rubbed his pounding temples. "Bloody hell. Either way, if I surrender to him, he will only return later with more threats, looking for more money. It will never end." He stood and moved to the mantel, rested his hands on it, and gazed down at the empty grate.

"What if I reveal everything myself," Nicholas suggested, "before the three days are up? Then he will have nothing with which to bargain."

"We could arrest him for your kidnapping," Randolph said.

Nicholas faced him. "If we arrest him, we will have to arrest Véronique as well. That cannot be an option."

His brother stared at him for a moment. "Do you realize what you are saying?"

"Yes, I intend to confess the truth about my legitimacy."

"You will lose your title," Randolph told him. "You will no longer be Prince Nicholas."

"What about the dukedom?" he asked, focusing on the particulars.

"That is a separate title I bestowed upon you," his brother replied. "I will not take it away, but you would no longer be a royal duke. Your rank would change."

"I can live with that," Nicholas said.

"The gossip will be fierce," his brother warned. "The newspapers will have a field day. The editors will jump for joy. They won't be kind. Even Véronique will be dragged into the slaughter, and will likely be cut to pieces. Will she be strong enough to weather it?"

Nicholas remembered the day she kicked Pierre in the nether regions, and the day she walked in on a man's suicide. . . .

"Yes, she's made of stern stuff, and she won't be sorry to see Pierre cut off at the knees. Metaphorically speaking, of course."

Randolph walked to the desk, where he stood for a long time with his back to Nicholas.

"What's wrong?" Nicholas asked.

His brother faced him at last. "I am thinking of our mother. Everyone always thought she was a shining example of purity and dignity. She was a beloved queen, but this will change that forever. The Royalists will say what they always do—that our family is not worthy of the crown."

Nicholas sighed. "Yes, but now we have you and Alexandra as our sovereigns. Alexandra is descended from the ancient Tremaine dynasty, so no one can ever dispute the legitimacy of your heir's rightful claim to the throne. The monarchy is safe at least." He paused. "But, Randolph, if you must wash your hands of me to protect your crown, I will not begrudge you for it."

"Wash my hands of you?" Randolph replied in shock and dismay. "I intend to stand by you, Nicholas, no matter what occurs."

His heart ached with love for his brother. "I don't want to bring you down."

Randolph laid a hand on his shoulder. "None of this is your fault, and perhaps it won't be as bad as all that. What Mother did . . . it was a long time ago. Perhaps the people will be forgiving. We will do our best to put the right spin on it. We will focus on your courage and honesty in coming forward."

Nicholas stared at him for an overlong moment. "It's going to be rough on all of us. I had best go and prepare Véronique."

He thought of her family just then, and hoped they would not regret giving him permission to marry their daughter.

When Véronique opened the door, Nicholas found himself exhaling. Dressed in a cheerful gown of peach silk with tiny floral sprays, she was indeed a sight for sore eyes.

She stepped aside and invited him in. "Thank goodness you are here. What happened? I haven't been able to sit still all afternoon."

She wrapped her arms around his neck and rose up on her toes. He curled his body into hers and held her tight, feeling as if the world might come to an end if he let go too soon.

"I think you should sit down," he said when she stepped out of his embrace.

Her nose crinkled at his words, as if she had caught a whiff of something unpleasant. She moved closer to sniff his jacket collar.

Oh God. His heart sank.

"I have something important to tell you," he explained.

She backed away from him, her face pulling into a frown.

"A few things, actually," he added, knowing that he must not hide what happened in the alehouse. He could not let Véronique imagine it was worse than what it was . . . though it was hardly an inconsequential matter. He suddenly wanted to dash from the room, change out of these dirty clothes, and scrub the stink of the stale liquor—and that woman's cheap perfume—from his person.

Véronique seemed to recognize the strain in his expression. "You don't need to say it. I already know. I can smell it on you, and I am not referring to the whiskey."

His brow furrowed with regret. "I am sorry, Véronique. I am not proud of what happened today, but you must let me explain."

Though he did not deserve her forgiveness. This was the third time, was it not? Or dammit . . . was it the fourth?

His wife moved to a chair by the fire and sat down. "I am listening."

He could feel the color slowly draining from his face. When he hesitated, she said, "I thought you were going to see Pierre."

"I did see him," he replied, thankful for this small detour from the more abhorrent sections of the day. Nicholas moved closer but did not sit down. "It was as we suspected. Pierre revealed his intention to blackmail me into signing over the deed to d'Entremont Manor. He threatened to reveal my mother's affair with the marquis, and the fact that I am illegitimate."

Véronique squeezed the ends of the armrests. "What are you going to do?"

Nicholas crossed to the window and looked at the snowy landscape. A full minute must have passed while he watched a pigeon on the ledge, huddling in the cold. Then at last he answered the question in a voice hardened by ruthlessness.

"I am going to crush Pierre and all his devious plans by revealing the truth myself. Randolph is at this moment drafting a formal statement, which he will read before Parliament and release to the newspapers. He will tell everyone that I am illegitimate, and he will have no choice but to strip me of my title of prince. I will no longer be addressed as His Royal Highness, and that will be the end of it. No more lies."

He heard the sound of the chair creak as his wife rose and approached. "Are you sure about all this?"

He faced her. "I don't intend to live a lie, Véronique, and I suspect you don't want that either."

She shook her head. "No, I do not. But I must ask— did you consider giving him what he wants?"

"Only briefly. Why? Is that what *you* think I should do?"

She pondered it for a moment. "No. If you must know, I have always felt it would be difficult to hide the truth forever. It would have come out eventually. These things always do."

"Which truth are you referring to, exactly?" he asked. "There must be another layer to this observation."

She inclined her head as if bewildered. "There is no other layer, Nicholas. I am referring only to the blackmail scheme."

"But what about the other women?" he asked matter-of-factly. "Clearly you can smell the perfume on my coat. You must know I was somewhere filthy today."

She gave a sigh of resignation. "I know something happened, and I am still waiting for you to explain it to me."

Nicholas frowned in disbelief. "It is the perfume of a prostitute in the Green District!" he said. "I stopped at a pub after my meeting with Pierre. She came to my table, slid her hands into my coat, and propositioned me. I declined, of course. Do you believe me?"

Her head drew back. "It almost seems as if you do not *want* me to believe you—as if you are challenging me to doubt you, so that you can say 'I told you so.'"

He sat down on the windowsill and folded his arms across his chest.

His challenge compelled Véronique to question him more thoroughly. "Fine. I will ask the question you clearly want me to ask. Did you kiss her?"

Though she did not really want to know the answer, for it would only cause her pain if it was a yes.

"She kissed *me*," he replied.

"Did you kiss her in return?"

He took too long to answer. Perhaps it was only a few seconds, but it was enough of a hesitation to expose the truth.

"I pushed her away," he explained. "Then I walked out."

Though she tried, Véronique could not erase the sickening image of another woman's lips upon her husband's. How long had the kiss lasted? She could not bear to think of it.

She turned away from him and moved slowly to her chair in a daze, sat down, and stared blankly at the floor. "Will women *always* be throwing themselves at you?"

He sighed, and his voice, at last, grew gentle. "If it helps," he replied, "I didn't invite her. I don't *want* to be unfaithful to you, Véronique."

She stared up at him. "You say that as if it is beyond your control. But it is not. I believe in you, Nicholas. I believe you love me, and you want to be a good husband, but for some reason, you continue to be influenced by your dead father's opinions of you. Do you not understand that? And do you not realize that he resented you because he knew your mother loved Lord d'Entremont just as much as—if not more than—she loved *him*? He wanted to punish you for her betrayal, and he wanted to see you fail while his own children, by blood, succeeded. He wanted to hurt you, as a way of retaliating against *her*."

Nicholas listened to all of it with a clear head and a willingness to accept what she was saying. Nevertheless . . .

"Even if that is true," he said, "I still do not understand how you can trust me. That woman in the alehouse . . . she kissed me, and for a few seconds, I kissed her back. You deserve better, Véronique. Surely I am not worthy of you."

"But you are," she insisted. "You have been my hero from the start."

Heaven help her, despite everything, she was still spellbound by him. No wonder women found him irresistible. She would have done anything in that moment to know that she would never lose him. She was no different from the others.

"I will stand by you through all this," she told him. "You're my husband."

He nodded, as if conceding that point to her. Then his chin lifted. "Very well, then," he said, as if something had been decided, but nothing about this was simple. "I suggest you prepare yourself for the tidal wave of gossip that is about to hit us all. The newspapers will be cruel. It will not be easy, Véronique, and I apologize in advance for whatever we must endure." He turned to walk out, but stopped at the door. "Incidentally, Randolph will not be stripping us of our ducal titles. We will remain the Duke and Duchess of Walbrydge, and the property will remain ours as well."

"What wonderful news," she replied with forced cheer as she watched her husband leave her bedchamber without looking back.

* * *

Feeling as if he were suffocating, Nicholas burst through the palace doors to the back terrace and strode quickly across the gray flagstones to the balustrade. Taking the cold air into his lungs, he shut his eyes and tried to calm the violent beating of his heart.

Very soon, everyone would know the truth. They would all know he was a bastard and a fraud. It would be ugly, and God knew what extra dirt they might dig up from his past.

Véronique would see and hear all of it.

What had he been thinking when he proposed to her all those weeks ago? Did he truly believe he could rescue her by making her his wife? It was quite the opposite now. Her reputation would be ruined.

Turning, he sank his weight onto the cement balustrade and looked up at the clean palace walls, the ornate sculptures, and the golden cornices. *God!* None of this wealth or opulence mattered to him. He didn't care about living in a royal palace, or the loss of his title, or the scorn he would endure from the people of Petersbourg. All that mattered was Véronique's happiness— her trust in him—but all that was at stake now.

He grabbed hold of his jacket collar, tugged it to his nose to smell the whore's perfume from the alehouse. He caught a whiff of it and shook his head in disgust.

Why the hell had he stopped in the Green District and gotten out there, of all places? Was he testing himself? Or was he taking dangerous risks because he *wanted* his marriage to fail?

Roughly wiping his sleeve across his mouth to rid himself of the memory of that foul kiss, he resolved to get through this. Somehow he would endure the gossip and censure, no matter how vulgar it became. He would take Véronique away and leave the country if he had to.

Ah, Véronique. . . .

Though he wanted to be good husband, he couldn't seem to quit stumbling—yet she never lost faith in him. A part of him hated her for it, for he was not sure he could succeed, and God knew, he did not want to fail. Not with her.

How odd and unfair that when he was finally ready to amend his tarnished soul, to become a better man, he would—in the very next instant—be exposed publicly as a bastard, unworthy of a royal title. They would call him irresponsible and degenerate, just like the old days. What would they say about Véronique? Would they punish her as well? Guilty by association? It sickened him that she would be dragged into this.

He wouldn't blame her if she left him. He'd certainly done his best to drive her away just now.

He realized suddenly that he couldn't let go of the belief that he would lose her one day. If not because of this, then for some other reason. Childbirth perhaps?

Part of him wanted to face the loss now and get it over with, before his feelings grew any deeper and he became so profoundly attached, it would be . . .

Unbearable.

Suddenly his thoughts drifted to the past.

"I am so proud of you, Nicholas. This is the best picture you have ever done."

His mother gathered him into her arms and held him close while she admired the rudimentary painting of a little boy holding his mother's hand. They stood beneath a yellow sun and a rainbow.

"I daresay you are destined for greatness. What a brilliant man you will grow up to be. I am so happy you are my son. Do you know you are everything to me?"

Nicholas gazed up at the sky and realized how fortunate he was to have found Véronique—a woman who, like his mother, believed in him. And by God, he *loved* her for it.

Did he deserve her? Perhaps, in some small way, he did. Perhaps she was right, and in truth, he was not the miserable, depraved scoundrel his father had always made him out to be. The realization struck Nicholas hard and left him strangely hopeful, in a way he had never been before.

How odd that he could feel so hopeful when he was about to be stripped of his royal title and labeled a bastard.

PART III
An Honest Life

Chapter Twenty-eight

The news of Nicholas's illegitimacy was read before the members of parliament by King Randolph, who revealed that his brother was not the true blood son of King Frederick, but illegitimately born after their mother's return from a yearlong visit to France. Nicholas's father was the Marquis d'Entremont, a known Bonapartist, recently deceased.

The announcement was received initially with quiet, confused murmurs as the members of parliament absorbed what seemed an impossible state of affairs. A short while later, they scattered like mice, eager to be first to spread the news.

A special edition of the *Petersbourg Chronicle* was published that night, while Véronique and Nicholas dined privately at the palace with Randolph and Alexandra.

To Véronique, it felt as if the city were ablaze outside the palace gates, while they were sheltered inside from the flames—at least for this one, final supper. Tomorrow, everyone would know the truth, and when she woke, nothing would ever be the same again. The people of Petersbourg would no longer throw roses at her coach when she passed. It was impossible to imagine what they might do. How tolerant or forgiving would they be?

"I am afraid to ask," Véronique said as she watched her husband enter her chamber with a gossip sheet in hand. "What is it now?"

Every writer in the city had been ruthless over the past week, using pens like skewers. Naturally, the incident with the prostitute in the alehouse found its way to the front page of every paper. The guard who had accompanied Nicholas that day was paid handsomely for his firsthand knowledge of the encounter—and was promptly fired by palace officials as soon as the headline broke.

Nicholas endured every possible insult. He was the subject of intense social and political debate in the public gathering spots and private drawing rooms of the city. He had been advised not to leave the palace and venture into the streets—a necessary precaution for his own safety and peace of mind, for it was generally expected that he would meet with hisses and verbal abuse, and no one wanted to give the papers any more fodder upon which to chew.

Véronique received her fair share of scratches as well, for everyone was suddenly questioning her basic morals, and asking why any woman would choose to marry a man with such a terrible reputation. Did she not see it? Was she a fortune-hunter or social climber?

Or had she been seduced like all the others? Perhaps even ravished?

Then, there were strange, preposterous rumors of a kidnapping. . . .

Nicholas tossed the newspaper onto her bed and spread his arms wide, as if surrendering completely to whatever dreadful fate was about to befall them next.

"See for yourself," he said. "Then sharpen your sword, darling, like everyone else, and take a swing. Cut me to pieces. Here I am."

Recognizing his frustration, she walked to the bed and picked up the paper.

PETERSBOURG PALACE DISGRACED AGAIN

Since the announcement of his illegitimacy, Bastard Prince Nicholas has been hiding behind the palace gates to avoid public censure. It has recently been discovered, however, that the wild young buck has been slipping out in the early mornings to exercise his freedoms.

May we take this time to remind our readers about a scandal from a previous year, when the notoriously rakish royal seduced and ruined a respected duke's beloved daughter at the Hanover Hotel?

The editors of this paper have lately discovered that the Bastard Prince secretly met with the young lady—who has come forward to expose his ungentlemanly conduct—both on the night of her seduction more than a year ago, and on another more recent occasion when he came upon her in the park during her morning ride.

Again, he attempted to charm and lure her into the forest, surely to engage her in scandalous activities that shall remain a mystery—for the young lady was fortunate enough to escape the notorious Bastard's clutches and gallop away as fast as her mount could take her.

Véronique immediately crossed to the hearth and tossed the gossip sheet into the flames. She watched it burn and crumple to ash; then her husband's hand came to rest on her shoulder.

She turned to look up at him. "How much of it is true?"

"Some of it," he replied. "I did have an affair with that particular woman at the Hanover Hotel more than a year ago, and there was a noisy scandal about it at the time. But who seduced whom remains a question that will go unanswered, for we later discovered that her family took bribes to help smear my family's name. It was a Royalist plot to set wheels in motion that would remove my brother from the throne, to be replaced by another. We believe the young lady played a part in it, and lured me to her room in the hotel, not the other way around."

"Did you really ruin her?" Véronique asked.

He chuckled bitterly. "I assure you, she had been ruined long before I entered the scene."

It was never a pleasant thought, to imagine her husband making love to another woman, but Véronique could not blame Nicholas for things that happened before they met.

"What about this week?" she asked. "I know you have gone riding alone in the mornings. Did you see her in the park?"

"No. That part of the story is pure fiction. I have gone riding, but I have neither seen nor spoken to anyone. Perhaps someone else saw me, however, and recognized an opportunity. This is all lies, Véronique, for the purpose of selling papers. Can you continue to weather it?"

She had to admit, after reading all the gossip printed about them over the past week, a small part of her was tempted to summon a carriage and travel straight back to France, where there would be no more spiteful stories about her husband's infidelities and ungentlemanly conduct, and her own immoral behavior.

Every word published stung her like a poisonous insect, and it took great strength of will to remember that these were the words of strangers, and no one knew the honest truth about her husband's heart, or the integrity of his character. Or hers.

She laid a hand on his cheek. "For you, I can weather anything, because I love you more than life itself."

He turned his face into her open palm and kissed it, then placed it over his heart.

Chapter Twenty-nine

Over the next seven days, Nicholas and Véronique went riding together in the park each morning. They galloped fast across the snow-covered meadows in plain view, shamelessly inviting anyone to secretly follow and write about their laughter and togetherness. Not surprisingly, no one seemed the least bit interested in their success as a married couple. There was no news in that. So Nicholas and Véronique simply enjoyed the crisp winter air on their cheeks and the opportunity to escape prying eyes for a part of each day that belonged solely to them.

On the eighth day, Nicholas was invited to a private breakfast alone with the prime minister, which he and Véronique discussed at great length the night before.

"What do you think he wants?" she asked. "You don't suppose it has anything to do with his niece, do you?"

Nicholas slipped into bed beside her. "God forbid, I cannot imagine Mrs. Kennedy would have allowed her uncle to discover the truth about her infidelities. But I suppose anything is possible in this age of scandal-rousing. The country seems obsessed."

"The war is over and Napoléon is gone," she said. "They have nothing else to write about. But if the prime minister does know, what will he do, Nicholas? Should we be worried?"

Nicholas gathered her into his arms. "Mr. Carlton is a good man, and I consider him a friend. If anything, I believe he may wish to offer a show of support. Perhaps he wants to help us emerge from this nightmare unscathed." He rolled on top of her, settled his hips snugly between her thighs, and lit her body on fire.

"I would hardly call this a nightmare," she breathlessly replied as he entered her.

Closing her eyes, Véronique arched her back and cupped her husband's muscular buttocks in her hands, pulling him deep inside. A spark of pleasure flared in her blood, while she reveled in the incomprehensible joy of this lovemaking.

In that moment, she didn't give a damn what the newspapers printed about either one of them. This was all that mattered.

Nicholas knocked on the door to the prime minister's private residence a few minutes before nine the following morning. The butler greeted him with a bow and invited him into the main hall, where he collected Nicholas's hat and coat. "If you will follow me this way, Your Grace, breakfast is being served in the green room."

The house, located in one of the fashionable new neighborhoods on the outskirts of the city, boasted large, south-facing windows. For that reason it was brightly lit by the sun reflecting off the fresh white snow that covered the grounds outside.

Nicholas followed the butler to the rear wing of the house, which overlooked the river, and through a set of double doors that opened to reveal a large table covered with bowls of ripe, colorful fruits; biscuits on platters; cheeses and meats. The delicious aroma of fresh coffee filled the air.

No one was present in the room to greet him, however, so the butler left him alone. He backed out and closed the double doors behind him.

Nicholas stood in silence; then the clock on the mantel began to chime the hour. It was nine o'clock. He was exactly on time, but where was Mr. Carlton?

His stomach growled with hunger as the scent of the warm biscuits reached his nostrils. At last the clock finished its ninth chime, and the door on the opposite side of the room opened.

"Good morning, Your Grace," his hostess greeted cheerfully.

Nicholas lowered his head. *Damn.*

"Good morning," he flatly replied before he looked up and watched Elizabeth Kennedy enter the room, take a seat, and gesture for him to join her at the table. "Where is your uncle?"

"He left for the country house yesterday," she replied. "Did no one tell you?"

"Of course no one told me," Nicholas testily replied. "I received his invitation only yesterday. Was there a change of plans?"

He knew, however, that there had been no change, for there had never been an invitation from Mr. Carlton to begin with. It had come from Lizzie, alone.

A clever scheme, he thought, but it would get her nowhere, for he had no intention of staying.

"I am sure you've realized by now," she said, "that I am the one who invited you. Please sit down, Nicholas. I had the cook prepare all your favorites. Look, there are raspberry cakes with chocolate."

"I'm not hungry," he snapped, then turned to leave.

He reached the door, but it was locked. Bloody hell. Clenching his jaw, he turned to face her. "Where is the key?"

She grinned shamelessly and pointed into her cleavage. "Come and get it, darling."

He flexed his fingers while the beat of his pulse intensified. "No," he firmly said. "You will fetch it yourself and open this door at once."

"Or else . . . *what*?" she asked. "Will you throw me over your knee and spank me? I really wish you would, Nicholas. Ever since you left for France, I've been a very naughty girl with very naughty thoughts."

He glared at her maliciously. "Are you going to unlock the door?"

She reclined back in the chair, parted her legs, and slowly lifted her skirts above her knees. "Surely you know me better than that. You know I won't surrender until I get what I want."

"Fine," he growled. Then he reached into his jacket pocket, withdrew his pistol, loaded it on the spot, and shot the lock and doorknob to bits.

Mrs. Kennedy screamed and leaped out of her chair. "What the devil are you doing?"

He swung around and bowed with a flourish. "Exactly what it looks like, madam. I am letting myself out. Please inform your uncle that I will cover the cost of the damages. Feel free to explain why I was forced to take such extreme measures. Good day to you."

With that, he pulled the door open and strode into the corridor.

"Wait! No! You cannot leave!" Elizabeth ran after him and grabbed hold of his arm.

He shook her off and continued toward the stairs.

"*Please!* Stay . . . just fifteen minutes more."

He stopped dead. "Why fifteen minutes?"

She stared at him with panic, and suddenly he understood exactly what was happening here. She hadn't invited him to tempt him into resuming their affair. This was a trap.

A rush of adrenaline burned in his muscles, and he shoved her up against the wall. "What's going on?"

Recognizing the dangerous fury in his eyes, she wisely revealed what she knew about a plan that was already in motion.

Nicholas immediately released her and dashed out of the house to return to the palace, where Véronique would soon be taking her morning ride. *Alone.*

With her groom, John, following close behind, Véronique trotted into the bridle path that would take her through the forest to the look-off point at the top of the ridge.

It was a quiet, windless morning. There was only an inch of snow on the ground, but it was coated in a thin sheet of ice that sparkled brilliantly in the sunlight.

As she was on her way up, she passed a few others on their way down, and greeted them with a smile. They responded courteously, but after they passed, she wondered what they would say behind her back. Perhaps they would report her husband's absence and speculate about his whereabouts.

She told herself it did not matter, for he had a perfect alibi. He was having breakfast with the prime minister, and surely some good would come of their meeting.

When she reached the clearing at the top of the ridge, she dismounted and handed the reins over to her groom, so that she could rest awhile and enjoy the view.

Her boots crunched over the crystalline snow as she walked, and she tugged her fur hat lower to cover her ears. Sniffing in the cold, she reached the edge and looked out over the grand cityscape below. The morning sun reflected off the snowy rooftops, and tendrils of smoke rose up from thousands of stone chimneys all over the city.

Véronique gently blew out a puff of air to watch her breath float away like steam. The world seemed completely still and quiet from this height on the mountain, and she relished the peace . . . until she heard the sound of her groom's voice.

Turning, she saw that John was addressing a man on a horse. Then he pointed at her.

Her thoughts darted back to the guard who had accompanied Nicholas into the alehouse, then subsequently sold information to the newspapers. She wondered if this stranger on the horse—or her groom, for that matter—could be trusted.

As the rider dismounted and began to approach her, however, she recognized his familiar gait and the set of his shoulders.

What in God's name was Pierre doing here?

He wore a friendly expression and held out his gloved hands, as if to assure her that he meant no harm. Her defenses rose up regardless, for she knew what he was capable of and wouldn't trust him for an instant.

She looked toward her groom, who remained with the horses, watching carefully.

"Good morning, Your Grace," Pierre said. "What a lovely winter morning."

Dispensing with the customary pleasantries, she faced him squarely. "What do you want, Pierre? And I warn you, my guard is armed."

Pierre glanced over his shoulder at the young man. "Well, that is a relief, I must say. I was a bit concerned for your safety when he allowed me to come and speak to you. I told him we were neighbors from France, and he didn't even ask my name."

She shivered in the cold. "You still haven't told me what you want."

"To talk to you. That is all. I have a proposition."

Véronique began trudging through the snow, back to her horse. "I have no interest in hearing it."

Pierre was wise not to grab hold of her, for surely—*surely*—her groom would have intervened.

"Please, Your Grace," he pleaded as she shouldered her way past him. "Hear me out, just for a moment."

Véronique hesitated. Not because she was compassionate or easily manipulated, but because she was curious. She wanted to know what card was hidden up his sleeve.

"The authorities have been looking for you," she said. "They want to ask you about your attempt to blackmail my husband. I am surprised you haven't left the country by now."

"But there is nothing for me to return to," Pierre explained, "which is why I have come to *you,* Your Grace."

She felt the cold air nip at her cheeks, and sniffed as she grew wary of Pierre's hand in his coat pocket. Was he carrying a weapon? A knife or a pistol?

"Your uncle willed you a property outside of Paris," she said, "but I understand that you sold it."

"That's right, because I wanted something more."

"D'Entremont Manor."

He nodded.

Véronique's gaze found John again. He was still watching, but she couldn't be sure if he could be trusted. Was he a loyal servant? Or had he been bought by some unscrupulous editor or, worse, by Pierre?

"You still haven't told me what you want," she reminded him.

He took a step closer.

She took an equal, measured step backwards.

Squinting at her in the bright winter sunshine, Pierre said, "There is no need to be skittish, Your Grace. I only want to ask for your help. I want you to say whatever it takes to convince your husband to give me the property. Surely you know how to influence him. You are his wife. You must have some . . . *power* over him."

"Power? How dare you."

"But I need your help."

Her anger flared. "Why in God's name would I help *you*? After what you tried to do to my sister—"

"Because it's the right thing to do," he replied. "You and I both know that Nicholas has no rightful claim to the estate, no personal attachment. I, on the other hand, was born and raised there. It should have been left to me, not him."

"But those were not the wishes of your uncle," she argued. "He made it clear in his will that he wanted Nicholas to have it."

"The marquis was grief-stricken over the loss of his son, and half-mad from the pain of his malady. He wasn't thinking clearly at the end."

Véronique fought to control her frustration—and her apprehension—for she was quite certain that Pierre could not be reasoned with. He was determined to have what he wanted, at any cost.

"That is not what the solicitor concluded," she said. "The written will stated—with legal witnesses—that Lord d'Entremont was of sound mind. So you must accept that, Pierre."

A muscle flicked at his jaw. "You are not hearing

me, Your Grace. I want the property, and you are going to convince your husband to give it to me, because he does not deserve to have it. You know it as well as I."

"I know nothing of the sort!" She turned to go, but this time Pierre grabbed hold of her arm.

"Are you not worried about your sister?" he asked with a threatening sneer.

She whirled around to face him. "What are you saying? Have you done something?"

She recalled what she had done to *him* the last time he tried to harm Gabrielle, and was fully prepared to do it again, right here and now.

"I haven't done anything yet," he quietly replied, "but if I don't get that property, I may lose my patience and pay a visit to Richelieu House. I'd wait until the baby was born, of course—and you of all people know I am not above kidnapping."

She recoiled in horror. "Did you not learn your lesson when you tried to blackmail my husband?" she asked. "Or are you foolish enough to try to blackmail *me* now?"

"Call it whatever you please," he replied. "I only want what is rightfully mine, and I'm sure you'll find a way to convince your husband that everyone will be better off if he simply submits and signs the property over to me."

Véronique tried to pull free, but his grip tightened on her arm. "John!" she called, turning desperately toward her groom. To her great relief, he came running.

Then a deafening shot rang out, and she jumped at the noise. John fell to the snowy ground, clutching his thigh and crying out in pain.

Véronique made a move to go to him, but Pierre quickly withdrew a rope and bound her wrists. She fought and struggled, kicked him in the legs, and cursed herself for not anticipating this—but she'd been distracted by the pistol shot.

"Are you all right, John?" she shouted.

"I am wounded, Your Grace," he bravely replied through clenched teeth as he squirmed on the ground.

Pierre dragged her toward his horse.

"Are you mad?" she asked. "A dozen people saw me ride up here this morning, and we will pass a dozen more on the way down."

"We won't be taking the bridle path," he explained as he led her to a fallen log to use as a mounting block. "We're going *that* way." He gestured toward the steep side of the ridge.

"It's the dead of winter," she argued as she stepped up. "The ground is frozen solid, covered in ice. We'll never make it. We'll be killed."

"Let me be the judge of that. Up you go, now."

She refused to cooperate.

He reloaded his pistol. "Get up in the saddle, Your Grace, or I will shoot your groom dead."

She glanced at John, who was clutching his bloody thigh.

"You won't get away with this," Véronique said.

"Maybe I don't *want* to get away with it," Pierre replied. "Maybe I just want to take something precious away from your husband. Maybe it's time he learned what it means to lose everything."

A memory of Lord d'Entremont's suicide flashed in her mind . . . the white death on his face, the dark puddles of blood on the floor. What if Pierre intended to do the same? He'd just admitted he wanted revenge against Nicholas. What if he planned to ride this horse straight over the edge of the mountain and kill them both?

"Fine," she said in a firm voice. "You win. I will talk

to Nicholas. I can get him to change his mind. He never wanted to go back to France anyway. He prefers it here. And now that we have Walbrydge Abbey—"

Pierre's eyes froze over with hate. "Get up on the horse."

"No, I will not."

They glared at each other fiercely.

Pierre pressed the cold barrel of the pistol against her forehead. Véronique squeezed her eyes shut.

"Maybe I should just shoot you now," he growled.

Cautiously, she opened her eyes to peer down at him. "I would prefer that you didn't."

"Then get up on the damn horse," he ordered.

Not sure how she was going to escape this, she nodded and put the toe of one boot into the stirrup while she stalled for time, fumbling with her heavy skirts.

The sound of approaching hooves caused them both to turn toward the path. Véronique nearly collapsed in relief when Nicholas emerged from the forest with four palace guards galloping behind him, all of them armed. She barely had a chance to call out to him, however, before Pierre pulled her off the log, wrapped an arm around her neck, and aimed the pistol at her temple. He dragged her toward the edge of the cliff.

"He's going to kill us both!" she shouted as she fought against his brutal hold.

Nicholas leaped off his horse and ran after them. He dropped his pistol into the snow and spread his arms wide. "What do you want, Pierre? Whatever it is, you may have it. Just do not harm her, I beg of you."

Pierre scoffed. "You beg of *me*? You are a bloody prince! I am the one who has spent a lifetime begging for respect. I never got it, and I never expect to. Not ever."

The guards behind Nicholas cocked and aimed their

weapons, closing in on them while Pierre dragged Véronique closer to the edge.

"Stop," Nicholas pleaded, his eyes blazing with desperation. "I will give you anything you want. Just please, do not take her from me."

Véronique met her husband's gaze and felt his love like an arrow in the heart. Overcome by a fresh wave of resolve, she bit Pierre's wrist, bent forward, and flipped him over onto his back. He landed in the snow with a thud, and she stared down at him in shock.

Without hesitation, he put the pistol in his mouth and fired.

"No!" Véronique covered her face in her hands and whirled around. Nicholas was suddenly at her side. She felt his arms around her.

"Don't look," he said, cupping her head in his hand. She buried her face in his chest. "Come with me now."

While the guards dealt with Pierre and John, Nicholas led her back to his horse, cut the ropes that bound her wrists, and pulled her into his arms again. "I almost lost you," he whispered. "What would I have done?"

"You didn't lose me," she said. "We are fine. Everything is fine. Pierre is gone now. He won't hurt us ever again."

Nicholas held her without saying a word. Then he lifted her onto his horse, swung up behind her, and took her swiftly back to the palace.

Later that morning, Nicholas entered Véronique's bedchamber and closed the door behind him. She'd needed time to change out of her riding habit, for there was blood on the skirt.

"This is not what I wanted for you," he said, "and I am sorry. It has been a disaster from the beginning."

"A disaster . . ." That was not the word she would use to describe it.

"I wouldn't blame you if you wanted to leave," he continued. "You *should,* you know. You should leave me now, go back to France, and try to live a normal life—"

"I beg your pardon?" Shocked by his words, Véronique stared up at him in disbelief. "Are you mad? Do not say such a ridiculous thing to me, Nicholas. I know you don't mean it. You're just afraid."

"Afraid?" His eyebrows lifted. "Me? Yes, by God, I am bloody well terrified. Terrified that one day something bad will happen to you, or you will grow to hate me because of what I have been all my life. But there's nothing to be done about it and—"

"Do you *really* want me to leave?" she asked. "Do you want your old life back? Is that what you are implying? Am I not enough for you?"

He flinched. "Good God, woman, you are more than I deserve. You have overwhelmed me in every way, and you have made me realize how little I could care for any woman but you. I don't know what you did to me, but whatever it was, there is no turning back. I don't care what the world thinks of me. All that matters is what *you* think and feel, but most important, that you are safe. And you are not safe here."

She stepped forward and clung to him in the quiet stillness of the room. A lump formed in the back of her throat and tears stung her eyes. She squeezed them shut and buried her face in his shoulder.

"I will not let you send me away." She looked up at him. "I know what you've been doing all this time. In all the years leading up to the day we met . . . women have been nothing but conquests to you, so that you can prove to yourself that you are in control and can walk away whenever you please. You enjoy being the one who leaves. That way, you are never the abandoned one. Now you are trying to control when *I* leave, as if it is an inevitable conclusion to our misguided, impulsive marriage. But I am not leaving you, Nicholas, no matter what you say . . . because I know you love me."

He shook his head and held up a hand. "That is not what I mean to suggest—"

"You *do* love me," she continued to argue. "You're just afraid it will end in disaster, like so many other painful things you have been forced to endure. Well. I am standing here now, telling you that I am not leaving, at least not by choice. You will have to throw me in the dungeon and chain me up to keep me away from you. That is how much I love you and desire you, and I will do anything to remain at your side. I don't care where we live, whether we are rich or poor, safe or in danger, or if people throw tomatoes at us. All I want is for you to love me and no other. Please, Nicholas, just let yourself love me, and trust that I will always believe in you and love you just as much in return."

Her last words were smothered by his kiss, and the ecstasy of his lips upon hers coursed through her body like fire.

"I believe it. You silly fool," he said, pulling her into his arms.

"You do?"

"Yes, but socially, we are quite ruined."

She let out a miserable laugh. "I don't care! I never wanted to be a royal! All I wanted was *you,* titled or not. I would be happy anywhere . . . as long as I had you in my bed each night . . . as long as I have your heart."

She saw his expression change to something that resembled amusement. "Stop," he said with a chuckle that took her by surprise. "As usual, you have made me your captive, but you don't need to convince me of anything. I know you are right about all of it. You helped me see that I lost the one person who believed in me at a very young age, and I didn't want that to happen again. But life is full of risks, is it not? And it is so brief, like a shooting star. We must make the most of it while we can and take pride in our lives. What exists between you and me is not just physical. It is not about temporary pleasure. It is deeper than that, and far more meaningful. I want to build a good life with you, a life full of honor and fidelity, and devotion to our families. I treasure you for showing me what kind of man I can be, for expecting more of me. My father expected very little and he pushed me into a life of empty debauchery. I believe he enjoyed watching me disappoint everyone. But you have proved him wrong."

"No, *you* have proved him wrong," she said. "I was only a witness to it."

"But you saw me as something more, and for that I am grateful. All I want to do is hold you forever and never let you go. If we leave here, we leave together."

His lips found hers again, and the kiss was deep and soul-reaching—hot, wet, and possessive—as if he were claiming her as his own once and for all, until the end of time.

She was his—there could be no doubt about it—and her senses reeled with passion and delight. "Oh, Nicholas," she sighed as he laid a fresh trail of kisses down the side of her neck. She relaxed, jubilant, simply to be in his arms.

Before she could utter another word, he swept her off her feet and carried her to the bed, where he laid her down on the soft feather mattress. In a foggy haze of yearning and desire, she watched him slowly untie his cravat while he kept his eyes fixed ardently upon hers.

"Did you really think I came in here to send you away?"

"I . . . I wasn't sure . . ."

"I do love you," he said with a smile, "and it is a love more profound than I ever imagined I was capable of." He began to unbutton his waistcoat. "I pray that I can make you happy, wife, because I will never forget the promises you made to me today, and how brave you were on that ridge. I will hold you to your promises, because I do not ever intend to be without you."

"You won't be," she assured him, watching with pleasure as he undressed and stood naked before her.

He smiled that slow, lazy grin, and as always, she melted like butter as he came down upon her in a tremendous rush of passion and the promise of a lifelong devotion.

Epilogue

D'Entremont Manor
Seven months later . . .

A soft, warm breeze blew the corner of the picnic blanket across Véronique's face, waking her from an afternoon slumber.

After flipping the blanket aside, she yawned and stretched her arms over her head, then lay for a moment, relaxing in the shade of the giant oak tree. From her vantage point, she could see the manor house in one direction, and the English Channel in the other. The branches overhead swayed in the wind as it whispered softly through the leaves.

An odd scraping sound caused her to sit up, which was no easy task, for her belly was growing larger each day. Her happy condition was part of the reason she sometimes fell asleep in the afternoons. She had never felt so fatigued in all her life, but it was a welcome sort of fatigue to which she was more than willing to surrender.

"What are you doing, darling?" she asked, seeing only half her husband's tall form on the other side of the wide tree trunk, which boasted a circumference of at least five feet.

He stepped into view to answer her question. "Carving our names," he replied, "but a chisel and hammer might have been a better option."

He disappeared behind the tree again. The scraping resumed.

"You are using a knife?"

"Yes, and I am almost done. Would you like to come and see?"

Véronique smiled. "I would love to, but I may need help getting up. I feel as big as a whale."

Nicholas was quick to offer a hand. As she rose to her feet, she paused to breathe in the fresh salty scent of the breezes blowing in off the Channel.

"It is so wonderful here," she mentioned. "Everything is so beautiful."

Her husband pressed his lips to hers, and she basked in the pleasure of his touch. She was the luckiest woman on earth.

"But there's more beauty to behold," he said. "Wait until you see my fine workmanship."

Nicholas escorted her around the wide tree trunk to the other side, where he had carved the words in a heart:

NICHOLAS
AND
VÉRONIQUE
FOREVER
IN LOVE

Joy bubbled up within her, and her smile broadened in approval. "It is indeed a stunning piece of work," she said, then wrapped her arms around his waist and rested her head on his shoulder. "I am so happy, Nicholas. I never dreamed it could be like this."

Seven months ago, when the scandals of Pierre's death and Nicholas's lost title as a royal were at their heights, she and Nicholas had decided to travel to France and take up residence at d'Entremont Manor.

To extend their honeymoon.

As soon as they arrived, they'd settled in as master and mistress of the house. Though the tenants and neighbors knew of the scandal, there was little talk of it beyond the first few days, for in the eyes of the locals, Nicholas was still the brother of King Randolph of Petersbourg, and a wealthy duke as well. The people of France were more than happy to welcome him and Véronique with open arms, and provide them with sanctuary from the ruthless wagging tongues of a foreign country.

Incidentally, the locals continued to refer to him as "the prince."

"Will we ever leave here?" she asked, for they had come simply with the intention of riding out the scandals, always imagining they would return to Petersbourg one day.

"Not anytime soon," Nicholas replied, kissing her temple with loving affection, "for you are in no condition to travel."

She felt a warm glow move through her and laid a hand on her belly. "But I will be eventually," she replied. "And then we will have a child who will require his or her proper presentation to a king and a queen."

Alexandra's letters had been frequent and lengthy. She reminded Véronique constantly of how eager she was for their son—the heir to the throne—to meet his new cousin. "What wonderful playmates they will be," Alexandra had written in the letter Véronique received just the other day.

According to Randolph, there had been more than a few social scandals to overshadow Nicholas's in the past few months, and the king felt it would soon be time for Nicholas to return and prove everyone wrong about their unfair judgments—with clear evidence of a happy marriage, and Nicholas's absolute devotion to his beautiful wife.

"Perhaps we could spend half the year *here*," Nicholas said, "and the other half *there*."

"That would be quite an enjoyable way to live," she replied, lifting her face to look up at him in the dappled shade of the oak tree.

As always, she was spellbound by his dark, arresting features, his strong chiseled jawline, and his tempting full lips.

He must have sensed her arousal, for he backed her up against the tree. "I don't care how, or where, we live. As long as we are together . . ."

Then he kissed her tenderly—almost teasingly—which ignited her passions to a feverish pitch. They clung to each other like lovers who had been torn apart and only just reunited on that very day.

Every moment must be treasured, Véronique thought, *as if it were the last. . . .*

His kiss ventured lower to her neck and the tops of her breasts, sending an endless ripple of desire straight down to her toes. Then he sank to his knees and slowly kissed her belly. "You are my angel," he whispered.

Just when she thought they might retire to the blanket and explore their passions more thoroughly, the sound of a carriage interrupted their reverie and Nicholas rose to his feet.

Peering around the side of the oak tree, he said, "It's Gabrielle and Robert, and it looks like your parents are with them."

Véronique turned and looked for herself. Indeed, her family was approaching in an open barouche. Gabrielle held baby Sarah in her arms. Véronique waved to them as she left the shade of the oak tree and approached the lane.

"Good afternoon!" Gabrielle called out. "We came to invite you both to dinner this evening. Perhaps we could play a few hands of cards."

"That sounds wonderful," Véronique replied while Nicholas opened the carriage door for her family.

When Gabrielle stepped out with her baby, Nicholas held out his arms. "May I?" he asked.

"Of course you may." Gabrielle grinned at Véronique as she placed little Sarah into his strong and capable hands.

He rocked Sarah gently for a moment, then turned toward the oak tree and said, "Come with me, little angel. I want to show you some very fine workmanship, just over this way."

He started off across the grass, while Véronique watched him with pounding, breathless love.

"He is so good with her," Gabrielle said.

Véronique was on the verge of tears. This pregnancy made her so emotional sometimes.

"He is an excellent uncle," Robert agreed as they all stood next to the barouche, watching Nicholas show Sarah the words and heart he had carved. She was just a newborn babe and probably couldn't see much farther than the length of her uncle's arm, but if she was like most women, she was probably floating on air, blissfully captivated by the mere sound of his voice.

"He is a fine husband," Véronique's mother said.

"Most definitely," her father added. "I couldn't imagine a better son-in-law. You chose well, dearest."

Véronique sighed happily and linked her arm through her father's. "Yes, I did."

As she continued to watch Nicholas pace by the tree, bouncing gently at the knees to rock Sarah in his arms, she laid a hand on her belly and anticipated the day when he would hold their own child in his arms. It wouldn't be long, now. A few more weeks, perhaps.

In that moment on the lane, like so many others since the day she'd married Nicholas, she was overcome by gratitude for all the gifts she had received in her life.

I am the luckiest woman on earth, she thought as she smiled appreciatively at her family. Then she walked back to the oak tree—to be with the man she loved.

Don't miss the first two novels in this heart-stopping
series from *USA Today* bestselling author

JULIANNE MACLEAN

BE MY PRINCE

PRINCESS IN LOVE

From St. Martin's Paperbacks